Whatever You Do, Don't Cry

"This story challenges the reader to keep hold of the ideals of peace, justice and love, even when everything around them is so dark and oppressive."

Whatever You Do, Don't Cry

Hannah Kawira

Hannah Kawira
Cover Art: Leona Beaver
2018

Copyright © 2018 by Hannah Kawira

All rights reserved. This book or any portion thereof may not be reproduced or used in any manner whatsoever without the express written permission of the publisher except for the use of brief quotations in a book review or scholarly journal.

First Printing: 2018

ISBN 978-0-244-07699-3

Hannah Kawira
hannahlindoewood@gmail.com
9 Blaen Y Myarth
Llangynidr,
Powys,
NP81NQ

Ordering Information:
Special discounts are available on quantity purchases by corporations, associations, educators, and others. For details, contact the publisher at the above listed address.

U.K. trade bookstores and wholesalers
Please contact
Hannah Kawira Lindoewood
Tel: 07581000407
Email hannahlindoewood@gmail.com

Dedication

To my family, who never stop reminding me that I am loved.

Acknowledgements

This book would not have been possible without the support, prayer, and encouragement of my friends and family. My heartfelt thanks and appreciation reaches out to the following people whom - among countless others who I couldn't possibly name in such a short space- were an integral part of me achieving this dream!

My incredible and artistic friend, Leona, for your amazing photoshop skills and cover art wizardry, as well as close friendship over the past few months!

My parents; mum for proofreading and picking out my silly little spelling errors, and dad for reading a work of fiction (!!) and asking those 'deep and meaningful questions'.

For my 'final draft' reader: Megan, whose valuable critique lead to those all-important last tweaks.

For the Lulu publishing team - and your incredibly helpful guides!

And finally, to God, who guided my heart to find the words to tell a story that needs to be told.

Prologue

I feel them first. Feel their cold, foreboding air that casts chilling shadows to forewarn their presence

Then, I hear them. The uniformed step of well-trained military poised for attack.

It can't be them. My thoughts ravage like wildfire, spreading despair and lost hope to the farthest corners of my mind. I thought I was safe. I thought they'd stopped chasing me.

I thought wrong.

The cluttered room around me, with its pale blue curtains and off-white peeling wallpaper that once symbolised naïve joy and innocence, seems to sway and pull closer, as if even the walls have turned against me in a fit of futile anger. They growl like terriers who lie obedient to their owner, but quickly turn on him at the beck of their true master.

The wooden dove, cold and fearful in my sweating palm, drops to the rough carpet worn by years of laughter and happiness, and splits cleanly into two pieces. Its peace shattered. Just as mine soon will be.

The dove. The symbol of the Resistance. The ideal of peace. The reason my children are alive. The reason I will soon be dead. The elegant creature with power and strength forgotten by the majority, its soft innocence cruelly hunted down and made extinct years ago. Will they forget me as I am hunted down and made extinct?

I stare at the shattered segments on the floor, as pale as a scream against the murky brown of the carpet, and fearfully await the three resounding knocks that will commence my fate.

There is nowhere to run anymore, no secret cavern or hole in the wall where they won't find me.

Nothing.

Nothing but to wait.

First knock.

Bile rises in my throat, the sound ringing in my ears like a thousand snarling dogs.

Second knock.

I begin to shake, a gasp escaping through my tight chest as cold, clammy sweat clings to my forehead.

I sense rather than hear the third knock.

My breath steadies, my eyes close, and I swallow, pretending that the fear does not exist. That it is only a game. A figment of my imagination that will vanish when I wake up. When I escape this cruel nightmare.

Slowly, I rise to my trembling feet and edge towards the door. My steps clatter against the floor as if walking is an unnatural movement. And my feet drag, rebelling against the weak will of my mind to reach the door with my pride still intact.

My palm scrapes the wall as my steps slow, supporting me as hatred writhes like a snarling snake in the pit of my stomach. The hating snake of evil that is the part of Them still breathing inside of me, longing for Their destruction. The fraction of me that I will never call my own and instead try to suppress and ignore, as if that way it will simply fade into nothingness. As if, if They will not die, then perhaps the part of Them within me will.

As I stand behind the door, all that lies between me and Them is an ancient slab of worm eaten wood.

I smell their rich, strong, perfume through the pores of the timber, and gag. The thick black smoke they exhale travels from their midnight lungs through the humble cracks of the oak, tasting of death and destruction. My hand rests on the doorknob, hesitating for a split second before I force myself to turn it. The movement seems laboured, as if I were pushing a boulder, my muscles tense and my brow furrows in concentration as the door seems to swing back of its own accord. It usually creaks, but now it is silent, muted in fear of They who stand before it.

They stand in their default triangular position, dark cloaks forming a black wall decorated with guns loaded with lethal bullets. They stand tall and menacing; sour faces wearing mirrored expressions of anger, hatred, and disgust

All fifteen. Fifteen perfectly rehearsed snarls. Fifteen dull, lifeless eyes that have seen death more than they have seen life. Fifteen fighters honed around their prey. The fourteen infamous Destructors create the walls of my prison, blocking out the light on either side as their leader, the First and most highly regarded of the Nobles that govern this Country, creates the razor-sharp point of the triangle. His shadow invades my soul, as I finally bring myself to stare into the deathly eyes of Rebato Antario.

"Hello son." He grimaces at the word. "I've missed you." The men either side of him step forward and pin my arms behind my back, as if I would even try to run. I know I've lost. I know I've failed. "Revicartus Antario." His voice remains monotonous, neither high nor low but with a darkness that cannot emerge from a pit nor fall from the skies to gather a more extreme malice. "Or would you prefer Moss Dell?"

I thought I was safe. I thought I'd outrun them. But you are never safe. Not from them. For five years I've lived peacefully here, selling wooden carvings and keeping my family alive and safe. But no more. I think about those five years, the laughs and loving smiles I have shared with my children. A happiness that I was starved of as a child. A hope that made each sunrise glitter with excitement and each sunset glow with promise.

" How....how did you find ...?" my voice is barely a whisper as the confidence that was strong and defensive in my mind translates into something submissive and feeble.

"I have my sources." He smiles, and in his glinting teeth I see a reflection of the pain exacted on his 'sources'. The pain that made them to betray me through no fault of their own. The pain that I'm afraid may soon make me to betray others.

"It's been a long time." He speaks calmly, casual in his condemnation. "Five years since you decided to abandon your family and defy the ruling of this Country. We found your tunnel, dug with a bucket and spade by the child that you are. Such an imaginative way of escaping your duty as one of Us."

The callous irony sails over my head. How can this be happening? My worst nightmare is becoming my reality. What will they do to me? I remember exploring the Emperor's mansion when I was a child. Discovering the hidden staircase. Hearing the screams.

"Where are my two darling granddaughters?" He refocuses my attention and I freeze, my bones warp and twist into icicles that pierce my heart. "You'll need some company in the dungeons."

I hoped he'd forgotten them, but he never forgets. Why can't he just take me and leave them alone?

"Willow and Maple, is it now? I must say, their Noble names were much more regal. Talemia and Amerina. They would have made fine leaders."

Leaders? Of what? A Country so corrupt it would rather watch children die than waste its food.

"Talemia might have even married the Emperor's heir. It's a shame their father is so… rebellious." He chooses his words carefully, scratching at the raw skin and biting into the wounds that only he knows exist.

"They're not here" I grunt through my teeth. Rubato cracks his knuckles and three men storm passed me into a cottage that I will never enter again. A small wave of relief that I was telling the truth washes over me. I couldn't bear it if they were ever to meet these men.

We stand in subdued silence; I avoid his gaze whilst he frowns at the dove shaped silver doorknob reflecting the June sunlight. The dove was the first ornament I crafted when the Resistance relocated me, every day it reminds me of why I keep on fighting, why I constantly put my life in danger for the sakes of others. The dove is defiance, it is rebellion, but most of all it is hope.

The three men emerge from the cottage shaking their heads and pushing me to one side as they conform to their default position. My father snarls like a wolf that has failed to catch his prey and turns to stare into my soul; his cold, unsympathetic eyes boring through me.

"Where are they?" He speaks softly but each word drips with threats. His voice is like a clay mask that is still wet with the paint of its intentions, and whose wearer still boasts of his vile personality through the mutated features. I watch him, silently showing nothing of the raging war going on inside of me. My face betrays only hatred as his nostrils flare and the muscles in his brow tense at my refusal to submit.

When I remain silent his temper fuses and the soft guise drips away, revealing a cruel, throat gargling shout that almost throws me backwards with its force.

"WHERE ARE THEY?" Sharp as razors, his words cut fear into my skin and every self-preserving bone in my body wants to tell him. Tell him that they're at the baker's in the village. Tell him that they're buying bread for the children in the slums whom he kidnapped a week ago and is currently starving to death. Tell him everything, just so he'll stop staring at me with those beady eyes that fire bullets into my heart and soul. But I don't tell him, I can't, and I mustn't.

That's when the first blow hits. It sends me sprawling on the ground and the corner of my face throbs, but I still won't answer his question. No matter what he does to me, I will never give him my daughters. More punches follow, each one striking fresh and cold. The Destructors are bloodthirsty and soon have me writhing and screaming on the cobbles. Blood plasters my face and I can do nothing to defend myself, nothing that won't cost me more blood.

Through my muted agony I battle to remember the cause. What I am fighting for. Why I long for a better future. However, my fear reminds me of what is to come. The chambers that scream and shake throughout the mansions, throughout the city that looms in pain. I remember the beatings I endured as a child. Even when I was one of Them my life was ruled by fear. Now? Now it will be much worse.

Black spots dance in the corners of my eyes and I shut them in fear that the hard wall behind them has cracked. Tears betray compassion. To them compassion is a weakness. For every weakness of mine, they have a strength. And every strength they can manipulate into a pain.

'Whatever you do,' I think to myself, a single thought shining small but strong in a foggy mental blur of unconsciousness 'don't cry'.

Chapter 1

A scream wakes me with a start and I open my eyes frantically, looking straight through the absolute darkness towards my small sister hyperventilating in her sleep. I swing my legs over the side of my bed, flinging the blankets onto the ground where they collapse in an untidy heap, and run to her, hardly noticing the cold floor searing my bare feet.

I reach her just before the tears start pouring down her soft cheeks, "don't go daddy" she mumbles "don't go".

Grasping her limp hand in mine, I whisper into her ear, her soft hair tickling my face. "Maple? May it's Willow here. It's alright, you're safe." Too soon I feel my own cheeks become wet and I collapse on the floor sobbing as hard as she is.

This night has always been a constant whirlwind of tears, a hurricane of grief that we will never outlive. Every year we weep together, remembering what happened those five long summers ago. May, asleep, trapped in a dream, unable to escape. Me, awake, kneeling by her bedside, clutching her hand as agonising memories plague my mind and refuse to subside.

My throat catches as the memory begins to unfold, trapping me in its cage until it has wrecked its havoc.

It was dad's birthday and Maple and I woke before dawn to bake him a cake. I was ten years old, she was seven and we were bouncing with excitement as we arranged it on the elegant tray that I had made for him from the wood of a willow tree.

The tray was my greatest achievement, cut from the bark of the tree with ridges and rings already embroidered by nature. Using a sharp knife, a kind lady from the village had helped me to engrave the tray with the outlines of extinct animals, my father's obsession.

Circling the outside of the tray lay an array of extinct land mammals, leopards, lions, tigers, pandas and more beautiful creatures of the past chased each other in a never-ending circle. Further in, there was a smaller ring of extinct sea creatures; dolphins, whales and beautiful fish almost jumped off the wood. Inside this was an even smaller circle of long gone birds; eagles, hawks, blue-tits and crows were frozen in mid-flight. Finally, in the centre of the tray, with his head held high and his ruffled tail feathers streaming behind him, a dove took his prime position, his beak stretched open as though he was singing and his eyes shining with peace.

I stared at it, proud of my amateur achievement but even more proud that it was to be a gift to my father. My fingers lingered for a second on the intricate carving of the dove before I carefully placed the chocolate sponge on top of it. The chocolate had been hard to find, it had cost almost all of my cleaning money and had taken weeks to arrive, but one look at the sweet brown squares told me that it was worth it, just the knowledge that it was for dad made it worth everything it cost, and more. Maple carefully went to lay her delicate, handmade locket beside the cake on the tray, but before it could touch the wood, I took it from her.

The silver chain glistened in the dawn sunlight as it dangled from my fingers, hanging in the shape of a maple leaf and painted in the glorified colours of autumn. My fingers traced the beautiful patterns as I sought out the clasp, where inside the locket lay a hand drawn picture of Maple and I. I gasped at its delicacy, talent incredible in a child so young. Staring out of the image were two, blissful faces, grinning with a girlish delight. My blonde hair hung loose over my bony shoulder whereas May's was tied in two graceful plaits that draped over her elegant body. Our bright blue eyes and rounded lips highlighted our similarities, but her frame was smaller, lighter and more dainty, her cheekbones more rounded and my collarbone more prominent.

The picture was a representation of our life and our happiness, with my arm draped around May's shoulders, holding her close, an eternal promise never to let her go.

"It's beautiful" I gasped, filled with so much pride and love that I was lost for words as I placed it on the tray.

Arm in arm, we made our way up the stairs to dad's bedroom on the east wing of the cottage, walking past the uncountable number of wooden animal sculptures that lined the pale green walls; rabbits, otters, frogs, blackbirds and hundreds more decorated the peaceful country cottage that was our home.

Without knocking we strode in to dad's room singing 'Happy birthday' out of tune at the tops of our voices. He sat bolt upright in bed, his stripy night cap hanging wonkily, but his initial confusion soon softened into a smile as he saw us laden with the cake and his presents. He laughed, a loud booming laugh that was energetic and melodic, as if he longed to make the wooden animals lining the cottage walls chuckle with him.

We sat at the foot of his bed, gorging on cake for breakfast as he examined the locket and the tray. He took the locket first, smiling at the picture inside of it before clasping it silently shut and carefully hanging it around his neck. As he studied the tray, his fingers traced each individual animal. I silently hoped that he wouldn't notice the wonky stripes on the tiger, or the hawk's oddly shaped beak, but when he finally looked up his eyes were brimming with pride.

"Thank you" He whispered, his voice catching on a stray tear. "They couldn't be more perfect."

We sat smiling, silent and blissful. The moment stretched for several seconds and the quiet was open and welcoming. Father smiled, his beam filling the room, enveloping Maple and I in his love and comfort as peace flooded the cottage, and we were a family, enthralled in togetherness that would, so it seemed, never unravel.

A loud knock on the front door pulled us out of our serenity. I grinned, volunteering immediately to receive our visitor and skipping along the corridor overflowing with childish energy, almost violently pulling open the creaky oak door.

"Willow!" Laughed a familiar voice.

"Sokk!" I exclaimed, thrilled to see our old friend. "Dad's in his room, he'll be excited to see you. How are you? Where have you been? What have you been doing?" My questions didn't leave a gap long enough for his answers as we leapt up the stairs and into dad's bedroom.

"Happy birthday Moss!" Sokk grinned as dad leapt out of bed to embrace his best friend, not at all self-conscious of his faded blue pyjamas that were now smeared with chocolate. "It's great to see you! Please sit down, the girls have made a cake!"

Sokk remained standing and looked towards me and May slightly awkwardly, suddenly seeming stiff and serious as he gave father a meaningful glance.

"Willow, Maple, why don't you go outside and play in the garden for a while?" Dad instructed, tension suddenly hidden in his voice.

Under our father's stern stare, Maple and I crept from the room, worried, but more curious as we sat on the stairs and pressed our ears to the door. However, nothing other than hushed, inaudible whispers penetrated the thick cottage walls, and we soon started playing pretend with the wooden pussycats who purred on the shelf above our heads.

After what seemed like an eternity, father and Sokk emerged from the room; but our plaguing questions about their private discussion were returned with a smile curling on Sokk's lips, as he tapped his nose and laughed. "If you knew everything there would be nothing to discover".

We sat in the living room as the morning idled itself away. Sokk and father chatted endlessly like old friends always do, whilst May and I tried to distract them with hyperbolic stories about the cove we had discovered on the beach that week.

As the sun seeped through the transparent window panes, dad sat back in his old wooden rocking chair, and with a smile reclining on his face, his eyes lulled shut.

"He's a brave man." Sokk whispered, almost to himself "and he loves you so very much". I smiled, not really understanding what he meant, and continued to chatter about the secret cavern that collected all our dreams.

Chapter 2

The sun was glittering brightly across the grassy stretch of garden as we sat around an old, hand carved wooden table. Simple sandwiches and homemade lemonade comprised our lunch, as Sokk and father laughed over memories that Maple and I were too young to remember.

After we had finished, Sokk suddenly stood up, pushing his wooden chair backwards so forcefully that it sounded like grinding teeth as he glanced at the ornate metal watch tied to his wrist.

"I have to go." He announced, hurriedly. "But thank you for lunch and I hope to catch up again soon." He darted out of the back gate, and heading down towards the silvery-sanded beach, his footsteps sent up little clouds of dust on the road in his wake.

"Why does he always disappear like that?" I sighed.

"It's not fair. He hardly ever visits us, and when he does he only ever stays for a couple of hours." Piped May.

Dad smiled knowingly, "Sokk is a busy man" He held out his arms for May, who obediently sat on his knee and rested her head in the crook of his neck. His arms wound around her small, elegant frame as I reached out my hand to stroke her long, tangled hair. For a moment, we were silent. A symbol of contentedness that was so true and perfect it was almost fictional.

Later that afternoon, when the sun's scorch had become too strong to even consider sitting outside, the high, shrill bell of a phone pulled us out of our respective daydreams in the nostalgic living room. Grasping the long cord that wound round the room, the metal receiver flew into my palm and immediately the desperate voice of Jenter Rintle squeaked out of it.

"We've found them" He almost wept "we've found the children."

My blood turned cold.

The children. The children who vanished from our little seaside village more than two weeks ago. The three year olds who made the villagers weep with their absence and the nine year olds who brought deep anger into the hearts of their parents. The children constantly targeted by the Nobles for the purposes of training exercises or human culls. The children of the slums.

"When?" I gasped. "Where?"

"Last night there was a blaze in the sewers, they had set a fire." His voice grew more urgent, more strained, as if the tone would affect the speed at which we rescued them.

"In the sewers?"

"The cavern the sewers lead to, near the river, they were tied to the ceiling with the water rushing just beneath their heads. But they're starving. They haven't eaten in over two weeks and they're trapped on the other side of a small crevice that none of us can squeeze through to give them anything." His voice was desperate, wrought with guilt and regret.

"I'll go," I whispered. "I'll be small enough."

I felt a firm grasp on my arm and turned to see my father, glaring down on me with serpent's eyes. "You will not" he barked, so fiercely I gasped.

"Please," I begged. "I won't try to free them. I know it's dangerous. But let me take them food. We can't let them starve to death!"

Slowly, he began to relax, and his paternal, overprotective shield disintegrated. A part of me almost felt like he was proud of me and my stubborn selflessness.

"Take May with you. His grudging agreement came with the sound knowledge that I would sacrifice any rescue attempt to protect my sister. "We will gather a full team of experts and rescue them later. There is no need to jeopardise your own safety. Do you understand?"

"Fine," I grunted "I'll buy a loaf of bread, climb through the crevice, and feed them."

"Nothing else?"

I stared up into his earnest eyes, that brimmed with worry and concern. "Nothing else." I promised.

I kissed him on the cheek as he fumbled in his wallet for money to buy the bread. He smiled, and handed me a crumpled note, now calm in the certainty of my vow.

"We'll be back before dark." I grinned, taking May's small hand in mine as we walked down the corridor lined with sculptures that seemed to beam a brilliant light, encouraging us as we left the small cottage and turned onto a smooth tarmac lane.

A thick mob of trees was all that separated the cottage and the village. Lush, green willows shielded us from the sun whilst maple trees, that in autumn turned the road into a sea of fiery leaves, towered high above; and moss, the smell fresh and clean with every breath, covered the rocks along the roadside in a warm, dreamlike blanket.

The trees faded away as the village materialised. May ran to retake my hand as our shoes scuffed against the dirty road, summoning little clouds of dust around our ankles. The streets were barren, and the sun glared down on villagers, tirelessly working. Most people fished in the reclusive sea, where they would stay until long past nightfall. The elderly clung to the business' that barely survived in the poor economy; and the children scavenged for whatever they could find to provide their daily bread.

We walked past the golden gates of the only red bricked, wealthy house in the village, where May and I worked almost every day of the year cleaning, polishing and wondering why some had so much and others had nothing. Finally, we reached the paved village square, surrounded by shops facing inward towards a large, gleaming screen that now my eyes avoided.

Maple skipped excitedly towards the bakery, pushing open the old wooden door and darting towards the sweet smell that forced us to pause for a moment, inhaling the freshly cooked bread.

Loaves were stacked high on each wall of the small shop, as many as possible crammed into the tiny space. Some were fresh and still warm from the fire which brought them into this world, perhaps a little charred and blackened at one end, but still thick and fulfilling. Others were old and stale, pleading one final time to be bought before they met their doom.

May reached for a long, thick baguette, barely relinquishing her hold on it as I paid the old baker who grinned at her childish excitement.

Together, we heaved it down the small hill to the mouth of the Pergi river. However, as we saw it, I stopped. Horrified. Frozen by the torrent of water.

"It's so high." whispered Maple beside me, her hands trembling as they clutched the bread.

"They might have drowned." My voice cracked as I hastily searched for the crevice between the rocks and struggled through, Maple on my heels.

"NO!" I yelled, looking back at her, "It's not safe." Thankfully, she reluctantly retreated as I lifted myself into the cavern.

Cold water lapped around my bare ankles as my eyes slowly became accustomed to the gloom and my ears began to search for inevitable cries.

"Help." a faint whisper. "Help."

Stumbling, I began to run towards the sound.

"Help. Help!" the voice was becoming more and more desperate.

I reached the child just in time to stop her falling into the water as the rope tying her to the roof of the cavern snapped. She dropped lightly into my arms, her starving stomach growling beneath my fingers and her skin so pale it was almost reflective in the darkness. Setting her on the ledge, she immediately collapsed, shivering.

"Where are the others?" I demanded.

Her trembling finger pointed towards the centre of the cavern where coarse ropes hung from the rocky ceiling and wound around the pale legs of a huddle of young children, their heads dangling just above the fast-flowing water.

Forgetting my promise, I delved into my pocket for my knife. Cutting the ropes that bound the girl who was now shivering on the ledge, I fastened them around my own waist and tied the other end to a rock, before I lowered myself into the swirling water.

Taking slow, even steps I made my way to the place where fifteen children hung on the verge of death.

Fifteen children all dying because they were from the slums.

Because the Nobles believe that the only way to vanquish poverty is to kill the poor.

Chapter 3

I slashed at the ropes with my pocket knife and dragged each child individually to the ledge, completing disregarding my promise to dad, these children needed saving, not just feeding.

Some were unconscious, and I carried them in my arms, others clung to my clothes, afraid of the endless tunnels but longing to embrace the welcomed daylight, desperate for release from the cavern.

On the emerald green bank Maple was sat waiting patiently, lost in thought as she stared into the river. Her mind was briefly visiting the beautiful paradise of childhood, where the sun is neither too hot nor too cold, and peace is the only word used to describe the gentle valleys and tumbling streams.

"May." I panted as I pushed the first child through the crevice.

She rushed to my side and together we lay the children on the ground, some were finally beginning to regain consciousness as their eyes flashed open for a few seconds before collapsing again into a dreamless exhaustion.

"How could the Nobles do this?" Maple's gentle voice was almost inaudible. "They're only children."

"Only children." I murmured. "Just like you and me." A silent, morbid tear ran down Maple's rosy cheek, and dripped onto the pale hand of a young boy. His eyes flickered like a faulty bulb, first confused, then afraid.

"Don't worry" I soothed, stroking the palm of my hand against his forehead "We're going to take you home."

His expression softened but he was still wary of me. He couldn't be more than ten years old, the same age as I was, though his cheeks were sallow, and his bony legs looked as if they could hardly support his weight.

"What's your name?" Asked Maple, her long hair falling from her shoulders to tickle his arm.

"Hantern" The boy stammered, as if the information requested was an order that he would be punished for withholding. "Hantern Whisker." He paused for a moment as fumbled memories began to dance in his mind. "What happened?"

"What do you remember?" I said, kneeling on the ground beside him.

"We...we were playin' in the fields behind the market, by our shacks. We were playin' hide an' seek, but then...then we couldn't find Bop. We all split up to look for him an' I had to look in the forest wit' Junce, my best friend," He raised his arm, gesturing to one of the boys lying near the river before the effort caused his arm to collapse and plummy to the grass by his side. "An' Fetha, my sister." He pointed to the girl who had been pleading for help in the cavern "It was horribly cold in the forest an' real eerie. As we were lookin' for him it felt like someone was followin' us but we knew it wasn't Bop, he'd be laughin' all of the time. I heard a scream comin' from the field an' we all started running, well I thought we all had but when I looked Junce had disappeared. Thankfully I still had Fetha with me, I knew she was there 'cause I could hear her pantin'. We stopped to rest behin' some logs but before we'd even sat down on the soil Fetha'd vanished, I was really scared that I might disappear too, so I headed back to the field." His face suddenly lost all of its energy and excitement at telling the story. Instantly sombre and grave.

"I got to my feet but as soon as I found the path I was frozen. There was a massive man, his arms were really muscular an' he had red blood on his hands, an' a huge sack. Then, I heard the screamin'. The sack seemed to move and writhe and through the opening in the top I heard someone shoutin' and I knew the voices. I heard Bop, an' Junce, an' Fetha; all three of them were in the sack but there was still room for one more. The horrible man smiled at me an' all 'is teeth were black, then, he lunged towards me so quickly I didn't have the chance to run. He grabbed my arm an' picked me up as if I were a pebble and stuffed me into the sack.

"I landed right on top of Bop and Junce but luckily Fetha moved out of the way. She was turned away from me an' the torn rags on her back were all I could see of her." The boy's voice became quiet and sensitive." '. Fetha?' I whispered. She slowly turned to face me, and I saw bruises coverin' her cheeks. 'Fetha?' I was cryin' then but she comforted me even though she was the one in pain.

"The sack jolted as the horrible man swung it around, we had no idea where we were goin' no idea who these terrible men were; the fabric of the sack was thin an' had holes in it, I managed to glue my eye to one. The horrible man was takin' us through the forest to this riverbank, when we arrived here he chucked us on the floor an' unfastened the strings that kept us in the sacks. We were plannin' to make a run for it but we were caught an' tied to a post and before we could even scream for help, our mouths were gagged. More children arrived in sacks, I recognised some of them, but I'd never seen most of 'em before in my life. Once we were all here, one of the horrible men moved that great big stone away and we were forced to go into that terrible cavern. Then, we were tied to the ceiling and left there, all on our own, to starve to death." His voice became stressed and agitated. "The water started risin' and it looked like we were going to drown. Most of us had given up 'ope of rescue, but Fetha, she never gives up. Every day for the past two weeks she shouted all day and night for someone to help us, an' it looks like someone did. "He beamed, his face filled with thankfulness and freedom fuelled energy as the baguette was passed to his lips. Savouring each morsel of dry bread, his eyes closed as he remembered his last meal that stood far back in the distance of time.

By the time Hantern had finished, most of the children were awake and sitting on the pea green grass around him, engrossed in his description of what they had experienced. The small Fetha wandered over, her body swaying slightly like a leaf in the wind as she walked and sat on her brother's lap. He began to stroke her scarred cheek that was half hidden by a fountain of wispy brown hair.

"Can we go home?" Asked a small, frail child; large, earnest brown eyes glazed over and worry lines creasing her forehead.

"Yes" I said after a long pause where silence grew into expectation, doubt, and fear "The Destructors will never play the same trick twice."

"The Destructors? Was it them?"

I nodded slowly. "I think so. The Destructors and Rebato Antario."

Antario, the first and most honoured of the seven Nobles, the highest ranking official besides the Emperor, and the leader of the fourteen Destructors. We all knew of the Destructors, their cruelty left evidence strewn across the

Country and blasted across the Screens of every town and village, to threaten the public into submission to the Nobles. Each of the seven Nobles trained their own menacing tribe, but Antario's was by far the most renowned and feared. They executed the 'important' commands.

We walked the now fed children, home to their dusty hovels where they were embraced by many relieved parents. Tears streamed from anxious eyes as Maple and I withdrew from the reunion, conscious of the slow falling dusk.

"Dad's going to kill us, isn't he?" Maple said as we walked slowly through the forest that now seemed ominous and haunting, towards home.

"Not us May. Me" I stared straight ahead, not daring to even glance at the impending trees to either side of me. "I should never have left you alone by the river. What if they had come back? You could have been killed, or worse!" There was no need to elaborate on what is worse than being killed. Where the Destructors are involved, death is a privilege.

"But I wasn't!" She argued, her voice becoming high pitched in frustration. "I'm fine, no I'm better than fine, I'm..."

"Shh." I cut her off harshly and pulled her to crouch beside me behind a large, moss covered rock, suddenly paralysed with blood curdling fear.

Only a few yards away from us sat the cottage, picturesque windows and dusty, red bricks had become the home that I had always adored. In front of the house, fifteen men clad in rough cloth so black that it disregarded the sunlight, were beating something.

One of the men stood a head taller than his comrades. He did not join his friends in the bloodbath, but instead glared down his pointed nose at his minions, supervising. Maple pressed close into my side as we watched in horror.

Roberto Antario. Snarling, almost elegantly as he relished in the pain and cruelty before him. Roberto Antario and his notorious minions. The Destructors.

Chapter 4

The next thing I remember is the sight of the limp, unconscious frame of my father dragged into a foreboding van the colour of pain. I screamed and tried to run after him as the van drove into the distance, but two anonymous arms restrained me, pulling me away from my perfect life that was rapidly vanishing into the mountains.

Dropping to my knees, the grip loosened as my eyes wept fat tears of fear, remorse and above all, loss. As the pool around me spread wider, I realised that it had three sources, my red, groggy, eyes, those of my sister, and I glanced upwards to see a third pair staring at the ground, fighting grief that was just too strong to withhold. Sokk.

It was the first time I'd seen a grown man cry. I admired it. The outburst of emotion that he had the bravery to display. In his sorrow, I felt stronger, understanding for the first time that weeping was not a weakness, but a strength. Another small, emotional act of rebellion against the Nobles.

"Come inside." Sokk whispered, grasping our hands and half dragging us towards the cottage. However, as we reached the house I froze and shook once again at the sight of thick, red bloodstains smearing the cobbles, the silver dove-shaped doorknob lying on the floor by my feet, scarred, but still intact. Slowly bending down, I held it in the palm of my hand, clutching it so hard my skin turned white.

Silently, Sokk opened the blood-soaked, oak door and we somehow managed to tread over the red threshold. I tiptoed along the familiar corridor as if it were an unknown place where danger might leap out of every corner. The wooden animals seemed to stare at us accusingly, their delicate smiles now menacing and cruel.

We reached the main, sitting room, that only that afternoon had been a place of laughter and bliss, but was now morose and foreboding, to find the fragments of a wooden dove, scattered across the floor.

I remained in the doorway, not daring to step into a place that was once a haven but would now be remembered forever as a room of fear and loss.

"Run upstairs and take one possession each." Sokk's voice was toneless, orderly and instructive. "I want you back here in five minutes, prepared to say goodbye to this life."

Maple clasped her hand in mine and we obediently climbed the steep and sorrowful stairs. The wooden animals, still on their delicate shelves, now seemed to stare remorsefully, as if they knew what was to take place over the following months and years of our lives and pitied us for it.

The door at the end of the corridor swung open with the lightest, trembling touch of my hand on the doorknob as the small bedroom that May and I shared loomed vast and distant before us. The room seemed to sway after each step that I took towards the makeshift dresser, where my fingers fumbled for the delicate silver ribbon that dad gave me for my birthday that year. May shakily walked to the trembling bunk beds, stacked like papers up against the far wall, and stroked the patchwork quilt before grasping the small, threadbare, teddy that had been given to her two years ago by a little boy on his deathbed.

The child had been no more than five years old. Sick with an easily curable disease, but the Nobles decree it illegal to use, or be in possession of, medicine, unless of course you are a Noble yourself. His parents had accessed an illegal network of secretly trained doctors and were travelling home from a remote farming town in the west with the precious medication vital for the survival of their only child, when they were stopped, searched, and shot.

Father, Maple and I took the child to an apple green field, decorated with playful flowers, and as he lay there in the last moments of his life, he was smiling. Handing Maple the small teddy bear, he told her that its name was Furr and she had to keep him safe "forever".

Sokk met us at the foot of the stairs and led us past the wooden sculptures that now looked on tenderly, a remorseful farewell that would render tears in their eyes if they were capable of crying. As we left the cottage the sun shone harshly and uncomfortably bright, and the bloodstains beneath my feet now seemed distant, a part of another life.

"Where are we going?" I asked, trying to conceal the fear in my voice.

"Somewhere safe." Sokk replied, protectively as if now he had assumed the role of our father. "Where They can't find you"

Sokk led us through the bottle green forest, where we would never again wander with excitement in our eyes, and energy in our steps, and through the back streets of the dusty village. We followed him down the winding ramp to the golden beach, and walking faster now, he brought us to the sea's front. The day had been long and tiring, and the water looked inviting as I briefly fantasised about delving underneath the cold ocean, but as the cool waves lapped around our ankles Sokk rapidly turned, and strode along the ocean line.

To the far left sat a small cove, shielded from the rest of the beach by a solid, rock wall that rose upwards to become the stubborn face of a cliff. A proud array of rocks, smoothened by constant erosion from the sea stood guard at the entranceway, claiming the cove as their own. As Sokk finally paused for a short moment, Maple and I collapsed, exhausted, our bodies crumbling on the sun-baked stones. He smiled at us sympathetically, before turning to face the solid wall of rock.

Sokk began to run his finger across one section of the cliff face and a small crack that was mostly hidden before, began to materialise. Tugging at the edges of the crack, he separated a large boulder from the rest of the mound, revealing a small, smooth tunnel within the rock face.

Before I could fully take this in, Sokk extended an arm to me, which I automatically took. Placing his strong arms around my waist, he hoisted me into the tunnel where I crawled forwards, afraid of tipping backwards and falling out. I felt Maple's fingers tickling my shoes as she was lifted in behind me, and at Sokk's command, I began to edge my way along the tunnel.

There was a scraping sound as the rock was replaced behind us and we were plunged into a darkness as black as the clouds before a storm.

All of a sudden, I felt alone and afraid. Where was I? Who was I? What was going on? I wanted to scream and shout. I needed to cry for my father, to shed my tears for the past, express my fear of the present, and demand an explanation for the future. But most of all, I was angry. An anger so fierce and alive that I longed to turn around, run the hundreds of miles to the Big City, and plunge a dagger into the Emperor's heart.

A bright shaft of light illuminated the tunnel ahead and dazzled my eyes for a moment, making me stop, almost afraid. Then, I began to crawl again, more quickly, desperate to reach the light, and the hope.

Finally, the tunnel opened up and the rock that was above me, forming the roof of the passageway, rose into obscurity so I could stand. Arching my back, I found myself perching on a narrow ledge above a vast cavern bathed in a gentle, azure light that touched the elegant stalactites hanging like mobiles from the ceiling. As I glanced downwards I saw, contrary to the vast, open space that I had imagined, a hectic workplace. Rooms with mechanical devices that I couldn't even begin to guess the use of, were divided by curtains hanging in brilliant white as people ran from room to room, busying themselves like bees in a hive. Before I could even begin to understand what was happening, I felt Sokk's hand on my shoulder as he gestured towards a ladder hanging from the edge of the small platform where we stood.

Once we were all safely settled on the ground, Sokk wasted no time in leading us through the maze of cubicles and machinery. The people we passed hardly noticed us as we were whisked into an almost bare room at the far end of the cavern.

The room contained three large chairs and a round table covered in an elegant, pale green cloth and presenting a plate of buttered bread. Staring at the food made me realise how hungry I was, and I involuntarily reached for it. My hand was half way through the air when I froze and glanced at Sokk, seeking permission.

"Go ahead." He laughed nervously, and within a minute, Maple and I were gorging ourselves.

After the plate had been emptied, Sokk gestured for us to sit on two of the three chairs. Exhausted we did so, though Sokk remained standing, anxiously looking down at his hands and biting his lip.

"Where are we?" Maple asked, as I ran my fingers through the knots in her blonde hair.

"This," Sokk replied, taking a deep breath "Is one of the many centres of the Resistance. The Resistance is a campaign for peace. We are preparing for a fight against the Nobles."

"A fight?"

"Your fathers arrest has forced us into more immediate action." He did not meet our eyes, but instead paced the room, the steady rhythm of his footsteps strict and formal, like a march.

I stared at him, confused and lost, unable to speak as my mind overflowed with questions.

"Children" Sokk began, his voice sombre and serious. "Rebato Antario is your grandfather."

Chapter 5

The silence of anticipation turned to one of shock as I struggled to hear and understand the words that had just come out of Sokk's solemn mouth.

"Your father was Roberto Antario's first son, his real name is Revicartus Antario."

Revicartus? The son of the first Noble? Married to the Emperor's daughter? Who the Nobles claimed had run away to join the evil forces against them? The man whose picture flashed on every 'wanted' screen across the country?

"How?" I mumbled so quietly, my voice was barely a whisper.

He stopped pacing, and stared at me, expectantly." Your nightmares, Willow. They're memories."

Dad had always dismissed them as dreams, figments of my imagination where my five-year-old self lurked crouching in the corner of a bare room, watching Malintaret, the Emperor's daughter, hurtling towards me with an iron mace in her hand. She swung it over her head and the next thing I knew was bright, white blinding pain. "Because I was talking to the servants." I whispered, a lump rising in my throat.

" Malintaret, is your mother."

The image of her luminous hair that is a different colour each time she appears in public; her painted teeth and nails filed like claws ready to kill, screeched across my mind.

My mother.

The overseer of the torture chambers and the most feared woman in the Country. "How?"

"Thirty years ago," Sokk began, finally slumping into the large wooden chair across from Maple and I. "Your father was a child, growing up in the house of the first Noble, Roberto Antario. Like the slaves who served him, he was born and brought up inside the walls of the Big City, with no opportunity to escape or witness the outer world."

There were always rumours circulating the Big City, the home of the Nobles and a place no one had ever both entered and escaped with their life. Within its walls, it was reported, lay a huge palladium of paradise where the seven Nobles each resided in their own mansion, with increasing finery the closer you were to the centre. It was supposed to be beautiful, with emerald green gardens and pools to dip your feet into during the summer heat waves; gems and jewels lining the streets and grand theatres and arcades, hospitals and schools, anything and everything to satisfy the Noble's slightest wish. The only City in the Country. The only place where luxury ruled over rags, where gluttony reigned over poverty, and where cruelty and selfishness were not only acceptable, but encouraged.

Sokk continued his story, hardly pausing for breath. "One of our women succeeded in creeping into the City, her goal to release, and escape with, the prisoners in the torture chambers. But she was caught and mistaken for a slave.

"Eventually, Menna was posted to work as your father's nanny. Unlike the other slaves, who had been trained to emotionlessly serve those above them, she was kind, and loving towards him. She also had the experiences that the other slaves lacked. She told him stories about the world outside the palace that he lived in. How the government oppressed people in the towns and villages, and how we all lived in fear for our lives. She exposed him to the knowledge of the massacre of thousands of children each year to prevent population growth; and your father became angry and upset, even more so when he learned of Menna's own story.

" When she was nine years old, her house was burned to the ground by the Nobles and her family were murdered. She had no choice other than to run. Angry and afraid, Menna wandered the countryside for weeks, almost delirious with grief and hunger. The child was almost dead when the Resistance discovered her unconscious body lying limp on the side of a road." Sokk stopped, staring sadly at the floor, as if he had forgotten that he was supposed to be speaking aloud. Finally, he lifted his head and sat back in his chair, attempting to relax as he continued the story. "We took her in, and relocated her with a new identity in a new home, and when Menna was old enough she began to work closely with the Resistance, to avenge her family.

"Your father was ten years old when the Nobles discovered who Menna really was. She was arrested, dragged away from the child she had mothered from infancy, and her face appeared on the Screen that month, drowned in a tank filled with blood."

Tears tickled the corners of Sokk's eyes as the harsh sting of the memory penetrated his heart.

"Did you...did you know her?" I stammered, longing for some gentle words to comfort him.

"Yes." He paused for a moment, longing to reveal a guarded secret, but saying nothing, only blinking rapidly and staring at the empty plate on the small table.

There was a thick silence as each of us were lost in our own grief. Maple and I finally began to understand this new world that we found ourselves in, heavily accepting the pain that would remain with us forever.

"Your father," Sokk continued, almost to himself "was so distressed by her death that he promised himself he would act upon her testimony and change the devastating conditions outside of the Big City.

"Time wore on and at seventeen, he was forced to marry Malintaret. She was a violent woman and saw children as an opportunity to rehearse her cruelty. Whatever you did or said she'd punish you; strike you, lock you in cages and cupboards. Your brother, Jamiant, died when she electrocuted him for coughing during one of the Emperor's speeches.

"Your father tried to protect you and your brother, but when Malintaret is angry there is no one who can stop her. Your Noble names are Talemia and Amerina, 'the Example Offspring'. You were used to show the Country how to deal with ignorant children." Sokk placed his hand on my arm and rolled up my sleeve to reveal a red scar that I had always thought was a birth mark. Now I saw a long, ugly, burn that stretched from my elbow to my wrist. "This, was screened across the Country" he whispered "a white-hot poker fastened to your arm for two days, replaced every hour."

"What did I do?" Bile rose in my throat.

"You stuck your tongue out at the Emperor." Sokk smiled weakly. "Your father had had enough. He spent the next three months secretly digging a tunnel underneath the electrified fence behind the Big City. One night, he ran away with you, and fleeing the Nobles chasing him across the Country, he finally discovered a Resistance base."

Pain and emotion hit me as if I were a punch bag, the object of someone else's anger. I felt betrayed. Why had no-one told me before? My own father lied to me about who he was. Who I was.

Who was I?

I didn't know who I was, even my name was not my own. Could I really have been born from people I hated? For if I was, then surely, I must hate myself, for being one of them.

"It took us a long time to trust him," Sokk's tone was edged with regret, "but he gave us important information, taught us to read and write so we could intercept Noble files, and became one of our closest workers. We relocated you here, and the two of you were injected with a serum that cleared your earliest memories, however it wasn't strong enough to permanently eliminate the pain." He glanced at me, and I met his eyes with an empty expression. "Since that time, the Nobles have been unaware of your hiding place."

"Until now." I murmured.

"Until now."

We sat in silence for what seemed like an eternity, Maple was weeping, with fat, seven-year-old tears rolling down her pale cheeks, but she made no sound.

I wanted to cry, to show some sign of emotion, but I couldn't. The tears wouldn't escape my eyes. They sat trapped inside of me, not daring to believe that they were required. It felt almost like a dream. Soon I would wake up and it would be this morning again. We would eat chocolate cake and laugh on dad's bed, Sokk would come, and stay for longer this time, and the nostalgic bubble would remain, and never burst.

This couldn't be real, it was too obscure, farfetched like the imaginary games that Maple and I played in the pea-green garden where everything was perfect.

"What happens now?" Maple stammered, sounding suddenly mature, as if she'd grown up several years in the last few minutes.

"We're going to Relocate you".

After another empty silence, Sokk cleared his throat. "Firstly, we're going to change you visually." Two women strode into the room, as if on cue, and stood either side of Sokk. "Maple," He gestured to the smiling woman on his left, "This is Glondina. And Willow," He nodded at the woman who perched on his right, with long red hair plaited and hanging over her shoulders. "This is Detti. These are our surgeons, they are going to change your appearance."

A surge of fear rose up within me and I grabbed Maple's hand, determined never to let her go.

"She'll still be your sister when you see each other again." Sokk smiled, calmly.

Maple stood up, releasing my hand. She smiled naively up at Glondina as I watched them skip through a small door that lead further into the depths of the cavern.

A few moments later, Detti and I followed her. We walked slowly through the hundreds of rooms and my heart began to race as I realised I was now alone, away from Sokk and Maple, the only people remaining who I could feel safe with.

I was shown into a bleached cubicle and sat upon what looked like a hospital examination bed. A tall, slender man clad in loose, white clothing with a clinical mask covering the lower part of his face walked towards me, carrying a large syringe full of dark green liquid. His rough hands gripped my arm and a gradual numbness was released through my body.

Chapter 6

When I woke up I couldn't remember where I was, instead of sleeping on a narrow bunk bed in a room with pale blue wallpaper patterned with faded flowers, I found myself lying on a double bed in a small, white washed room with no windows.

Then, everything flooded back, like a wave of pain that made me wish that I could have remained forever in the previous moments of oblivion.

Shaking now, I climbed to the edge of the bed, only to freeze when I caught sight of a stranger in the mirror.

Relocation. I didn't quite understand what Sokk had meant before, but now it was painstakingly clear.

My hair, which had once been long and blonde, was now died chestnut brown and cut untidily half way down my back with a full fringe covering my forehead. My skin seemed paler than it had been, and my lips were thinner, with a subtler, peach-coloured tone, sitting on a more rounded face. My shoulders were broader, and my body seemed thicker, small rolls of fat under the skin on my arms and legs. I looked more ordinary, less like the short, twig with hair constantly knotted and a smile which was bright and childish, and more like just another child in just another village, nothing special or different about me, one of a hundred identical faces.

Slowly, I lifted one hand to my face to reveal my stretched fingers and the unfamiliar pattern of my palm.

Every part of my body had been pulled, twisted, and moulded; my nose, ears, even my elbows seemed less bony than they had been. I was different, strange and not my own, everything changed except for my eyes; they remained bright, blue, and shining. The burn also still stretched across my arm, paler but still painfully visible. Too strong and embedded to eradicate.

Draped over one corner of the mirror was a dark green, long sleeved dress. The material felt soft in my arms as I fitted it onto my new body, it hung to my knees and clung to my waist and hips, so I looked older. I was uncomfortable as I sat on the soft blankets on the bed, trapped and alone in the strange surroundings and my new body. I felt anonymous. No one on this earth would recognise me now. Even dad wouldn't know who I was. My heart twinges as his memory passes through my mind, and I bite my lip as my artificial cheek feels the sharp wetness of its first tear.

Sometime later, I heard five short, sharp taps on the door. Recognising the rhythm from childhood games May and I used to play, I leapt to the door and opened it on a little girl.

"May?" I asked looking for some sign of identification in her unrecognisable. 'relocated' body. Then, she removed the dark rimmed glasses that framed her face and I came to stare into the only part of this May that I knew. Her eyes, like mine, remained unchanged, bright blue, and glittering.

Her once blond hair was now the same chestnut shade as mine, but where mine draped untidily down my back, hers was cut to frame her slightly sharper face. Her lips were redder, and she seemed taller, her fingers slightly more slender and her legs longer. Once she had looked youthful with puppy fat protecting her body; but now it had been replaced by a graceful elegance that disregarded her age and made her look far older than she actually was.

She threw her arms around me and I held her close, becoming reacquainted with my little sister and my best friend. It was some time before I heard her stifled sobs on my shoulder. The tears began to seep through the fabric of the dress as I carried her to the bed, trying my best to comfort the small, seven-year-old who had been through so much in the last twenty-four hours.

As I cradled her in my arms, I could only blame one person. It was Sokk who had brought us to this cavern which now felt like a prison. He had taken us away from our home and he had given the order for us to be morphed into these foreign creatures.

In a spurt of fiery rage, I marched out of the room to look for him. Maple, oblivious to my plan, ran into the corridor after me, but I could not turn around when she called me. I had to find him. What right did he have to cause so much havoc in our lives? May was only seven years old, afraid and lost in this new world of pain where she didn't belong. Why had he brought us here?

Running through the endless corridors I checked behind each door before I finally found him in what looked like a dining room. It contained a long table laden with all sorts of food that glared at me out of beady eyes. Sokk sat contentedly in the second wooden chair on the left side of the table happily eating what looked like a potato pie.

"Hello Willow." He said lightly, without even glancing up.

"Look at me." I growled darkly, standing opposite him on the other side of the table. "Look at me!"

He finally moved his attention from his plate and smiled. "Aren't they brilliant?" He chuckled to himself.

"I don't look like me anymore!"

"Of course you don't." Sokk still spoke calmly, the laughter gone from his voice. "If you looked anything like the way you used to, the Nobles would find you instantly." He grinned, and began once again to eat.

Slowly I began to understand, and as I relaxed, I was suddenly embarrassed. I slumped in a chair, and hastily grabbed a bread roll from the wooden bowl in the centre of the table, staring at my fingernails and biting my lip as May crept into the room, smiling nervously and perching on the wooden chair beside me.

After the meal Sokk lead us to yet another room in the maze of the cavern. Embedded deep within the rock face on the far left, this room was dim, illuminated by a lonely lamp that cast a weak glow, creating more dark shadows than it did useful light. It was crammed with bookcases and filing cabinets. The floor was littered with pieces of paper, and the centre of the room occupied by three large brown armchairs that Sokk hastily swept of dust which had settled upon them like a blanket of snow, creating just enough space to sit down. As May and I picked our way through the mounds of documents, searching with our feet for the sparse squares of carpet that acted like stepping stones through the sea of clutter, Sokk was rummaging through a draw, discarding useless manuscripts as he did so, and creating more mess.

Finally, he produced two large brown envelopes, handing one to each of us before he began to speak so quickly it was as if his words were competing in a race

"We are relocating you to a small town called Rente. It is in the heart of the Great Range"

"The Great Range?" May asked.

"Mountains. A range of mountains in the very centre of the Country. Inside of the largest mountain is the core base camp for the Resistance and most of the citizens living in Rente work with us so you will be well protected. Near the town, there is a factory that makes laser-eye guns for the Big City. I have contacted them and they will be happy to take on two more children."

Guns? Why would they make weapons of destruction for the people they were seeking to destroy? Surely the guns themselves would be used in turn to murder the Resistance.

"They produce guns to maintain our disguise. Who would suspect that a small town living plaintively in the countryside, creating valuable supplies for the Big City could be the cause of its undermining? We also have unlimited access to the weapons ourselves, though we prefer more peaceful methods of rebellion.

"You each have new identities. As well as your changes in appearance, your names are now Heather Will Nillon, and Clover May Nillon. You may tell people that you prefer to be called Will and May, and Willow and Maple can be nicknames, but never officially, or in earshot of anyone unknown. Your parents were shot in a Destructor training exercise and you will be living with your grandmother, Dothelle Nillon."

I opened my slightly creased envelope and took out an ID card, birth certificate, and several other documents and possessions that I would need to fabricate my new life. My fingers brushed a worn photograph of a couple who look like older versions of the new May and I. Our dead parents. Both had pale blue eyes and chestnut hair with delicate, frail, smiles that the slightest breeze might shatter. The man wore a large flat cap that covered most of his face in a dark shadow, and the women leant on an old wooden crutch, her dress caught in the wind, frozen in the photograph as it floated mid-air.

" Barnak and Jeena Nillon." Said Sokk, and after a short moment of staring at the tattered picture and wondering who these people really were, and what had become of them, I stood up and followed Sokk and May, who were already treading their way back through the jungle of litter, to our new life.

Chapter 7

The first shafts of light are now seeping through the window, illuminating the small bedroom that my sister and I share in a pale-yellow glow. The anniversaries' night of treacherous memories is over at last and May's sleeping frame has finally begun to relax. I Stroke her tearstained cheek and fight the urge to look away. I can't bear to see her so pained. Just the sound of her feeble whimpers torture me, knowing that I am powerless against the nightmares that terrorize her.

May has endured so much, but she's still too young, too sweet and innocent to be fit for the harsh world that she inhabits. I stroke the place where her heart has been torn to shreds and painstakingly taped back together again. But as I do, I remember once again that despite her youth and innocence, she is strong, so much stronger than I am.

When we first arrived in Rente, I sat alone in the corner of the dark and gloomy room for days, rocking forwards and backwards to the melody of the nightmare I had just lived, which would now never cease to torment me. As I sat, there, alone and too afraid to let anyone else in, it was little May who had organised our work, visited our neighbours, and spent hours each day trying to coax me out of my unresponsive state.

It took months for me to adjust to the new, unfamiliar surroundings, to enter into the strange community and be a part of the bustling and lively world that the townsfolk inhabited. But May held my hand and lead me through the pain and the heartache, urging me to break down the barriers of fear and grief and participate in what I now know to be a joyful, encouraging community overflowing with lifelong friends and humble, undying loyalty. After five years in the town's welcoming arms I can almost pretend I've forgotten. May is twelve, growing up far too quickly and my fifteen years make me feel as if I have lived a century, yet still a millennium lies before me. Our world is quiet, soft and quaint, and we are almost happy, working towards a life that values only love and peace, living in a utopian bubble of hope that defeats and replaces the darkness.

I look out of the window, over the rooftops of our friends and neighbours and smile. We have both come to love this town, it is full of honest people who base their lives on kindness and forgiveness. They believe in Someone with a pure heart and beautiful soul who loves them, and many years ago died for their freedom. No matter who you are or what you have done, He will forgive you, and refresh your life. And when you die, those who believe in, and trust in Him will live forever, in joy and peace.

As I kneel at May's bedside, she starts shivering. Her face creases as her dreams enslave her to more fear, hurt, and confusion. I pull her head to my chest, and hold her tight, rocking her like a baby, soothing her as if my feeble whispers in her ear could defeat all of the hatred and cruelty attacking her mind. Quietly, I begin to sing the slow, comforting lullaby that father would always sing to us in his gentle, baritone voice when we cried. Now, the simple tune and lyrics seem like our only shred of hope. The only chance that we have of survival in a world where danger lurks in every corner.

"Someday soon, your worries will be forgotten,
On that day, there will be no more pain,
On that day, no harsh words will be spoken,
Someday soon, you will smile again.

And the dove, will signal the revolution,
With feathers as white as snow.
He will sing his song to restore our freedom
His love, and peace we all shall know."

May leans on the headboard of the bed, her brilliant blue eyes now awake, glittering in the pale dawn light. A contagious smile links with mine as she grasps my hands to sing the final verse as a duet of optimism.

"Someday soon, there'll be an emerald green meadow,
On that day, brooks will laugh whilst children play.
On that day, there will be no more sorrow,
Someday soon, your worries will fade away."

We laugh, releasing what we can of the ensnaring pain before the moment withers and the reality of the nightmare returns. May's small, sharp mouth now smiles weakly, before she bursts into a fresh bout of sobs and buries her small face in my shoulder.

It's not long before I feel a reassuring hand squeezing my shoulder, Grandma Dothy stands behind me, smiling encouragingly, but remaining silent; respecting our need to suffer through each thought.

When I first met the elderly woman, I was cold and unfriendly, frustrated that we were not allowed to live by ourselves and determined to survive without any help or care. May on the other hand, loved her, jumping into her inviting arms and embracing her new grandmother who would guide her through the rest of her childhood. I was almost jealous of the old lady. It had always been just me and May, we had each other. Dothy had stolen my precious sister away from me and I hated her for it, resenting how she pottered around her little house, clanging her pots and pans together and filling the endless silence where I wanted to mourn and wallow without the never-ending torrent of meaningless noise.

As I remember, a surge of guilt rushes through me, for now I realize how kind and loving Grandma Dothy is. Sokk couldn't have chosen a better old woman to take care of us than the small, round lady with plump, rosy cheeks and a stubborn smile that is both joyful and comforting. She never hesitates to give, and is prepared for any crisis, no matter how large or small. She spends her days knitting and baking for people in the community, visiting the sick, sweeping the roads, and sacrificing her time and energy to the whole town which would come to a complete standstill without her loving kindness. Never in my life have I met anybody as selfless as Dothy, and I doubt my path will ever cross someone like her again.

Today she is wearing a long, colourful, floral skirt with an off-white apron. Her faded blue slippers match her cleanly ironed blouse and her grey hair is pinned into a lose bun that has already permitted a few stray hairs to escape its haphazard binds. Her face is angelic, smiling despite the lines of worry and care that crease her forehead as the seconds of stillness stretch into minutes, and the gentle light of dawn floods the room, bathing us in its soft comfort.

The small, ancient, alarm clock that usually wakes us from our deep dreamless slumber now wrenches us out of our melancholy trance and sets us into the slow, robotic motions of preparing for yet another backbreaking day at the factory.

Somehow dressed in my plain, bleakly grey oversized shirt and creased, dull matching trousers - the standard, Noble approved uniform for all factory workers across the Country, - May and I silently trudge down the stairs and into the floral, brightly-lit kitchen, an almost incomprehensible contrast with our life-draining attire.

Neither of us can eat breakfast and so, clutching our small lunch boxes, made lovingly by Grandma Dothy, we head out of the house to face the three-mile stagger to the bleak, foreboding factory.

I look at May's weak frame and wonder once again why she must spend each day in a dusky room, and not playing on the green mountain slopes outside as children should. But the law recited at the beginning of each working day echoes around my mind in response:

'All citizens from the age of seven to seventy must be employed unless they possess a EOD (Exclusion of Occupation Document). Unemployment is a punishable offence, facing the challenger with thirty lashes of a sharp tailed whip as a mandatory public display.'

EOD's are highly valued but agonizingly difficult to obtain, only granted to the terminally ill, and those considered a danger to the community. The rich are also exempted from the toils of employment for no reason other than the biased favouritism of the Nobles.

Arriving at the dark, greedy factory, a buzz encompasses the treacherous building. As workers gather in friendship groups, eager to trade local gossip and reminisce with each other about blissful times gone by in an attempt to distract themselves from their dismal situations, I can't help but want to scream at them for treating this ghastly day like any other.

Capturing my words before they explode from my lips, I remind myself that this is not their fault. They don't know how cruel today is, nor what heart-breaking deeds took place those years ago, that broke my soul and destroyed my life.

A low, deafening gong resounds, drowning out the noise and summoning silence. By the time the final remnants of the sound have vanished, the whole factory has undergone a change from light, friendly and cheerful; to grim, morose and sombre.

Chapter 8

The factory is divided into several large ominous buildings, each designated to the creation of a different type of gun. The buildings are separated into long, corridor like rooms with high arched roofs and sparse windows; shrouded in thin, grey curtains that shield those inside from any hope that the outer world might betray. Each room has a different duty in creating the gun and the workers in each room are determined by age, with the youngest and the eldest completing the easiest tasks, and the more physically able facing the treacherous, often life-threatening work.

Maple and I work in the Laser Gun building, creating weapons used by the Nobles to shoot victims in the eye with a poisonous gas that pushes a bright light into their brain, causing them to slowly turn blind and die. When we first arrived, May was put into the youngest group where she would spend her days feeding square slabs of metal through a blazingly hot iron. On her tenth birthday, she progressed to the following room, where, for two years now, she measures out the metal used to make the gun, pouring the molten liquid into delicate moulds.

Pecking me on the cheek, May runs to the stairs that lead to her workroom on the second floor of the 'Laser Gun' building, where already children from the ages of ten to thirteen are forming an orderly queue, waiting to be admitted for another day of perilous measuring and pouring. Stopping just long enough to disguise the raw emotion that accompanies today's anniversary, I smile bravely and make my way to the far side of the Laser gun building, wearing a mask that would impress the Emperor himself.

"Hello Will!" The optimistic face of my trusted friend smiles blissfully, her eyes glinting in the early morning sunlight.

"Hi, Sheil" I reply with as much enthusiasm as I can manage.

"How are you?"

"Ok thanks." I lie, speaking too quickly "and you?"

"Great thanks" Thankfully she hasn't notice the worry in my voice, or the catch in my throat. "Well, as good as anyone can be today."

"Why? What's happening today?" Panic stirs inside me as the words almost choke me, closing my throat as my imagination begins to explore the numerous terrors that this life might present.

"It's the Screening this afternoon." She recites, dutifully, as if she is frustrated with tirelessly having to remind me.

The Screening? A fresh bout of fear envelopes me as I sway with a sick, terrified emotion that sends rocks to the pit of my stomach like weights.

"Oh well," She sighs, unaware of the severity of this monthly terror, "at least we get the rest of the afternoon off." Sheil smiles annoyingly as she follows the throng of teenagers through the heavy iron doors.

Numbly, I pursue her into the long, dark room that smothers all talk with its silence. My stiff grey boots tread carefully around the shards of broken glass that litter the floor like stars in the sky as I take my place on the long, splinter ridden workbench which I will be forbidden to rise from for several hours.

A gong resounds, its commanding tone removing all hope of happiness for this day, ordering the factory to serve the Nobles without question. Our harsh overseer firstly recites the Law of Occupation, then commences to pace the room, forbidding anything other than subdued work under punishment of lashes by the long whip that hangs from his belt.

Here, we take charge of the red laser production with a fear-filled grasp. It is a dangerous job, given to young lives that are worth little to the Nobles, and results in at least fifteen deaths per year. I remember with a shiver that only last week a fourteen-year-old boy was electrocuted. As no one was allowed to leave their seat to drag him away from the dangerous machine, his heart stopped, and he lay dead on the workbench. Gone the next day. Never seen again.

The table in front of where I sit is covered in a sheet of white paper, for testing the lasers.

First, I take a long, thin silver piece of corrugated iron that has already been moulded into the shape of a long tube by another group. Too full of fear and grief to think and concentrate alone, I robotically imitate what those around me are doing, still relying on them for guidance after five years working here.

Firstly, I create the laser, filling the tube with a strange soft, dry material. Following that I place orbs of electricity that sit like little bombs threatening to explode, into it, embedding them in the cloth. When that is complete, a layer of glass is positioned on top of the substance, about half way up the tube.

I place a flat, clear circle of something burning hot on the surface of the glass, using tongs to settle it into its delicate position. Then, sealing the tube by carefully gluing a small square of iron to its rim, I shake it once to test the laser against the thick paper on the table. Satisfied with the burnt hole that is surrounded by charcoal black scorch marks, I pass the laser down the table towards a large, metal bucket where it is placed into one of the many compartments, waiting to travel to another room and be united with the other components of the gun.

I repeat the same process endlessly, losing track of time and not taking any care over what I am doing. The novelty of having such a dangerous task has long since worn off and, unlike the anxious newcomers into the group; I find it dull and lifeless.

Finally, the gong sounds once again, signalling lunch. Sheil, myself and a few other girls from the group head to the bank where we collapse on the polluted grass.

"I hate lasers." Angie declares.

"Quiet, they'll hear you!" Lise giggles, playfully, obviously not fully aware of the real consequences of being heard.

"I don't care! I've had enough of making murder weapons!"

Though the statement is a serious and punishable one, it is clear that the girls are joking. Despite my morose mood, the careless atmosphere has engulfed me, and I am soon laughing with them, relaxing in the glaring summer sunlight.

Opening my small, packed lunch, a wave of memories wash over me again, and I feel guilty about having spent the previous moments smiling.

Grandma Dothy has made a special effort with my lunch today, packing not only the usual barren sandwiches, but also a large, chemically grown apple and two small, dry biscuits. I eat the food slowly, but it's taste is lost on my tongue.

The afternoon gong that usually redirects us to hard hours of work, today sentences our formation in the bleak courtyard. Once assembled in age groups, we prepare to march to the town square where the dreaded Screening awaits us.

The factory lies three miles from the town, and it is a long and tiring journey. All nine hundred factory workers weave single file with fear fuelled discipline, as the terrors of what we will soon be forced to witness are absorbed into the minds of every man, woman and child who marches with their head forward and their eyes low.

For May, I, and any other families who have loved ones in the power of the Nobles, the fear is magnified as we brace ourselves to watch a helpless prisoner face slaughter by whatever means the Noble's see fit. Sometimes, it is over quickly, a hanging, or just a straight shot; but those kinds of death are rare. The Nobles prefer to use their warped imaginations to drag the murder out for longer, torturing not only the victim sentenced to death, but also the public.

When we reach the town square, we are given permission to disperse, and we rapidly dissipate into the thick crowd gathering below the large, silver screen in paralysing anticipation. Grandma Dothy runs towards me, holding the hand of a fear-stricken May with a lip bitten so hard that it bleeds. Clutching her hand, we stare at the screen with sickening nerves, praying that the face displayed to the whole Country, is not my father's.

Chapter 9

The town square is surrounded by soldiers who multiply in number as the emotionless murderers return from completing their rounds. Hand reared in the Big City, the soldier's sole purpose in life is to deliver a compulsory influx of fear to the citizens of the Country, or rather slaves to the Nobles - vulnerable guinea pigs, exploited and subjected to the tortures of the Big City. Attendance at the monthly screening is a mandatory event. Nobody escapes its cold grasp that serves as a constant reminder of the consequences of hope in action.

Every house is fully searched for any poor soul who may be hiding from the imperative horrors, even those so sick that they are unable to move are carried to the square. The punishment for not attending is a brutal, thirty lashes of the long, evil whip that remains at the side of the highest-ranking sergeant who now stands on the tall platform before the screen, every so often, slicing his weapon randomly through the crowd.

After a solemn nod from a red-cloaked soldier, the rifle bunter- dressed in a similar blood coloured uniform - points his eager pistol into the air and snarls as he shoots a joy-shattering bullet at the innocent clouds. The throng of hopeless victims fall silent and morbid as they shrink closer into their loved ones. May falls desperately towards me, and catching her in a comforting grip, I can feel her heart's frenzied palpitations mirroring my own.

The silence seems to shroud us forever, a never-ending nothingness that screams as loudly as the gunshot which just pierced the overcast sky mocking us. The soldiers stand menacingly tall, like hawks guarding their prey, knowing that all anyone longs for is for this to be over, so they can forget that it was anything more than a dream, and resume their daily lives suffering under the Noble's harsh, but survivable oppression.

Our eyes are trained on the silver screen, half hoping that it will remain blank, but still selfishly longing for the painfully accented colours to flicker on and for the ceremony to begin and end this torturing wait. After the agonizing tension has goaded me to the stage where I want to scream and face the barrel of a soldier's gun, the enormous screen hanging from the town hall comes to life, growing into bloom like a flower, first slowly, and then rapidly spreading its petals to boast of its full and intimidating glory.

The ominous death cage fills the entirety of the screen, the only sector of the Big City that anyone breathing outside of it has ever witnessed. We look upon a large courtyard with high, spiked walls outlining the painfully precise square shape that resembles a prison window, enslaving its charge in thick panes of confinement.

A winding ripple of snakes with luminescent skin gleaming in the artificial sunlight crawl along the beige cobbles, anxious to be released from the coarse ropes that prevent them from reaching their long-awaited meal that will soon lie fearfully in the centre of the courtyard.

The courtyard is made up of a kind of basin with three stepped levels, like a grand staircase descending into desolation. Upon the highest level, the snakes writhe with a keen longing to sink their venomous teeth into their tasty banquet. The second level is slightly lower, inside the first and stepping down into the third square of concrete that imprisons the victims of the Nobles Wrath.

The lowest level is crafted from limestone and boasts of a mosaic of thousands of peasants serving a taller, elegant gentleman dressed in grandeur that most could only dream of- the Emperor, and seven others like him in a formal line, overseeing the work with pompous laughter decorating their eyes- the seven Nobles. Some of the humble peasants are cleaning the sun-streaked floor of the mirage and others heave heavy stones to a place where a large mansion is under construction. I know this image too well. It used to embellish every bare fragment of wall, every billboard, and every public space to serve as a constant reminder of how we have no purpose other than to serve the Nobles and the Emperor, and that we will always remain under their power.

The very centre of the courtyard's basin is a pit as deep as the fear that engulfs me every day. Within the pit lies a menacing, bloodstained cage, the cobbles around it shining a threatening red in the fiercely concentrated sunlight. The cage is crafted from winding metal bars that have rusted over the years, and it currently stands empty with the door swinging open on ancient hinges and an inhospitable promise of pain.

Once the camera has completed its task of devouring the scenery, it reverts to the uppermost level where it encompasses the face of the famously detested Emperor who governs the Country. Alastair Greatest.

"Hello, citizens" He snarls, spitting his utter disgust at the words. "It seems that the time has come once again for you to be reminded of the perils that face the rebellious amongst you. I would like to welcome you warmheartedly to the August Screening of Justice"

Justice. That's what they call it, labelling the brutality as something honest and true. It will never qualify as true justice when the deed is committed for no reason other than a lust for murder.

"As you are aware," He continues, baring his gleaming white, superficial teeth. "I am your acclaimed Emperor, and so it's correct to assume that my judgment overrides all. You, are my servants, nothing more; as a more prized individual you have no purpose other than to serve me. I am your master; you must respect me, and be prepared to sacrifice your life for me, for by right, all of your lives are mine." He walks, slowly towards where the snakes strain on their leads, every step seems to cause a tremble in the earth both on the screen and here, in the town square of Rente, where hundreds of oppressed citizens quake with fear. "However, sometimes people begin to assume that they are worth much more than they truly are. These people become enthralled in the idea of living with liberty. They are so absorbed in their childish dream, that they overlook the obvious difficulties that accompany freedom." His voice becomes, soft and patronizing, as if he were addressing a naive child. "How would you survive without strict discipline and constant regulations? If there were no slaughter, then how could you understand the consequences of disobedience? The Country would die in your hands." His dark, absorbing eyes revel in the attention of a nation focussed solely on him; my heart bursts with a longing to rebel, scream and shout in a whirlwind fight against his constant torrent of lies that form the basis of our Country. "So, you see, the troublemakers must be eliminated, and we must do what we can to discourage new rebels from rising. This is why we will now show you the punishment that faces anyone who dares to disobey our command"

The Emperor walks to take his default position on the far right of the courtyard, confident that the camera, and the Country, will follow him. The camera now reveals the regimented line of Nobles and their families, watching the proceedings with smug contempt.

At the far left stands the seventh Noble, Maninta Genzashu who takes charge of periodically instilling fear into each town and village. Beside him stands the sixth Noble Trentaku Frinalle, the supposed co-ordinator of the Country's economy who seizes the majority of the Countries produce and ensures that the public have barely enough to feed themselves. The fifth, fourth and third Nobles, Rengini Egnigina, head of intelligence; Hardnida Delvaaint, master of weaponry; and Yepole Carrinte, leader of the terrorist group the Grangers; stand in that order with their wives and children wearing blank faces, staring past the camera with a mixture of misguided hatred and naivety, into the unknown realm of the Big City before them. The second Noble who controls the security of the Big City, Jerapo Bellona, is staring covertly towards the first Noble, Rebato Antario, my grandfather.

Antario, the leader of the infamous Destructors who stole my father from me, is standing so that his chin almost rests in the Emperor's ear. His mouth is twisted into a wry smile that curls at the corners like the coiled tails of snakes, hardly able to disguise his sickly excitement at what is to come.

May burrows into me, both of us holding our breath in ghastly bouts of sickening anxiety as we expect only the worst. My heart still clings to the singular shred of knowledge that we have always clutched at like a dispersing cloud; if his tortured face that we no longer remember clearly, does not haunt the Screening, he lives. My father would be the perfect example of a Screening victim, his crime blasted across the Country as proof that they would not hesitate to turn even on one who was once their own. Every month we writhe in helpless fear that only increases as the ceremony swells to the sickening moment when the victim is revealed.

The Destructors march into the cruel view of the camera, each man holding a long rope which holds the victim currently concealed in their midst like a painting at a gallery, preparing for a stunning revelation. May and I do not dare to glance away, controlled by the torrent of fear that consumes us, hoping with strength like a dying breath, that it will not be him, that he is still alive. The Destructors turn away in a well-choreographed movement, still clutching at their coarse ropes as they expose the victim.

A wave of relief floods over me, almost pushing me to my knees when a young girl pulls away to free herself of the silver collar that clings to her like a vine. But as soon as the relief of my father's life has released me from its warm grasp, fresh horror grips me as the girl's wide, tear brimmed eyes that glitter with intensity and desperation stare directly into my soul.

She looks a similar age to me, fifteen, perhaps younger. Her burnt auburn hair has been torn at, leaving great, ugly bald patches and exposing he paper pale scalp. Her eyes bulge and her lips are dry and flaking, her body, covered only in rags, is so pale she could easily be mistaken for a sculpture. Her abused figure is bent, looking so withered the merest gust of wind could blow her miles into the horrors that consume her life. Malnourished and deprived of light, her appearance is nothing like the stunning, heroic image fairy-tales entertain of martyrs. Her skin is baggy, and infected, red marks scorch her back like the decoration on a mosaic. The numerous scars that cover her body announce to the world that she has undergone torture for years and felt pain that should not be real. The question bearing on everyone's mind screams in the silence of desperation. What was her crime?

Allowing the features of the girl to impress on each mind, the Emperor's loud voice booms across the Country once again.

"This is what we do to those who dare to steal."

Her case needs no more explanation, she cannot speak on her own behalf, forbidden to explain that she was starving, or forced into it by her family. Silenced for a crime her perpetrators forced her to commit in a world ruled by injustice.

The Destructors lead her down the many levels of the basin, into the pit from which she will return with a heart that has ceased to beat the steady rhythm of pain. They reach the cage where the cold, metal, electric collar is taken from her, and the ropes are untied. The door of the cage swings shut with a tone of mourning and finality, as a heavy key turns in the lock.

She stands in the centre, readying herself, knowing that nothing can be done to save her life but still prepared to fight.

"Three." The Emperors voice reverberates, counting down to the release of the pitiless snakes. "Two." The Nobles look on with exited smiles unnaturally littering their faces. "One."

The slaves holding the snakes, who have learnt that possessing kindness will only lead to their place in the wake of death, release their grip, allowing the venomous creatures to dart through the slits in the cage and compete for their prize. The girl begins to fight her bars to escape. The first few, leap at her from below, missing her bare, soiled feet by inches, but learning from the mistakes of their brothers, the other snakes slide up the bars and surround her from different angles, where all hope of life collapses. One slithers onto her white knuckles where she clings onto the bar, causing her to lose her grip and collapse to the floor in a laboured heap. Still, she struggles against the thirst driven snakes, longing for just one sip of her anaemic blood. Her arms flailing, and her mouth tightly closed against the screams that would grant the Emperor the most detestable satisfaction, she does not stop until a ravenous killer creeps up her spine and punctures two small holes in the base of her sallow neck.

"Bravo my child." The Emperor addresses the lifeless pile of translucent skin, and brittle bones on the floor of the cage. "It seems you have taught us yet another lesson today." He turns to stare directly into the camera, personally addressing each of the viewers. "Never think to fight us, we will always win."

I almost smile in contempt, as his narrow, selfish perspective misreads the girl's bravery. Yes, she has taught us a message, but not the one he explained. She knew she was going to die, if it were her life she wanted to preserve, she would have submitted to death, letting it finish quickly with less pain. She fought for another reason, in her last moments of life she still had hope. If she had died quietly, it would have been surrender to the Nobles. Instead, she chose to fight. Fight until her dying moment.

Chapter 10

"Concentrate!" Sokk almost screams at me in frustration as he holds the sharp blade of a sword to my neck. "If I were a Destructor, you would be dead; sprawled on the floor within one minute of the fight."

It feels like years that I've spent trapped within the walls of this mountain, training for the battle that Sokk ensures me soon will come, but still seems as far away as it was when we first began. Nothing is happening. No protests, no rebellion, no sign that freedom might be near. The oppression of the Noble's is worse than it ever has been but Sokk and the rest of the Resistance still live in this foolish hope of revolution, a dream that will only make it hurt more when we fail.

Despite this, I am glad of the work, of the intense training that might all be for nothing. I feel useful, like I'm helping in some small way to avenge the thousands dead or tortured at the command of the Nobles. To avenge my father.

I mumble a brief apology and prepare myself to fight again, trying to achieve the fear and adrenaline that would course through my veins if I were really faced with a Destructor. Flattening the creases in my pale green dress and retying my hair into its typical plait that tickles as it follows the line of my spine down my back, I hold the knife, clutching it tightly in the palm of my hand as he lunges at me, grinning with a playful spirit that I know will never truly hurt me. I try to fight back with the well-rehearsed strokes that he has spent years drilling into me like a nail into wood, but suddenly, my palms start to sweat, and my head begins to spin. I drop the knife and collapse, knocking my skull against the hard mountain wall so hard, a dull ringing erupts, underscoring a whirlpool of dizziness in my mind.

When Sokk announced my physical training on the morning of my thirteenth birthday, I was burning with excitement, embracing the chance to be a part of a fight that I had dreamed of for so long. But after two years, the novelty has worn off and the repeated exercises have become monotonous, dull and useless. Sokk pleads with me to keep on, that the revolution will come soon, but how soon, he won't say. It could be another month, another year, or even another hundred years before the people of this Country can smile without facing the barrel of a gun.

I don't know what will happen in the future, what might become of May and I. We are prey, being hunted by an elite group that gain miles as we travel metres. Sometimes my heart and soul are filled with hope that we might reach the green meadow, but often it seems as if the end is inevitable, and we may as well turn and walk into the fire, lying submissive to the flames and the pain that follows them.

Sometimes, I feel Sokk's gaze on me, and it's as if he knows; as if all of this training is for a time in the future where I will be left to fight alone, with no Resistance workers by my side, and only those who long to see our bodies lying dead on the cobbles ahead. It's as if he knows that my story will not be a fight among an army of hundreds, but an individual battle which targets my sister and I as its victims; and nothing else can happen until this does. The war will not progress until I have faced my family.

"What's wrong Willow?" Sokk kneels down beside me, concern etching compassionate lines of worry over his face.

"Why are you training me? What's this all for?" There's no need for him to speak, Sokk's eyes see the question in mine and fight to show me the answer that deep inside, I already know.

"I think we'll finish training early for today." I get to my feet without glancing at him, angry at being seen as a child; left in the dark to guess at the future that he won't tell me.

As I leave the Resistance base behind, the bright sun almost blinds me after the dim, electrical lights inside of the mountain. I slowly begin to make my way down the grassy slope, carefully avoiding the buttercups that gleam a sickly yellow as if they are saluting the sky.

After such a violent session, I worry about how May will cope when she begins training. Her thirteenth birthday is in less a month and each time she thinks about learning to fight and becoming a full member of the Resistance, her face lights up in excitement. She has always been jealous of my time with Sokk, but I don't know how she'll survive as a part of an organisation with no alternative other than to seize hope through violence.

May has a heart as big as the mountains which surround Rente. She sees the best in everything and is quick to forgive. She would help anyone and everyone, friend or foe, and would never dream of hurting another human being. If she is on the battlefield, her place will be with the injured, caring for both our soldiers and those of the enemy, reciting like a war chant: 'Forgiveness is the first step towards peace.'

How could I even allow her to see the horrors that surround us in this world? She has been hurt too much already. She doesn't belong here; she is too gentle and kind to understand the motives behind hatred. Yet I know that she will be an invaluable beacon in our struggle. Just her smile could light a thousand candles with hope in a Country that bows down in sorrow.

The cottage is closer now, almost visible beyond the green trees that sway in the afternoon breeze; soon I will be sitting by the fire, cradling a hot drink, relaxed and satisfied that the day has achieved all that it can. Peace is so rare; when it comes, I relish it like the taste of sweet fruit on a summer's day. I start to walk faster as the trees begin to thin, like a veil revealing the slope that rolls down the mountain.

The sight of the pale cottage makes me gasp. My muscles tie me to the ground and my breath is enslaved by fear that stops me from screaming.

A black van stains the picturesque greenery of the countryside. A black van with cruel features that casts a beam of hatred, murdering the air around it. A black van that has haunted my dreams for the last five years.

Hidden by a thin maple tree, I can only watch as the gothic arrow of Destructors march back towards the vehicle. I take a single, deep breath, as the unsavoury meeting before me draws to a close.

They open the back of the van and push something, or someone inside. Closing the doors with a deafening 'bang' that can be heard for miles; the Destructors file into the front of the vehicle and the engine roars as if amplified through a megaphone.

I start to run, sprinting towards the cottage that now stands alone. I reach the gate just in time to see the pale face of my little sister, staring out of a small, dusty window in the back of the van.

Her lip is bleeding and her hair has been yanked from the roots. Our eye's meet and I see that hers are shadowed by the mark of a punch.

Staring at each other through the murky glass, I try to put all of the words I need to say, everything that I must tell her, into the emotion of my eyes. 'Be brave May. Don't scream. Don't cry. Be strong. Find dad. Don't think about me.'

Then I make a promise that I will move mountains to keep

'I will come and get you.'

May nods, understanding. She tries to tell me something, mouthing the words, but the van is already curling along the bare road, towards the mountains that separate us from the Big City.

I stand stone still on the grey tarmac outside for what seems like an eternity, staring at the place where she was, the faint spill of oil left by the Destructor's van. My heart hopes, too painfully in me, waiting for them to return and tell me that it hasn't happened; it's just some horrible joke. My knees are weak and tremble as if they aren't really there, a hallucination fading before I wake up from this dream, this nightmare that is plaguing me like a swarm of wasps on my heart.

But it's not a nightmare. It's not a cruel prank. May isn't going to jump into my arms and tell me it's just a game. It's here. Right here before me. My worst nightmare has escaped my dreams and decided to torture my wake as well as my sleep.

I sink to the floor, gripping my chest, fumbling for the place where my heart is being torn at by demons. A piece of me has been cut away and now screams with my sister in the depths of the black van; wrestled from me and now driving towards that unreachable horizon, facing a world full of darkness and hurt.

What will they do to her?

Images plague my head of dark, blood stained rooms with cruel weapons and soul piercing instruments. I close my eyes, trying to shut out the murderous scenes that spin in a dizzy whirlpool that I cannot escape, but in my mind they're even clearer.

Then I hear her screams- her cries for help that I won't be there to give. I press my hands over my ears, but the pitiful yells still reverberate, bouncing off the walls of my skull. The sound crescendos until there is nothing left but her pain and her screams overloading every sense.

I rock myself back and forth, cradling my head which has been hijacked by a desperate urge to break me like the tender twig of a willow tree, old and tired from a life of weeping.

It takes all my strength, will and determination to seal my final vow.

Whatever it takes, even if it costs me my life, I will save my May.

Chapter 11

Slowly, I rise out of the pool of tears collecting Slowly, I rise out of the pool of tears collecting on the cold road that now stinks of pain and grief. Rain patters on the tender cobbles and creates little whirlpools of splashes that remind me too much of the watershed still falling behind my eyes. Each step trembles like a nervous animal as I walk towards the house, keeping well to one side so that I do not go near the place where they stood.

The door swings wide open, its hinges lost, as a new fear wrenches my heart.

Grandma Dothy.

I run through the house screaming her name, my voice raw and afraid. Where is she? Could she be another victim now crouching in the Destructor's van? She is innocent. A woman who only wanted to help two lost children. She has nothing to do with my family, or my father.

The Resistance - She is a retired Resistance advocate. They would have guessed that. They're taking her to the Big City and they'll hurt her, torture her for information that could lead to even more pain, even more deaths.

No. They can't. They wouldn't. Not an innocent old lady? But May is just an innocent little girl and they didn't think twice about taking her.

My voice is hoarse from shouting and my eyes are steaming their second river of tears as I pause for breath in the now surreal, unfamiliar corridor, determined to keep screaming if only to drive away the thoughts that the silence would yell into my mind.

I pause to take a breath, and in that the brief moment of nothing, my body jolts at the sound of a low moan. It is quiet like the gentle echoes of a noise lost in a cavern, and I'm sure that I am deluding myself, my mind playing tricks on my heart that longs for some sign of life to hold me close and whisper words of love and comfort into my ear. But then it comes again, a soft, almost inaudible whimper with the tone of a requiem of birds.

I follow the sound to an old cupboard embedded in the hall, where usually shoes and coats sleep in the dust created by the almost extinct wood.

Tentatively, I push the door open, my hands shaking like a feather quivering in the wind.

The sickly moan comes again, this time more agitated, louder and full of fear as I notice a trail of sticky red blood that gleams luminescent against the carpet.

Nervously, I follow the path to the very back of the cupboard, my eyes squinting in the heavy darkness that is like a blanket layered on top of the thick atmosphere.

My palms stroke the hard brick wall. There is nobody there and I start to think that the cry was just a figment of my imagination.

I turn to escape the forest of coats and darkness when the cry comes again, more real than ever as my heart pounds like a piece of machinery verging on malfunction. The sound falls from above like smoke pouring from some great height and a lump rises in my throat as my eyes tilt upwards.

Hanging above me like an apple on a tree, I see the battered, broken body of woman close to death tied upside-down to a beam on the ceiling. The darkness clouds Grandma

Dothy's wounds, but blood falls in steady drips from her arms, legs and neck where I know gaping scars will prove the Noble's strength and power over this Nation yet again.

I clamber onto the long bar that supports the coat hooks, balancing precariously as I pull my penknife from my boot, and reach out to cut her ropes. Cradling her limp, light body in one arm, and clutching my old, rusted knife in my other hand, I slash at her binds and drop her gently onto the floor where she lies unconscious, her face contorted with pain.

As my feet land heavily on the floor, I haul her over my shoulder and bring her into the corridor, slowly tiptoeing across the blood-stained carpet that becomes wooden flooring as the door into the living room creeks open. I don't dare to even glance at my grandmother until she is lying on the sofa.

Slowly, I trail my eyes over her limp body. Her hair has been plucked out of its roots, leaving large, ugly red marks on her scalp and a gash in her temple oozes infected blood. Her left eye is swollen shut and twice its normal size, and her nose is bent at an awkward angle, broken and disengaged from the rest of her body.

Dothy's dry lips are flaking and from one corner of her mouth drips a steady stream of blood. My eyes find her arms, gasping at how one of them hangs dislocated and limp. Her other hand lies over her stomach where blood seeps through her fingers, disguising a wound which I can't bring myself to unveil. Her legs are stretched from hanging like a captured rabbit on the ceiling, and the burns etched into her skin make me want to vomit as my heart screams to help her.

The souls of her feet have been ripped off, revealing a layer of blood-soaked flesh unmasked by skin. I gag as the blood slowly trickles onto the cream carpet that the old woman used to spend hours each day cleaning.

I want to run to the mountains and hide amongst the greenery, far away from the pain of the real world to begin a make-believe life. I need to forget; forget everything that has happened, everything I have seen in this world decorated with pain and heartbreak that colours the unnatural stain of blood streaming onto the carpet.

But I can't. My heart screams for escape but my head knows that I must keep calm; I must stay strong in my soldier's post, withholding the wind, the rain and the storms. Not for myself. If it were only me then I would put up my hands and let them take me. I'm here, still fighting in this whirlwind of a war for my father, for Sokk, Dothy, and for all the oppressed citizens of this nation who deserve more than to be trampled on by rulers of hatred, but more than ever now, I'm fighting this battle for May.

"For May." I whisper under my breath as I turn my head away from Grandma Dothy's howling feet and begin to stumble towards where the medicine cupboard hangs on rusty hinges from the wall that is now spiked and threatening.

The roll of bandage feels strange and unfamiliar in my hands. Delicately tying the dressing around grandma Dothy's feet, I slowly begin to do all that I can to treat more of the serious wounds that cry for medical attention which I am unable to give. I kneel by her head and clutch her withered palm in mine, unable to do any more to heal her, and hating myself for my helplessness as I watch her die.

"Will?" The sound of her voice makes me jump as the no longer unconscious woman slowly moves her dry lips. "Is May...?" Her voice is ragged and tired, withered like a fading memory.

"No." I gulp, emotion rising up from my heart to my throat. "They took her. I'm sorry."

Grandma Dothy's shoulders sink in bitter disappointment as we both acknowledge the arrest of her favourite child. The air hangs heavily, screaming on behalf of the old woman's heart that, though she would never confess it, wishes it were me who had been taken.

"Grandma Dothy." I whisper, my voice urgent and tear choked. "What happened?"

"They came at four." She began, her voice fading but somehow energised with a longing to leave a legacy. "I could feel them. Their presence was so evil, so prominent. I tried to warn her, but May was too quick to answer the door. The moment she saw them she screamed, I heard a thud, and then nothing but breathes and gasps as they tied her." Grandma Dothy's brow creases in pain at the memory. "I wasn't thinking as I ran to the door to stand by her side. I knew, even if I only held her hand for a moment, my sacrifice would be worthwhile.

"They asked May who I was, and still playing the game, she told them that I was her grandmother. Then they hit her. The black eye swelled like a monocle on her face. She was so innocent, so young, how could they have done that? They asked her again and when she gave the same reply their fists found her lip; there was bleeding but the sound of the crunch of her teeth was more painful. Then they began to ask about you, Willow. Where you were, what you had been doing, and why you were living a life in defiance of your Country. We said that we didn't know and finally they stopped. But then the constant questions became a thunderclap silence.

"Their plan was to sit and wait for you to return, keeping May and I as hostages; but Roberto, your grandfather, received a call from the Big City and left almost immediately afterwards, locking May in the back of their lorry as if she were a dog, and he were the dog catcher. He would return for you later, he said." Grandma Dothy's poor face becomes taught with emotion and fear. "He turned to stare at me. He said... he said that they should... that they should apologize for having missed you, and to compensate, they would leave you a gift. Your grandfather snapped his fingers and four of the Destructors marched towards me, dragging me into the house.

"They pushed me into the cupboard and....and cut me before they tied me to the ceiling and left me strung up like a dead rabbit for you to find."

As she finishes her story Grandma Dothy's voice is deteriorating, her breath is becoming laboured and she struggles to maintain consciousness amidst the cloud of grief that surrounds her.

"Willow." She has to repeat my name several times to make herself heard through the screams of silence. "Don't worry about me" Her last ounces of strength ooze into the words. " But find May. She doesn't deserve this. Please"

Her body loses consciousness and her breath slows, deep and pale like waves rolling over the sands of a beach. Her hand falls away from her stomach, a curtain revealing a priceless painting, to uncover a large, open hole that spills rivers of dark red blood onto the white carpet that's past purity now seems ironic.

The only open eye, slides shut. The old woman's breathing is cut short as if with a knife. And the hand, which I am still clutching in rapidly dying hope, goes cold.

Chapter 12

I kneel, trembling on the stained carpet beside the sofa, for what seems like forever. I feel almost dead myself as Dothy lies like a limp fish on the sofa, innocent of any crime but murdered none the less, with patterned cushions supporting her head that lies motionless in contrast to my never-ending flow of grief.

The innocent are murdered for the pleasure of the wicked. Why? Is it for the victim's pain, lasting a brief fragment of their life before they are free of their torturer forever? Or is it purely a torment for those who love them? Who must live with the pain of a broken heart that will never fully heal? The Nobles understand love. I know this the way a horse knows its master by his whip. They may not feel love, or goodness, or compassion but they recognize it, know how to manipulate it so that your heart pounds against your ribcage like a hammer, screaming to escape the confinements of your body. Love that longs only for peace and joy and tortures your emotions until its wish is fulfilled. Each time I see someone smile I want to scream. They are vulnerable. The love in their smile will only turn to hurt. It will wait in anxious anticipation before morphing into a pain that pummels into them the way my heart now attacks me.

I see, through weeping eyes, Grandma Dothy's limp, lifeless frame lying like a blanket on the sofa. I'm sorry. My emotions scream an apology, acknowledging that this is my fault. She was a gift intended for me, not for the purposes of her pain, but for mine. If only I had been there, to defend her and force the Nobles to leave her in elderly peace. Then I would have been taken and she would be safe, sad perhaps, but safe.

Safety is a privilege. Something to be hoped for, but rarely truly grasped. Nobody can live a life completely free from the Nobles. Grandma Dothy was safe until her final hour. May and I have known safety for the past five years, but now it has become alien once again and danger greets us with an all too familiar grin.

As I think of danger I think of fear, and my emotions run wild for May. My sister so beautiful and innocent, undeserving of the peril that lies before her like some wild animal. Where is she? Have the ominous gates of the Big City already been closed behind her? I glance at the ebony clock on the mantelpiece that still ticks like a lulling nightmare, constant through the malignant horrors and unaffected by the tears shed in its sight. It is almost evening and the cuckoo will soon end the hour with a noise too shrill and excited to bear.

I need to move and escape this death cottage before night traps me in its screams.

As I get up from the floor, I glance once again at my devout carer for the last five years. Who will find her like this? Lying in a sea of blood with death, pain, and sacrifice written all over her face?

Whoever discovers her shouldn't see this much pain. They should see a heroine, an act of defiance against the Nobles. They should see someone so strong, so brave that she was willing to sacrifice her life for the sake of others.

Someone who fought the good fight until her dying breath, clinging throughout her life to peace, love, and hope.

I walk to the garden, my legs shaking as I lean on the wooden fence for support. Rows of perfectly kept roses, tulips, marigolds, and other sun kissed flowers stare at me blissfully, unaware that they will soon be dead, wilted with no caring gardener to ward off the dangers of weeds and neglect that would otherwise choke them.

Treading my way through the beautiful sea of colour, I pick as many different types of flowers, herbs, and anything else I can find that was born of Grandma Dothy's tender touch. After carrying them, like children, to the living room, I lift the old woman, surprised at how light and delicate she feels in my arms, and slowly take her up the stairs to her bedroom.

I lay her upon the neatly arranged blankets on the bed, her closed eyes and dried lips facing the ceiling. My shaking hands place the flowers like a frame around her still body, surrounding the resting martyr, with the bright pigment of the blooms forming the grave of a good soul.

As if lost in a dream, my hands slip under the folds of the mattress and close around the small, rectangular package of contraband. My fingers stroke the pale, off white paper and the old and beautiful biro pen as rebellion suddenly excites me. I begin to write, my handwriting messy and shaking at first, but gaining confidence with the strength of my words.

The woman, who you see, lying here today, is the victim of a great evil among us.

I debate, for a moment whether to protect my identity.

She selflessly helped two children who were endangered by the law because of their birth. She never had children of her own, and so poured her soul into caring for those who had never known the warmth of a mother's love.

One day, cruel men came to the door, with the vindictive intention of taking her children, for she did consider them her children, to be tortured and imprisoned through no fault of their own. Only doing her motherly duty she defended the youngest, who was too gentle and innocent to be confronted by those who knew only hatred.

She chose to fight. She could have hidden in the shadows, in silence, and watched the children that were not her own face arrest and receive their punishment. But instead, she was committed to peace, donating her own final breath so that another's could go on.

Dothelle paid the ultimate price for daring to defend an innocent. But regret never once blazed in her eyes. She would rather have died, than have lived under the oppression of people who destroy lives for a living. But her death will not be in vain. I will avenge her, and all the other victims of the Noble's thirst for blood.

I read the letter again and again, reciting it to myself like a mantra, before I fold it into the shape of a dove, a final attempt to illustrate how peaceful Grandma Dothy was. As I place it gently on the soft rolls of the blanket, I hope that I haven't surrendered too much information, but then, I smile, remembering that the only people who can read are the Resistance workers.

The ability to read and write is illegal in this County. Only government officials, the Nobles and the Emperor have the skill officially. However, May and I began our education whilst still living in the Big City, and dad continued it with us in secret, after we fled. He also taught several Resistance workers how to read and write, a skill that has allowed them to intercept and interpret important information, helping them to prevent some of the Noble's major schemes. However, if anyone is caught with even the smallest piece of evidence that they are literate, the consequences are severe.

I remember, with too much heartache, a cold, December day; close to the elegant festival the townspeople celebrate called 'Christmas'. We were called out of work and made to march to the town square. Everybody presumed it was for an emergency screening, something the Emperor wanted to threaten us with, which demanded the immediate attention of the nation.

We were all shocked to see that the screen, hanging like a vulture in the sky was blank, but on the platform in front, one of the fourth Noble's soldiers held a man dressed in rags by the scruff of his neck, and pressed a gun against his temple. The soldier's voice echoed across the courtyard, as he told us that they had found an old, gnarled book in the poor man's home.

He had claimed it was an antique, and that he couldn't understand a word of it, only liked to stroke its soft leather binding, but the Nobles 'disregard all lies'. The man was tied to a wooden post, and the gunshot echoed like the crackling of a vicious fire. His insides stained the cobbles, and when the soldier carried his limp frame away, the silhouette of his body stood out against the red sheet of blood.

Shivering at the memory, I quickly leave the room, hoping that the closed door will hide the fear. I head into my own bedroom but stop short. Cast on the floor, like dead leaves in the centre of the room, lie Grandma Dothy's old, hand woven shawl, and May's threadbare teddy which she has slept with every night for the past five years.

The lives of two people were destroyed today. One of them is gone forever. But the other, my sister, still breathes somewhere on this earth, a chance of survival lighting the smallest candle of hope for her.

I take a rucksack, preparing for a rescue mission with a thin, hand woven blanket that smells warm and comforting, like Dothy; a small flask of water; a packet of dried fruit; and my knife, a recent birthday present from Sokk to protect me from the hatred in this world.

As I leave the room, my eyes rest on the old, worn photograph of Barnak and Jeena Nillon, my counterfeit parents smiling out of a silver frame. I'll miss this life. I'll miss the friendly smiles of the townsfolk who relish in the opportunity to show kindness to one another, the naive optimism of the workers at the factory, and the sheer joy that gives light and purpose to these people in Rente. I'll miss the way they love each other, the smiles which accompany their forgiveness of those who hate them, the way that they care for each other because Somebody cares for them. They are happy. In this world full of pain and weeping, joy finds a foothold in every step.

"Goodbye." I whisper to my fabricated, paper family, the witnesses to my final words. "Thank you for loving me."

My hand is resting on the oak doorknob when I remember May's teddy, the one, thread-bear item that she chose to bring into her new life in Rente, all those years ago. I carefully place it at the very top of my rucksack and with a deep breath, I take the first, dangerous steps out of the door.

Chapter 13

Turning left along the windy road, I walk quickly, deserting the home and comfort I have known for the last five years.

Trying to clear my head of the hundreds of taunting thoughts and regrets, I start to run, racing against the emotions torturing my soul. But still, the strongest of them pull me into the dizzying maze of helpless fear that has no escape.

You should have been there for her.

You should have run after her, been caught and taken with her. At least then you'd be together.

It's your duty to protect her.

It's your fault she's gone. You should have stopped them taking her. Just like you should have stopped them taking him.

They're both screaming in pain right now. She doesn't deserve to be tortured because of you.

She doesn't deserve to be tortured because of you.

The thoughts and tearing emotions empower my brain until they completely control me. Every terrible thing that has happened in this warped Country is because of me. It is my fault my loved ones are being tortured. It's my fault Grandma Dothy is dead. Even the Noble's reign is my fault because I am related to them.

Everything cruel and hateful in this Country is because of the Nobles, and therefore because of me, a descendant of their evil.

Cold drops of rain seep through my clothes and my mood is mirrored in the thick blankets of clouds that begin to tip a steady stream of raindrops onto the earth. I don't know how, but I'm sure that the rain is somehow my fault too.

The sky slowly darkens, and soon even looking a few metres ahead of me is almost impossible. Paranoid, I whirl around in circles, searching for shelter from the drizzle that has quickly escalated into a storm. Something snake-like crawls up my back and hooks itself around my neck. It is wet and slimy. I scream and pull it away. But it's only a broken tree branch covered in wet, dead leaves.

I don't know where I am going as I scramble aimlessly off the road and up a hill that feels as steep as a cliff face. My arms grope the empty air in front of me, but all I can see is the blackness of a storm and the dark blue texture of the night. My hands feel nothing but the cold enveloping them and threatening to rip them to shreds. I close my eyes and here nothing but the screams of the wind and the constant, violent patter of raindrops. I open my mouth but in seconds my taste buds have been numbed by the downpour. My nose smells raw earth and the cold air pushing into my skin, is enforced by the wind.

The wind controls my limbs as it pulls me further and further away from the road, into the dark unknown. Unable to think, I collapse on the waterlogged, wild grass that soaks me to the skin and throws my body into a fit of convulsive shivers before fatigue and tiredness pushes my eyelids shut, gently numbing the rest of my body as I drift away from consciousness.

I wake to find myself staring up into morning sunlight seeping between two green, palm tree leaves. My clothes are bone dry and I am lying on what looks like a mattress of grass and leaves. Confused, I suddenly yelp as I notice a small head looming inches above mine.

"She's awake!" The face belongs to a small boy who looks about twelve years old. He has lank, dark hair that has been cut untidily short and his face is small and oval shaped. His curved lips turn at the corners as if he is always smiling, and his eyes, green and glimmering, lock with mine. "She's awake!"

The child runs away and disappears in the mass of surrounding trees, as I slowly manage to sit up.

I'm in a small forest clearing, sitting on top of a dense pile of grass and leaves. The clearing is circular with a brown, earthy floor under a canopy of webbed branches and deep green leaves. Wispy grass and a scattering of wild flowers surround a large tree in the centre.

Animals dart in every direction. Not the genetically engineered creatures that you see in towns and villages, but natural, rural animals, untouched by man's lust to mutilate.

At my feet runs what looks like the original Badgit. A badger? Unlike it's genetically engineered equivalent, created to drag large storage carts across towns, this creature is much smaller and had a more streetwise, knowledgeable expression. Whereas the Badgit has high and defined shoulder bones, the badger's body runs straight into his head. This animal has a longer snout than its descendant and seems to burrow deep into the ground as it scoots past me.

Above me, standing proudly on a tree branch, is what must be nightingale. It looks almost identical to the purposeless Nale, created in a lab experiment where all they succeeded in changing, was its song. The song of the Nale is harsh, and is often used to warn someone of their death. But the nightingale's voice sounds like life itself.

I sway a little to the sound of the music, melodic and delicate. It reminds me of hope, ignorant and naïve, but still hope nonetheless.

I am just about to lie back down and listen to the calming bird-song when I hear a rustling in the trees. My muscles tense as I watch the movement in the dark green leaves. But then, the child reveals himself, holding the hand of a boy who looks only a little older than me.

I catch my breath as I glimpse his tanned face. His eyes, like the boy's, glimmer the colour of emeralds and his features are so finely carved, he could be a sculpture.

His hair is jet black and glistens in the leafy sunlight. It hangs long and free, past his shoulders, all the way down to his waist where it curls upwards slightly.

He is wearing a pair of dark brown shorts, but his chest is bare, revealing dense, knotted muscles and olive skin.

Smiling, his jaded eyes meet mine. "I'm sorry if my brother woke you."

Chapter 14

My mouth opens but no sound comes out. I try to speak but my voice catches in my throat. He laughs, not mocking but kind of encouraging.

Shaking my head, I sit up further, arching my back.

"No" I smile, relieved that words seemed to have returned to me. "He didn't."

I look sheepishly down at my lap and suddenly realise how ragged I look, in an old storm wrecked anorak with thick boots caked in a brown sludge I only hope is mud. I hold out my hand, horrified at the jagged scars that ooze beady blood, and rake it through my greasy, knotted hair to find twigs and leaves sticking out from clots of mud.

"You chose a great night for an evening walk." The strange boy refocuses my attention as he makes his way towards me. "That was one of the worst storms I've seen in years."

"Where am I?" I feel like I should be afraid of him, but can't turn away from his cheeky smile as he settles himself beside me.

"You know it as Claw's Wood. But I prefer the name Pelopod."

Claw's Wood? The infamous forest rumoured to have swallowed trained soldiers into its midst? Trapping them in its endless circles of dark, taunting creatures until they were chased into the centre, where an old, evil miser would capture them for manic, scientific experiments?

"Pelopod?" I gulp, wondering what this other name could mean.

"Him." He whistles to the patch of forest on the right, and a small, genetically modified jaguar gallops like a horse towards him. This is a Pelopod." He explains. "My father's first successful animal experiment."

"Your father?"

Laughing the boy looks at me almost sympathetically. "Yes. The 'manic' scientist." He sees my anxious expression and hurriedly continues "Not the man in the legend. He's just like any other scientist. Only with a different aim." He pauses, planning carefully what he is about to say." He's more adventurous. He believes that anything is possible."

Suddenly I look around and realise that where I am, is not the natural paradise it seemed to be a few moments ago. Though the odd organic element remains, the place is filled with manmade organisms that I can only guess at the origins of.

"Then where did the stories come from?"

"The Big City" He says bluntly. "Where else? My father's scientific skills are so unique that the Emperor wanted them for himself. But my father refused and ran away to live here in the woods before the Nobles could capture him. The Emperor knew that his soldiers would be useless against my father's powerful creatures, so he chose to isolate him and socially severed our family from the community. He told the towns that my father was a merciless, murderous scientist, and spread rumours that ensured no one would come near this wood, hoping that someday, the humiliation would make my father surrender. But he never has." He smiles, staring into the distance. "And he never will."

Without giving me a second to register his explanation, the boy rapidly jumps into another conversation. " I'm Bant, by the way, and this is my little brother, Gront." The younger boy skips across the clearing and sits on Bant's knee where he strokes his older brother's long hair.

"Willow" I say, deciding that there is no point using my Rente name when, after my sudden flight, my story will soon escape anyway.

"So, Willow," He pauses, smiling a little, a soft smile that is not happy, but neither mocking," How did you find yourself wondering in our woods in the middle of a storm?"

I hesitate but decide the honesty and openness he has given me should be returned. I also doubt that I can lie convincingly to his soft green eyes that brim with concern.

Slowly, I unravel my whole tale. Revisiting places I had tried my hardest to forget and opening boxes of emotion that have been shut for such a long time that what is inside them cuts me with fresh horror.

By the time I am finished, my eyes are brimming, and I am kneeling on the floor with my head turned away from Bant, so he can't see the emotion that I haven't let myself feel for a long time.

"It's ok." He whispers as I start to bawl "You're safe."

His breath is hot on my neck and his words are sincere as I struggle to hold in my tears. Blushing, and embarrassed, I try to forget what I have just begun to remember. But my heartstrings still thrum, understanding that some things are too important to forget.

"May!" I whisper, getting to my feet. "I have to find May!"

My legs shake as I stand up. I blunder towards the thinnest part of the forest, determined to escape this jungle and find the road again, but I fall and crash against the hard earth as the Pelopod jumps on me and knocks me to the ground.

"Where are you off to so quickly?" Bant smiles, his words almost patronising, with an edge of menace that makes me feel uncomfortable.

"My sister...." I mumble "They're going to hurt her!"

"Calm down" He helps me up from the floor but when I try to find my balance a swooping creature that looks like a cross between a falcon and a swan sends me flying backwards again.

I suddenly realise that behind me is a thicket of brambles and brace myself for the sharp contact. But instead of harsh spikes I am caught in a pair of strong, muscular arms and the rich stench of my own blood is replaced by his proximity.

"I'm afraid, if you're that scared of a Swancon you'll stand no chance in the Big City."

I giggle, a high pitched, girlish giggle that I don't recognise.

He stands me up straight and takes my hand. Turning to look me straight in the eyes he pleads. "Please stay. We don't get much company out here, and even if we do, they're never as beautiful as you are."

I laugh again, embarrassed, and can't help abandoning, or at least putting aside, all thoughts of rescuing my sister. All I can think about is Bant, and the kindness and beauty in his sparkling eyes as he puts a gentle arm around my waist and leads be back to the centre of the clearing.

Chapter 15

I'm not used to undivided attention, and don't really know how to respond, holding my breath as Bant strokes my matted hair.

When he is satisfied that I can at least walk without falling over, he holds my hand and silently leads me to where the forest seems most dense.

We make our way into an endless blur of greenery. He is clutching my hand but racing ahead, dragging me behind him through what seems like an endlessly regenerating maze.

Brambles, bracken and berry bushes scratch my already broken skin as he pulls me faster through the trees. The forest is a complex web of chemical and natural plants, all combined in one huge jumble of greenery with splurges of indigos, reds, and even bright pinks decorating branches and flooding the grass at our feet.

Each part of the forest seems to be an identical copy of what came before it and I even wonder if Bant knows where we are going. It feels like we have been walking aimlessly for hours, with no change, as far as I can see, to anything around us or ahead.

Worried, I cling to the only lifeline I have, Bant. I know that if I slip out of his firm grasp I will be isolated in this daunting forest, forever.

We begin to move uphill and I find it difficult to keep up with him, Bant is stronger than me and he moves too quickly, weaving in and out of trees that are as tall as two-story houses. Occasionally he turns to glance back at me with an exhilarated smile that reaches the corners of his eyes; I smile back as if the journey is a pleasant wander through a park, I cannot appear weak in front of him.

We go on like this for what might only be minutes, but feels like hours. The forest has taken my anorak, and my boots are littered with so many holes there is barely any material left.

My feet ache and I'm freezing cold, dripping blood from the superficial wounds all over my body. I want to scream at Bant, tell him that we're lost forever and may as well just turn and surrender to the mercy of the elements, when he slows. I notice for the first time that the forest doesn't seem so dense here and I can almost see light filtering in through the branches above my head. It shines a pathway to where two trees bow towards each other, hanging a curtain of oval-shaped leaves that conceals what may be beyond.

Bant turns to me and tells me to close my eyes in his sweet, honeysuckle voice and all of a sudden it's just a game. The perilous journey fades into the distance until it is almost forgotten, as I focus on his voice, a gentle calm amidst the storm.

I hear the sound of Bant drawing back the leaves, and then he gently leads me through what must be the archway into whatever lies beyond the trees. Without my sight, I focus on the feeling of him guiding me. His gentle but strong hand on my back flexes, tickling my spine. His other hand is on my arm, gentle, but firm as he guides me. I surrender all my willpower to him and let him lead me blindly forward.

The first thing I notice is the sound, a soft hum gentle, but noticeable.

Bant lets go of me and I can hear his footsteps disappearing into the distance. For a moment I think he has abandoned me, left me alone with my eyes firmly clamped shut like gullible bait. But the trust I felt for him just a few moments ago soon overpowers this.

"You can open your eyes now"

The distant, laughing voice startles me. But my face floods with relief as I realise he is still here, still with me.

Slowly, I open my eyes, blinking a few times to adjust to the fresh sunlight that greets them.

I can only gasp at what lies before me.

I am in another natural clearing in the forest, but this one is bigger than the last and shaped like a large eye. It is delicate and quaint, soft and watchful as the rays of sunlight seem to play within it, dancing for joy in their freedom.

The grass at my feet seems to be sprayed with multicoloured flowers that cover the whole beautiful area with a fairy-tale-like beauty and I think that this scene, could easily be the setting of a children's storybook.

In the centre of the clearing lies a beautiful crystal-clear pool of litmus blue water. The glistening sun reflects in it's perfectly unbroken surface. Curves in the water seem white and glowing, basking in its own glory.

Between trees dotted around the clearing, hang hammocks, swings, and animal perches in colours that laugh and communicate to each other in a constant buzz of energy.

The cause of the humming sound soon emerges as a family of bright pink, fluffy birds chase each other around the clearing, diving into the pool, reminding me of young children playing carefree in the summer mornings.

"Do you like it?"

His voice startles me. I glance around, wandering where he is hiding among this breath-taking beauty.

Finally, I spot him standing in the cleft of a large rock that I hadn't noticed until now, his muscular body is glorified by the light shining onto it.

Once he is certain I have seen him, he quickly climbs nimbly off the rock and disappears, only to tap me lightly on the shoulder a few moments later. He looks at my torn appearance and says shyly "I thought you might want to bathe, and freshen up." He whistles and almost immediately Gront runs to me carrying a bundle of fresh clothes. "We hope these fit."

Bant takes his brother's hand and gently leads him into the dense trees behind me.

I look, edgily around the clearing before quickly walking towards the pool in the centre. I slowly peel off my mud drenched clothes and slip into the water. It is cool but not cold, and refreshes me in the baking hot sun. The waters remain calm and tranquil as I fully plunge into its welcome depths, pushing my head completely under and letting my hair, now loose and free, flow around my head.

The mud, which before caked each exposed inch of my body, now begins to ooze out of my system. As the water erodes it from the pores in my skin it seems paler and strangely vulnerable.

When we lived with dad, before he was arrested, he taught me to swim in the winding rivers that surrounded the village. Sometimes, he even took me into the sea, though never very far, as the Nobles won't allow anyone to swim more than three hundred metres away from the coast. Besides, the rapids were too wild. Now, slowly, the skill returns to my aching muscles and I'm slicing through the water like I always used to.

Swimming in the clear pool, I feel careless, confident, and happy. It reminds me of when it was me, May, and dad. When tears were a rare occasion, and fear was a stranger. When we were always careless, confident and happy.

Chapter 16

When I notice that the light has begun to fade, I swim leisurely towards the side of the pool, lingering in the water and reluctant to leave its comforting body as my hands stroke the hard earth on the bank.

I finally summon the willpower to push myself up and out of the crystal water, and notice that the pile of dirty clothes I was wearing has disappeared. I'm suddenly self-conscious, embarrassed by the thought of someone entering the clearing whilst I was swimming naked.

I quickly dart towards the pile of fresh clothes Gront brought me, smiling as I think of the small child, he seems so sweet and naive. He reminds me of how May was before they arrested father.

The clothes aren't what I expected them to be. I don't really know what I did expect from people who have spent their lives living amongst the trees; fabrics woven from grass and flowers? Instead, I unravel a long, scarlet dress with short sleeves cut in waves so beautifully woven I have to stop for a moment just to stare at it.

I pull the dress over my head and it fits as if it were made for me. It feels soft and smells of wild roses. Natural roses, not the rosne flowers that were generated in a lab to absorb dangerous and poisonous chemicals that had built up in the atmosphere.

Winding patterns line the dress in glittering gold, two long, shining strings fold themselves into each other creating beautiful flowers. The pattern weaves from the low collar across the shoulders to the sleeves where it creates a delicate border, winding through the curves of the dress like a mountain brook. It runs down the bodice and follows the shape of the dress, coming in tightly at the waist where it forms a ring with a magnificent, large rose in the centre that seems almost real. The dress curves slightly outwards as its silky creases tickle my calves at its hem.

I walk to the water's edge, enjoying every step in the free material, and study my reflection in the clear blue pool. My skin is darker, tanned by the summer sunlight, and my hair has grown since I was re-located, now evenly hanging at my waist. I try to ring out some of the excess water from it before running my hand through the matted locks.

Slipping my feet into elegant slippers that are as beautiful as those worn by the Nobles, I feel graceful and mature, almost beautiful. I try to smile at my reflection but there's a tugging in my heart. I stop, realising what's missing. There's no little girl in my arms.

Tears well in my eyes but I fight them off and push my sister far from my mind. Thankfully, a distraction places a hand on each shoulder and playfully whispers "boo!"

Bant turns my body to face him and examines my dress as if I were a priceless piece of art.

"It fits perfectly" He smiles, and his emerald green eyes star directly into mine, creating a spellbinding connection that I never want to be severed.

"I knew it would. You look...." he struggles to find the right word, "breath-taking."

I smile, bashfully biting my lip and looking down at my feet.

"It was my mother's," He continues.

"Your mother's?" I ask, tilting my head upwards and surprised at his pained expression. "Is she here?"

"No" The words seem forced, as if it is a struggle for them to escape his mouth. "When my father was still living in civilisation; and the Nobles were chasing him," He looks at me nervously "they kidnapped her and sent us a video of them...torturing her."

Silence hangs, and I think about how the Noble's most powerful method of torture is to persecute our loved ones. Why else did they want me? Why else did they take May?

Rapidly changing the conversation Bant leads me towards a hammock on the far-left side of the clearing, "I thought we could sleep out here tonight". He motions for me to sit beside him in its crest "It's cooler than the castle, and more peaceful."

"Castle?" I ask, confused.

"It's like a mansion" He explains "But far older. This castle is the last one left in the Country, made thousands of years ago. My father renovated it when we came here and that's where we live. We have modernised the inside, to make it more comfortable. But the outside and the four tall towers are kept as they were, back when they used fire for light and heat."

"Can I see it?"

"Of course! But I will show you in the morning. When the sun is rising directly behind it and it is at its most magnificent."

We sit side by side on the large hammock that is big enough to sleep four and I notice it is made of the same material as my dress. I trace the patterns with my finger and he places his hand on top of mine. I look up at him and smile. My other hand strokes his arm, running across his dense muscle that is toned and almost gleaming in the last shards of light. I realise that he is now wearing a pale blue T-shirt with his long brown shorts, his feet are bear and his toes flex as the sun sets, stretching. His shoulders are sharp and graceful bones are visible beneath the tanned skin of his hands. Every part of his body is elegantly carved and beautifully chiselled by a fine hand.

"When will I meet your father?" I ask, still tracing his muscles with my fingers.

"In the morning, he is away on business tonight."

"Away?" I'd thought the family never left the forest.

"We need things, Willow. The food in this forest may seem abundant, but when you're feeding three mouths all year round, it quickly disappears. We can't survive without clothes and technology. There are some necessities in life that it is impractical to be without."

"But you can't buy things at night"

"*We* can't buy things in the day. We're too recognisable. What we need, we have to take"

I stare at him as I suddenly understand. I'm almost disgusted at the idea of stealing, something I've been brought up to know is wrong. But as I look into his apologetic eyes, I can't help but forgive him with a raw passion that might make mountains tremble. I wrap my arms around him, pulling him close. "I'm sorry" I whisper.

He pushes me away. "What for?"

"For your life. For your isolation. For everything"

"It's OK, it's for the best. My father's cause is great, I would do anything for him. Besides, you're here now. That makes it all worthwhile."

I lean against him, my tired limbs aching, and he moves so that I am lying on the hammock. He lies next to me and holds my hand in his.

"Please don't go away. Stay with me. Forever"

"Forever" I smile as he leans over, and our lips meet in a kiss.

Chapter 17

Gleaming rays of golden sunlight rouse me from my deep slumber. Lifting my heavy eyelids, last night suddenly rushes back to me, the golden coated fairy-tale scene that makes my heart smile. Looking at the empty space on the hammock next to me I wonder where Bant is, worrying for a second that he has abandoned me, before an unexplainable sense of calmness and trust returns, and I know that those loving eyes will never leave me for long. I bask in the morning sunlight for a few moments before swinging my legs over the edge of the hammock and letting my feet rest on the soft, plush leaves beneath them.

Washing my face in the clear pool, I resist the urge to dive into the cold water and swim, instead, sitting on the edge and letting my feet dangle in the enveloping coolness. Birds sing around me as fish play cheerfully in the water. I watch a small rabbit dart across the clearing, excitedly chased by its laboratory equivalent, the robir. Though I don't like laboratory animals, I can't help but admire the grace and tactical mind of the robir as he easily catches the rabbit and nuzzles her lovingly. If they could speak, I think that they would be laughing as they roll on top of each other on the soft grass.

Wanting to leave the couple in peace, I decide to search for Bant. I delicately venture out of the clearing and weave through the trees, not knowing where I am going but not really caring either.

After walking and scrambling over the natural paths, I catch sight of a large turret ahead of me, standing even taller than the giant trees. Excited, I run towards it, intrigued and curious as I push away the branches and brambles.

Soon I find myself standing in front of a huge building, what I assume Bant meant by the Castle. However, it is much larger and grander than a mansion, made out of hard, silver stone that rises upwards for what seems like miles. The castle is surrounded by a wide moat full of dirty, murky water, and on the side of the monument there is a wrought drawbridge pulled tightly up against the wall that I can only guess reveals a doorway when it is lowered, allowing entry to the castle.

The large, bleak walls are as high as the treetops and at each corner tall, round towers rise even higher. I cannot see any windows in the stone but instead several slits are embedded as thin as arrows and as long as a bow.

The beauty of the castle grips me as I gape at its elegant features and wonder about the people who once lived there. But it also seems ominous, and for some, unknown reason fear and foreboding wrap themselves around me, clamping my heart.

I suddenly hear footsteps and freeze. Darting behind a tree, I hold my breath like startled prey hiding from her predator.

I peek around the edge to catch sight of Bant followed by a sinister looking man with a permanent snarl and a bent nose. His pale skin stands out behind his dark clothes as bony fingers clutch a withering cigar.

"You have done well my son" He says in a voice as crooked as his nose. "Now tell me, how did you come to find this girl?"

My heart skips a beat. They are talking about me?

"She was lying on top of the mountain" Bant chortles "Unconscious. Caught in the storm!"

"What was she doing out at night?" Bant's father laughs.

"Going to the Big City. So she says!"

"At least, in that case no one will miss her. They'll know she's dead."

Behind the tree, my stomach starts to churn, why are they laughing? What do they mean? My heart flutters in my chest so loudly I think they hear me!

"Is she suitable?" Bant asks, staring earnestly into his father's eyes, eager for his approval.

"She's perfect!" His snarling mouth creeps into a sinister snarl. "She's young, lost, and by the sound of it will do anything you say. At last I can put my theories into practice. Then I can finally prove to the Nobles that humans can be modified, just as animals. We just needed one."

He laughs sinisterly as I double over in fear, my stomach tying itself in knots. One what? What are they going to do to me?

I stare at Bant, noticing that he seems slightly uneasy. Maybe he's going to say something, stand up for me, tell his father that he would rather die than let him perform his horrific experiments on me.

"Come on son!" The old man adds. "Think of it like this. Once we've succeeded with her, we can take her to the Nobles and they'll release Ternia! Your mother, Bant! She'll be with us, safe and happy. We'll be a family again! This is the only thing we can do to get her back. I don't want to do it either, but I have to."

Bant's small shreds of humanity disintegrate and he grasps his father's wrist, all feelings for me vanished. "What should I do first?"

"Take her to the lab." He whispers so quietly I can barely hear him. "Be her divine love till you reach it, then tie her to the operating table before you say a word. She seems headstrong, and her reaction will be violent, so be careful." He smiles menacingly as I try to fight the urge to vomit. "Strip her, then take the whip from the wall and strike her until she is too weak to struggle. After that, I'll come to perform my first experiment."

Before I hear Bant's response I am running through the forest, gasping for air as I try to take in what I have just witnessed. How could he? He told me he loved me! Were all those kisses, all those words, a lie?

I've been so stupid. So idiotic to believe his facade. His kindness, his gentleness and sympathy, it was all a ploy! A stupid plan put in place so he could torture me.

Human experiments. Rumours of his father pound my head. Rumours that should have kept me away from him. That should have sent me running a million miles from him and his seducing charade.

The pounding of my heart echoes in my ears at the volume of a stampede of elephants as I keep running, faster and harder, trying to escape my own thoughts and emotions, scared of what might happen if I stop for even an instant.

I understand what it is like to lose a family member like Bant has. And I know the pain and passion that would do anything to get them back. But not this. Never this.

Amidst the hatred and anger a part of me can't help feeling sorry for little Gront. He is so young, so innocent, and yet too soon, he'll grow up into the menaces his father and his brother now are.

Frustrated, afraid, and angry I run faster, concentrating on weaving through the jeering trees, trying to stop myself thinking about the painful past, the bitter present, the gaping future.

Chapter 18

The volcano of emotions inside me finally erupts as I collapse in a heap, writhing and weeping on the forest floor. Loathing, disgust and shivering, naked fear take over my entire body, transforming me into a disfigured creature of pain.

My hands cover my ears, but I still can't shut out the echoes of Bant and his father.

".... Is she suitable?"

"....my first experiment..."

"...We only need one..."

The shining patterns on the dress that once seemed like elegant swirls are now vicious pythons, like the ropes that they plan to use to bind and torment me.

I vomit. The torturous words push the food, given with secret spite, out of my system and leaving me hollow and alone.

The trees around me seem close and ominous, and I feel claustrophobic. Rain starts to patter, forcing me to get up from my uncomfortable, earthy respite and look for shelter.

I shiver when I finally reach my feet, my limbs weak and tired. I press my eyes tightly shut as the sick green of the forest makes me dizzy. Walking blindly in a random direction, the drizzle turns into a heavy downpour. The water makes my clothes cling to my skin and plasters my hair to my face as my eyes flash open to see lightning falling from the sky only one hundred meters away. Thunder claps in my ears as I run, longing for somewhere to hide from the raging storm.

I trip, and fall on my face, drenched dirt filling my mouth. Exhausted, I lie there for a few moments before scrabbling to my feet once again. My ankle becomes tangled in brambles, but as I shake it free, it meets something cold, metal and man-made. Rummaging in the bush with my hands I find a lever, and without thinking I pull it. With a jolt, the ground beneath me gives way.

I let go of the leaver in surprise and fall into a gaping hole. The solid earth closes up above me as I am plunged into darkness.

Gravity whirls my body in circles, so I can't tell which way I'm falling. My arms are flailing, trying to find something to cling to but grasping only thin emptiness. My head reels as the world spins dizzyingly in the dark.

I hit the floor with a heavy thud, a current of sheer pain exploding in my head and rippling down my spine. As I attempt to move, a light flickers on and almost blinds me with clinical brightness.

Looking straight upwards, I see a wide, long, circular tunnel. Down one side is a rope ladder and what looks like complicated scientific formulas are scrawled on the walls that loom all around me.

I drag myself onto my feet, my head and back still searing with pain. Leaning against the wall I struggle towards the centre of the room that I guess must be a secret cavern underneath the forest floor.

The formulas and equations on the walls all seem complicated nonsense to me, a foreign language that is alien and intimidating. I suddenly catch sight of a silver operating table and my heart stops, frozen in fear.

This is the Laboratory.

Panicked, I slowly stumble towards the table. It is gleaming in the synthetic light, unnervingly clean without even a fingerprint smudging its shining surface. Four metal shackles snake from the corners of the table, dangling open, their cold grasp ready for fresh flesh. A thick metal band comes across the middle of the table, to pull down my waist. Mounted high upon the wall is the whip. Nine tails as sharp as razors look threateningly down on me. Blood stains the handle from a previous use. My chest aches in sympathy for the poor victim.

A transparent table beckons me forebodingly towards it. I stare, paralysed in fear, at a glistening set of metal tools. Three scalpels lie vertically side by side, each one a little larger than the last. Scissors, tongs and tweezers are lined up neatly, looking sharp and dangerous. A queue of test tubes and glass beakers are so in line with each other it would have taken hours to place them there.

My eyes almost can't accept the hundreds of implements, some that I have never seen before, nor do I want to see again. On the far right, different metal tools stick out of a metal ball on the end of a long, thin spike and rotate slowly, like a tiny windmill with lethal wings. A knife lies next to it with seven blades, and beside that a spoon the size of an eyeball, with jagged edges - the teeth of a wild animal.

I turn away, towards a glass cabinet full of strange, brightly coloured potions, each labelled with clear writing that Bant's father must have learnt in secret, or a long time ago.

"SPINE COLLAPSE"
"MENTAL SHUTDOWN"
"STOMACH FIRE"

I run from the luminescent, violently coloured bottles as if the words have pushed me away, to a table on the far end of the room where I notice a book bound with heavy black leather.

Fleetingly, I wonder again how Bant's father learnt to read and write, but it is not my main concern and my stomach backflips at the title of the book.

EXPERIMENTS

Tentatively, I turn over the front cover and scan the first page.

MENTAL SHUTDOWN

BEFORE PERFORMING ANY PHYSICAL EXPERIMENTS, YOU MUST DISENGAGE THE MENTALITY OF THE VICTIM.

FIRST, WHEN THEY ARE SAFELY CHAINED AND SECURED, FORCE THEM TO SWALLOW HALF A BOTTLE OF THE GREEN LIQUID LABELLED 'MENTAL SHUTDOWN'. THE POTION WILL INFECT THE BRAIN WITH A DISEASE IMMOBILISING EVERY PART, EXCEPT THOSE USED FOR BREATHING, EATING, DRINKING, SLEEPING AND MINIMAL SPEECH AND MOVEMENT. THIS PROCEDURE WILL REMOVE ANY HUMAN THOUGHTS FROM THE VICTIM, ENABLING THEM TO BE USED AS A MIND SLAVE AS WELL AS RENDERING THEM INCAPABLE OF RUNNING OR FREEING THEMSELVES FROM YOU. THE VICTIM WILL ALSO BE ABLE TO FEEL AND PROCESS PAIN, AND REGULAR INSTALMENTS OF TORTURE SHOULD BE USED TO REINFORCE THE MENTAL SHUTDOWN.

<u>WARNING</u>: DURING THE PROCEDURE OF MENTAL SHUTDOWN, IT IS IMPORTANT TO KEEP THE VICTIM BOUND AS THE POTION WILL CAUSE

EXTREME ANGUISH, THE VICTIM IS ALMOST GUARANTEED TO WRITHE AND SCREAM IN PAIN FOR SEVERAL HOURS. ENSURE YOU ARE A GOOD DISTANCE AWAY TO PREVENT YOURSELF FROM INJURY.

Chapter 19

The book is full of detailed diagrams of how to perform hundreds of terrifying experiments. Each diagram is clearly labelled and annotated with descriptions that send shivers down my spine. Some seem to change a person mentally and others horrifically maim and transform them physically.

One experiment describes wiring an electronic system into the still active portion of the brain, forcing them to obey any command given. Another describes how wings can be attached to the shoulder blades via intense surgery that links new nervous impulses to the brain. There is a footnote describing how to ensure the victim uses and manipulates the wings immediately, even under the intense pain they cause.

I look away for a moment and close my eyes, trying to slow my jagged breathing.

"So, you're the runaway girl, are you?"

The voice sends a cold shiver down my spine as my heart stops. I am still facing the wall behind the table, eyes closed, frozen. Panic paralyses my bones as the voice gets closer.

"We've been looking for you. I'm glad you've found your new home."

I don't need to look to recognise the voice of Bant's father. Sick terror rises from my stomach to my throat as I have no other choice but to listen.

"Let me introduce myself. My name is Meniar. Have you heard of me?" He laughs. "I see you've discovered my Tome.

Do you like the human in the diagrams? I think it's quite a good resemblance. As if it was meant to be."

His voice is right in my ear and a cold, bony hand grips my shoulder.

"Come on Willow." He snarls. "this way."

Somehow breaking through the fear that keeps me rooted to the spot, I pull myself free from the elderly man's grasp and run towards the tunnel. I reach for the step-ladder, climbing two rungs before it is violently shaken, and I lose my grip, falling into Meniar's arms.

Seeing him closely, Bant's father, is just as repulsive as his personality. Age lines crease his elderly face as I realise he must be well over seventy. He is strong however, and although I pull against him with all of my might, he slings me over his shoulder as if I were a sack, gripping tightly to my legs and ignoring the aggressive punches I throw at his back.

Pushing me down onto the operating table, he struggles with my wrists to shackle them in place. Sharp pain only makes me struggle more fiercely as I kick his ribs, winding him.

"Bant" He screams breathlessly, knowing that he's not strong enough to finish me. "BANT!"

I kick him again and he flies backwards. His head smacks against the floor and his eyes close, consciousness suddenly escaping into the chasm.

Relief sweeps through me but is replaced quickly with more fear. My wrists are still chained to the table. The key is six feet away in Meniar's right hand. And Bant is coming.

I lie there in fear and dread that is just as binding as the metal cuffs, for what seems like an eternity. Struggling against the shackles does nothing, but I still try, just because it's something that drives away the thoughts that will overrun my mind if I stay still for even a moment.

I see a shadow below the ladder and my blood turns cold. The silhouette grows, becoming larger and larger as the person climbs further down. Bant drops with a thud, wearing a face I've never seen on him before. Loathing, hatred, and disgust.

He looks from me; half chained to the table, to his father; lying motionless on the floor. He takes the key from his father's hand to lock the remaining two shackles around my ankles. As he crosses the room, he stares at my feet, not daring to find my eyes. So, when he is close enough I kick him, forcing him to look at me, the person he one claimed to love.

He finally acknowledges my eyes, brimming with fear, defeat, and defiance and I see his heart soften, though his face still remains cold and hard.

"Please" I whisper.

Slowly, not breaking eye contact, he comes to my wrists, bleeding from the fight against the chains, and twists the key in the lock. Relief shoots through me like a rocket as he reaches over and unlocks the other cuff. I leap up from the table, running towards the ladder and the tunnel. But Bant is right behind me, and before I start to climb I look back at him, my heart filled with pity.

"Thank you."

Running up the ladder, I think what might have happened, and intense gratitude makes me gasp for breath, as I remember with a shiver the images and descriptions in the leather-bound book.

When I reach the forest, tears l stream down my face, and I am running once again through the trees, only this time with a clearer determination - to get out.

Maybe if I can just escape this forest, I will wake up and it will just be another hideous dream. May will be holding my hand, Grandma Dothy will be frying eggs in the kitchen, and everything will be all right.

But I know that this isn't a dream, it's all too real, too close and too dangerous.

My hair gets caught in the brambles and my feet are cut and scarred by the dead leaves and twigs on the harsh floor, but physical pain now seems distant and meaningless. The real agony writhes inside of me, my emotions tearing me to shreds and screaming so loudly that they drown out the deafening sounds of the forest.

When I feel as if I have been running for hours, a bright light and an open space confronts me through a gap between two solemn trees.

I stop. Shocked. Panting and wheezing. But suddenly hoping.

I take slow, laboured steps towards the opening as the shards of light creep closer and closer. Finally, I break through, and I'm free of the forest, free of Bant and his evil father and free of a future of pain and torture. As the stress and the fear leaves my body, I collapse into a shrivelled heap of leaves, exhausted.

After several shaky drums of tears escape my body, I manage to find my feet and stand up, wobbling slightly as my legs struggle to support my weight. I am on a hill, the same hill that I climbed during that first storm that delivered me into the clutches of the wood.

I glare down at the road beneath me, untouched and peaceful, identical to the way it was before. I want to scream and shout at it, order it to understand my pain, to show some sympathy. Or to have changed somehow the way I have changed, be afraid the way I am now more afraid, more damaged and alone like I am damaged and alone. Something to show me that what I have just experience has been somehow acknowledged, and understood by some, small part of the universe.

A lonely figure strolls along the road, agitated and determined, but disheartened and almost giving up as I notice his hunched shoulders and bowed head longing to return to the town.

I run down the hill to warn him about the forest, to send him far away from Meniar and his experiments. But I am still a little way off when he turns towards me and I stop suddenly. The sad, careworn face of Sokk reflects the same disbelief as mine as I am now sprinting towards him, tears racing down my cheeks.

"Willow" He whispers as I collapse in his arms. Not trusting myself to speak I fling my arms around him and bury my head in his shoulder.

Slowly, he leads me along the road, almost carrying me as we make the slow and agonising journey back to Rente.

"Shhh" He whispers in my ear as I sob into his shoulder. "We're going home."

Chapter 20

I wake days later in a small room with brown walls that create a dome above my head. I am lying on an old, worn mattress and when I shake off the soft duvet and sling my feet over the side of the creaking double bed, a storm of ragged, artificial feathers leak out of a tattered hole.

I stroke my fingers across the wall, and my hand comes away dirty, a few crumbs of solid earth falling through my fingers.

I am in the Resistance base. Inside of the mountain.

A door on my left leads me into a tiny bathroom with green and white tiles lining the floor and ceiling. A grimy porcelain toilet, sink and a rusty shower remind me how filthy I am, and I look away in embarrassment at the face in the broken mirror, almost unrecognisable through layers of crispy mud and dried tears.

I quickly plunge into the shower, not caring that the water is icy cold and sends shivers down my spine. Afterwards, I take a faded cream towel and wrap myself in it tightly, quickly returning to the main room where I rummage in the beautifully carved chest of wooden draws, and find a faded blue shirt and some baggy, dark trousers.

Tying my hair up with a ribbon I found on the side of the basin in the bathroom, I sit on the end of the bed, and rub crusty sleep out of my eyes.

The bed is made of natural oak, the ornate headboard carved with swirls that weave in and out of the creases in the ancient material. The frame itself is old, but sturdy, taking my weight without any creaking complaints.

The walls are simply solid earth, windowless and blankly brown. I press my hands into the low ceiling above me and they come away covered in damp mud, my handprint embedded into the heart of the mountain.

In the corner of the room is a small, tatty cradle and a tiny chest of drawers sits opposite the bed, carved from a now extinct wood that smells like pine. The draws themselves are engraved with circles that surround tiny knobs cut into the delicate shape of doves. Above the chest, somehow mounted on the earth wall, is a tiny mirror bordered with the same winding patterns as the bed and small cracks drape across the dusty glass like helpless waves seeking a resting place among a raging, icy sea.

Every surface in the room is caked with a layer of dust an inch thick, betraying that it hasn't been used for a long time. I slowly walk over to the chest of draws, noticing that the floor is rough beneath my bare feet, and look down to see a worn carpet, the burnt orange colour of fallen leaves in autumn.

The moment I touch the top of the draws, the dust explodes into a thick cloud, almost chocking me. With my shirtsleeve plastered against my mouth and nose, I wipe away more dust until I finally clear a small space and make out the letter E etched into the wood.

I wipe away more dust, curiosity overcoming the pungent flakes of dirt flying into my mouth and nose and discover two words neatly carved into the wood.

MOSS DELL

Dad? When was he here? Why?

My hands shake, somehow afraid to find out more about my father. But this is the first contact I've had with him for too many years and even touching the engraved wood sends bursts of excitement, as I imagine him carving the words with his skilful hands many years ago. I suddenly feel close to him, closer than I have been to him for almost six years.

Fuelled by the one, short burst of excitement, I am now suddenly desperate for more. I root through each of the drawers and finally my fingers wrap around a bundle of paper, tied together with thick, fraying ribbon.

I wrestle the tight knot and finally manage to snap the worn material as the parchment falls onto the floor with a heavy thud. Quickly picking up the pieces and perching on the end of the bed, I turn to the first page where I see a badly drawn key and some shaky lettering.

SECRET DIARY OF
REVICARTUS ANTARIO
MOSS DELL

I turn the page. The first entry is short, written untidily, the letters cramped together on the page. I glance at the date, realising that the childish scrawl was printed over twenty years ago, when dad was ten years old.

I read it hastily.

I'VE DECIDED TO WRITE A SECRET DIARY! MY NANNY SAID THIS IS WHAT THEY USED TO DO, HUNDREDS AND HUNDREDS OF YEARS AGO. NANNY'S TAUGHT ME SO MANY NEW THINGS. I WANT HER TO BE MY NANNY FOREVER!

I smile at his innocence and turn to another page.

OH NO!!! THEY'VE TAKEN NANNY AWAY! WHAT ARE THEY GOING TO DO TO HER? CAN'T WRITE MUCH, I NEED TO SAVE HER!!!

I clamp my eyes shut as my chest tightens with sympathy. I quickly turn to a page in the centre of the pile of papers. Here, dad's handwriting is neater, dated five years later. He is now fifteen.

I CAN'T BELIEVE IT! I AM BEING FORCED TO MARRY MALINTARET. SHE IS DISGUSTING AND REPULSIVE. I WOULD RATHER DIE. I SAID AS MUCH TO FATHER, BUT HE DIDN'T CARE, HIS PRIORITY IS THAT I CLIMB THE NOBLE LADDER. HE TELLS ME THAT IF I DO MARRY HER, THEN ONE OF MY CHILDREN MAY BECOME THE EMPEROR, SOMETHING I COULDN'T STAND! NEVERTHELESS, THE WEDDING IS TOMORROW AND FATHER HAS THREATENED TO PUT ME IN THE TORTURE CHAMBERS IF I DO NOT GO WILLINGLY.

My heart aches for him as I quickly turn to a page at the back of the stash of paper, dated six years later.

FINALLY! WE HAVE ESCAPED! I MANAGED TO DIG A HOLE UNDERNEATH THE ELECTRIC FENCE AND TONIGHT I TOOK TALEMIA AND AMERINA AWAY WITH ME. WE ARE FINALLY FREE FROM THE BIG CITY! BUT TALEMIA IS STILL IN SO MUCH PAIN FROM THE METAL ROD THEY BOUND TO HER, AND WE HAVE NOWHERE TO GO. I REMEMBER THAT JUST BEFORE SHE DIED, MY NANNY TOLD ME THERE WERE PEOPLE TRYING TO FIGHT THE NOBLES WORKING INSIDE THE WOODS. I'M HOPING TO FIND AND JOIN THEM.

Finally, I turn to the very last piece of paper in the stack.

THANK GOODNESS! I HAVE A FRIEND AT LAST! THE RESISTANCE HAS BEEN WARY OF ME EVER SINCE I TURNED UP IN THE WOODS TWO WEEKS AGO. THEY THINK THAT I AM A SPY! BUT I ASSURED THEM THAT I

HATE MY FAMILY AS MUCH AS THEY DO, AND THEY DECIDED TO MOVE ME HERE, TO THE MAIN RESISTANCE BASE WHERE I'VE FINALLY FOUND ONE PERSON WHO BELIEVES ME! HIS NAME IS SOKK AND HE TELLS ME HE KNEW MY NANNY BEFORE SHE WENT TO THE BIG CITY.

HE HAS PROMISED ME THAT PEOPLE WILL ACCEPT ME AND MY DAUGHTERS EVENTUALLY, AND I AM NOW WORKING CLOSELY WITH HIM, GIVING HIM, AND THE REST OF THE RESISTANCE, INFORMATION ABOUT MY FAMILY.

THEIR SURGEONS HAVE CHANGED US ALL PHYSICALLY, AND WHEN THE FUSS OVER OUR ESCAPE HAS DIED DOWN, WE WILL BE INTEGRATED INTO THE CIVILIAN COMMUNITY. I AM CURRENTLY BEING TAUGHT ABOUT THE CULTURE AND WAYS OF THE REAL WORLD, AS I, IN TURN, AM TEACHING THE RESISTANCE MEMBERS TO READ AND WRITE.

FINALLY, I THINK THAT MY LIFE MAY BE LOOKING UP.

Chapter 21

As I finish reading the last diary entry, the solid oak door behind me creeps open and Sokk comes into the room. As soon as I see him, I leap off the bed and fling my arms around his neck.

"Hey!" He exclaims laughing and pushing me away. "Glad to see you're awake at last!"

"How long did I sleep?"

"Two days!" He chortles. "You needed it."

I smile and glance nervously at the dusty furniture decorating the walls around us, a million questions burning in my mind.

"This room... was it dad's?" I already know the answer.

"Yes. We brought him here as soon as we decided to believe his story. Before we began the relocation process."

"What was he like.... then?"

"He shocked everyone. He spoke like an aristocrat, but somehow, he had none of the Noble's arrogance and pompousness. Despite his upbringing, he was kind and compassionate, and so patient with us while we decided whether or not we could trust him. During his life in the Big City, his power as a Noble heir was never really exercised, and underneath the layers of his family facade was a frightened little boy who never really grew up. It was almost like he was meant to be one of us, destined to fight against the evil he was born into by accident. The only thing that ever differentiated him as a Noble was his looks."

His words warm my heart. Since I discovered the truth about who my father really was, small doubts had begun to swim around my head. Was he really a good man? If he was a Noble, did he act and feel the same way as his family? Finally, after so long, I feel at peace with myself, knowing that dad was the kind and true father I remember. I smile, enjoying a moments peace that sweeps over me for the first time since I saw the Destructor's van almost six years ago.

I look up, staring earnestly into Sokk's round eyes. He grins.

"By the way, happy birthday Willow" From the depths of his pocket he retrieves a small package, wrapped in yellow tissue paper.

At first, I stare at him in confusion. Birthdays are associated with happiness, something I haven't known for so long I've almost forgotten what it is. But as generosity puts its golden package into my palm, I can't help but welcome it back into my life with open arms.

"Sixteen, Huh?"

Sixteen. When I was nine years old, living in the little cottage by the sea, sixteen meant I would be free to go out into the world, marry the prince of my dreams and live in a fairy-tale house to start a family of my own. Then, after dad was arrested, sixteen was the age where I could be properly initiated in the Resistance, and eventually attack the Big City, rescuing my father. But now? Now the number seems bleak and empty. Just a sign that time is passing, not only for me, but also for dad, and for May.

"May." I whisper, pushing past Sokk and running for the door. "I have to rescue May!"

"Wait!" Sokk pulls me back towards the bed. "You're not going anywhere. It's too dangerous!"

"But I have to save her." I wail "She's been there so long already!"

"We will save her! But not now. You remember what happened the last time you tried! You didn't get two miles before you were almost mutilated!"

I sit on the bed in silence, knowing that what he says is true, but not wanting to accept it.

"She will be rescued, with your father, soon. I promise." He sighs. "When it's time, the whole Resistance will attack the Big City. We will defeat the Noble's, and then, they will be safe, and there will be peace."

Sokk takes my hand and leads me out of the room. We walk through several long corridors that I vaguely recognise, before we arrive in a large, dark open space that caves in on one side. A giant screen takes up all of one earth wall, and artificial light floods the room as it senses our movement.

Sokk motions me to sit down on one of the long, brown sofas in-front of the screen. He then taps a small button on the side of it, making the dusty panel flicker into life.

Photographs of the twelve nobles flash before me, the Emperor hovering above them, looking menacingly at us down his long, pointed nose.

"You can't attack the Nobles until you know more about them." Sokk says. "Now choose one to start with."

I stare at the loathsome pictures, far too recognisable faces frozen in cruelty.

Fear automatically churning inside me fights anger and hatred as I mutter under my breath. "Antario."

Slightly surprised, Sokk taps the crystal picture of my grandfather. The image magnifies, and the other photographs are replaced with ones of his immediate family. Several facts also appear on the screen, circling his snarling face.

"Roberto Antario, overseer of the Destructors." Sokk reads. "Married the late Ansita Antario, who died thirty one years ago in childbirth."

Where the pictures of offspring should be, there are instead faded photographs of a young man and two small girls with luminous red crosses obliterating their bodies. I struggle to understand why I can't recognise myself, my sister, or my own father in the pictures before I realise that these were taken before we were all relocated.

"Roberto enjoys exercising the Destructors by terrorising communities. The Destructors are also used to control inflation and reduce poverty." Sokk grimaces as he reads this, our disgust mutual as I look away from the screen.

"Where did you get these files?" I ask, scanning the reels of information about the first Noble.

"Your father helped us develop them. We now have detailed profiles for almost every member of the Noble family."

I breath in slowly, understanding how important this information is. I close my eyes. "Can I see my mother now please?"

When my eyelids flutter open, a woman snarls into the camera, plastic surgery making her figure cold and hard.

" Malintaret Greatest, previously known by her married name, Antario, the eldest of the Emperor's two daughters. Her role is to oversee the torture chambers in the Big City. She lives in the Emperor's mansion, where most of her work takes place in the dungeons beneath the building." I sense Sokk's eyes on me, but I stare, firmly at the screen, listening to his toneless voice. "She has publicly stated that she despises all compassion and hope and resides on the board that decides who is to be screened each month."

"Stop" I whisper, and my voice breaks as my heart jumps into my throat, making me feel sick. "STOP!"

I clasp my hands over my ears and start to scream, crumbling on the floor as Sokk runs towards me.

"Shush" He says in a comforting tone that sounds too much like my father's. "It's alright. You're safe here."

Chapter 22

Sokk seems to have given up on training me. After my melt down in the information room I can't blame him. Instead, he keeps me busy with other things, and I've spent the last three weeks helping Resistance workers research and track the Noble's movements.

The sheer amount of horrors the Nobles wreak across the Country almost paralyses me with fear. Murders, maiming and several 'playful' torture practices terrorise towns and villages each day. Several times in the past few weeks, I've had to sit down and close my eyes, pushing the pain, the fear and the destruction away from my heart and trying to hold life at arm's length, where it can't hurt me.

I am now working with an elderly women called Shesha. She is shy and reserved, but friendly, with tattered grey streaks streaming through her pale chestnut hair. Shesha tells me she has been working closely with the Resistance in Rente since her husband and two sons were brutally stabbed to death by the Destructors over ten years ago. I don't know why or where, but from experience I understand that asking her will only revive more pain for the poor woman.

We soon discover that the Grangers, another public abuse team headed by the third Noble, Yepole Carrinte, have bombed a small, knitting factory in the west, believing that a Resistance base was planted there. Several innocent men and women have been killed, and since the ban of medical practices twelve years ago, more will die if the law is not broken soon.

I begin to shake, and cry when I read the report, but Shesha, having spent her life discovering incidents like these, quickly organises a team of Resistance workers and underground doctors to rescue and treat as many people as they can. I admire her strength and courage, but I can see how deeply it still affects her.

Slightly embarrassed at my incapability to hold myself together, I slip out of the room and begin to wander around the base, understanding that I am useless in this situation, and it would be better for me to keep out of the way.

The mountain base is divided into several chambers, separated by long, earth clad corridors. Walking aimlessly, I can't help but wonder how the mountain remains intact above our heads, and how it was built, and still exists, completely concealed from the Nobles.

Nobles. Nobles! Why do they rule our lives? What do they have that makes them so supreme? What makes them worthy of crushing us as if we were minuscule, unimportant crumbs of dirt?

I close my eyes and try to imagine a world without the Nobles, a world of peace and harmony. The world in the nursery rhyme father used to sing to me, and I used to sing to May.

Someday soon, there'll be an emerald green meadow,
On that day, brooks will laugh whilst children play,
On that day, there will be no more sorrow,
Someday soon, your worries will fade away.

Comforted by the childish words, I walk more briskly, energised by the ideal of a life full of happiness, generosity and innocence. A life with no pain, no sorrow, and no darkness.

I walk past a small room I have never been into before, and stop short. Through the closed door I hear, and instantly recognise the snarling, loath filled voice of my grandfather. I silently push the gnarled wood open a fraction and see a silver screen, portraying Rebato sitting, sternly upright on a cold, black sofa.

"Good evening, viewers." His voice has a sickly sweet tone with a flavour of uncanny menace. "This is a special message to some personal friends of mine" He laughs menacingly. "However, if you would like to listen in, be my honoured guest." His whole body turns, and the screen shows him through a different, closer camera. "Hello Rebels. Or as a little girl once told me you like to call yourselves, the Resistance."

Little girl? May! She's alive. Relief washes through my body. But it is soon replaced with fresh, prickling fear. What could they have done to make her tell them that? I creep slowly into the room, trembling, as if he were in there with me, and wasn't just a pixel on the wall. Shaking, I stare at him, straight into his black and beady eyes, as my ears quiver with what they are hearing.

"I'll keep this brief" His sickly sweetness sours into a cold, heartless voice. "There's a young child here who has been a great source of entertainment for her dear mother and our specialist team. I myself love to hear her sweet screams, they sound adorably painstaking. However, she is incredibly lonely. She keeps telling us that someone will come to rescue her. That someone will find her and bring her home to safety. So, will you come Heather Willow Nillon? Your sister is waiting for you."

The sound of my false name makes a monster of fear jump inside of me, growing so large it fights against the inside of my body, tearing me to pieces in an attempt to escape.

A scream I know only too well accompanies the screen as it fades to black. I stand, rooted to the spot for a few moments before I turn and start to run. Out of the room, I sprint through dozens of corridors, searching for the way out, the way to the surface, longing to escape this horrible maze.

Blinded by tears, I don't see the Resistance workers on either side stopping and staring at me. Blood pumping in my ears deafens me to the sound of Sokk chasing after me until he throws his strong arms around my waist. Two large and muscular men stand in front of me, preventing me from running anywhere.

"She was screaming!" I weep. "I need to rescue her. I need to find her!"

"You won't rescue her Willow, you'll only get yourself caught!" Sokk barks.

"I won't. I'll rescue her, and then bring her back here, or to the forest. Anywhere! They're torturing her!"

"Of course, they're torturing her. But not as much as they'll torture you if they catch you."

"I don't care. I don't care!!"

Crying uncontrollably, I try to fight against Sokk as he slowly leads me back towards my room, numb to my punches as I struggle against him. He lays me down on my bed and sits beside me.

"I saw it too Willow. But it's all a lie. It's all part of his plan to capture you. He wants to torture you to break your father. Your dad is a strong man. It will take a lot to make him talk. But if he saw you both, heard both of your screams echoing together, it would break his heart."

I close my eyes, not wanting him to see the stubbornness that still lies within them. Eventually, he gets up, and walks out of the room, I hear the key turn in the lock and my eyes flash open.

In my head, May's screams echo over and over. Rebato's words vibrate in my ears, sending me into a frenzy, punching the bedclothes in time with the constant thrumming of my heart. Guilt overwhelms me as I imagine my sister sitting alone in a prison cell. If she was lonely, then where was dad? Surely, they would at least let her be with her own father?

Memories flicker through my head. Memories from long ago. When we were a family. I remember sitting on the beach, looking out at the dark ocean and wondering if the Noble's teaching that this was only land on the planet was true. That was why we are called The Country, and not named as the individual towns and villages are. Now, I really hope that there are other, uncorrupted, countries. That not everyone lives like this.

I start to scream, trying to block out my memories and my fears. I need my sister here. She needs me. Soon my voice is hoarse, and I lie still on the bed, silently sobbing into the damp quilt.

I have to find her. I don't care what Sokk, nor anyone else says, I have promised too many people, including myself, that I would never let anything happen to my Maple.

As I stare quietly into the darkness, I know that I will not rest until May is safe in my arms.

Chapter 23

Hours later, I fling myself off the bed, unable to stay still as I battle the fears raging in my mind. Darting across the room, I struggle with the locked door, knowing that I will never prize the unbreakable magnet from its snug binding, but desperately wishing for a miracle to free me from my underground prison.

Frustrated, I collapse back onto the bed and stare up at the mud clad ceiling, images of May flickering in front of my wet eyelids. In the pit of my stomach, vulgar self-hatred makes me snarl inwardly, like a hyena waiting to pounce on one of its own children.

Glistening with tears as clear as raindrops but as cruel as snakes, my eye snags on the solemn handprint embedded in the brown, sickly coloured earth above my head. The one I created the day I first woke up here.

I kneel up on the bed, remembering how easily the earth had given way. I place my palm inside of the handprint, pushing it into the earth, and immediately, the print deepens several inches and a plan forms in my mind.

I leap off my bed and hurry to the small, en-suite bathroom, searching for the ancient shovel I found a couple of days ago. I didn't think anything of it at the time but now I can't believe how stupid I was!

I grope in the darkest corners of a cupboard that may never have felt a fresh air before, and finally grasp what must have once been shiny and glistening underneath its thick layer of molten mould and rust.

Coughing out the dust that seems to permanently linger in my lungs, I have to pause for a moment to let the breath inside of me rattle in and out until it returns once again to a steady rhythm.

I use a corner of my thick, already murky, jumper, to try and scrape some of the dirt off the shovel. It's so old it's almost an antique and the dust that cakes it is as thick as the door between the bedroom and the bathroom. I don't think it's been used for a long time, if ever, and I can't help but wonder why it was made. Shovels were replaced by electronic spades and robotic machines years ago, leaving no use for the hard, laborious tool that I doubt most of the Country has even heard of.

As the dust begins to flower into clouds of billowing smoke that hide the small spade from view, my fingers, invisible behind the fog, clutch something cold and smooth on the rough handle.

I bring the shovel so close to my eye I can see nothing else and make out a tiny white pearl embedded in the elegant wooden handle. The fog of smoke clears, and I read the regal, capitalised initials R.A. inked onto the precious stone.

Another of dad's souvenirs! This must have been the shovel he used to dig his way out of the Big City. It is silent and small, never regarded as anything more than an artefact so would have been perfect to slip under the Nobles noses. I stare at it in awe, feeling so much closer to him just by holding it and letting my fingers curl around the oval wood. I think about how it helped my father to escape his prison and feel somehow connected to him as it now helps me escape mine.

I gently close the door to the cupboard and fuelled by the heirloom of a man who had risked everything for me, I leave the bathroom and clamber onto the bed. Slightly afraid to stand on it, I wince when the old, but sturdy, wood bows beneath my weight.

Lifting the shovel above my head where I can reach the low ceiling, I push it firmly into the soil. The earth is dry and with one, jagged movement dirt rains down on me, heavily landing on my head and shoulders where I automatically shake it away, adding to the thick pile already mounting on the bed.

I begin to dig diagonally, ignoring the earth falling into my face as much as I can. The further into the ceiling I get, the more difficult it is to dig and the harder and more compact the soil becomes. Doubts rise in my mind as I ask myself if this is actually possible.

I have no idea how far I will have to dig to reach the outside of the mountain. Though I know that there are hundreds of steps from the bottom of the mound to reach this room, and it is relatively high compared to the rest of the base, it could still a long way below the grassy slopes. If I can even dig the tunnel wide enough, who's to say it will hold my weight and not cave in and drop me back into the room? I imagine landing on the hard floor, knocked unconscious, injured or even dead. I look down at the mess beneath my feet with a well-known cringe contorting my stomach. What if Sokk found me? Even if he saw me now I would be punished. I've already tried to escape once, and he knows more than anyone else that I would never just give up and accept my quarantine. I would be treated as a prisoner and moved into a more secure room with a guard at my door. There would be no way to run away, and I would have to live in the constant nightmarish knowledge of my father and sister's horrid torture.

If I give up now, I'll still be punished, and so, if only to flee the embarrassment of those consequences, I keep going. Once I can't reach to dig the tunnel from the bed, I haul myself up into the hole, tensing as I perch in the mouth of compact earth. I sigh with relief when I don't plummet downwards and destroy my work, and sit for a moment, dangling my legs into the room below.

I glance at my hands and realise that where I have been clutching the shovel, my palm has been imprinted with the silhouette of the gem. A raised emblem on top of the stone has also pressed itself into my skin. I hadn't noticed it on the shovel but now I can trace the soft figure of a dove. I should have guessed, dad was always crazy about the birds. He loved their beauty and their grace, and the way they flew with a natural elegance that was as light as the air. But the symbolism was more important to him, the idea that the extinct creature could bring peace and happiness to everyone. The thought lingers in my mind as I remember how the doves vanished immediately after the Nobles had seized power. The end of all hope.

I start digging at the earth again, letting the constant scraping of the shovel and the dull thud of dirt landing on the floor drown out my demoralising thoughts.

After what feels like hours of constant digging, deeper and deeper into the muddy gloom, my shovel suddenly gives way into the earth above me. I almost squeal with excitement as I overturn grass; green, wispy and comforting.

I scrabble to uncover more dirt that reveals a tangle of roots and moisture, and finally pull myself through a small gap, into an outdoor world that I feel as if I have never seen before.

Chapter 24

A smooth torrent of fresh air makes me gasp, smelling like delicate food I have finally been allowed to taste. Pulling myself up and out into the night sky, I absentmindedly brush off some of the mud caking my filthy clothes. As I stand on the mountain top, I gaze into the blackness shrouding the world, isolating, and disorientating. In the Resistance base, I lost all awareness of night and day, only vaguely conscious of my sleeping and eating patterns to tell me when the sun rose, and when it set.

I look down at the opening I have just dug through the mountain, half-discouraged by how short a distance I have come in hours of work. Even from here, I can still clearly make out the small, shady room and the bed now layered with thick mud less than twenty feet below. I realise that the room must be one of the highest in the mountain, probably also the least safe and most exposed to intruders. But I still doubt that Sokk would have even considered my escape through the solid earth, and the idea of him discovering the way I have defied him fills me with a guilty, childish pride.

The moon, silver and bright, peeks out from behind a cloud. I stare in awe, unable to pull my eyes from its spellbinding beauty. To see the moon in all its glory with no lamps or electric cable lights to obscure it, is illegal. One of the many laws that I am only beginning to understand as I break them. The moon looks dreamy, almost wistful. It seems like an emblem of hope, and I'm sure even the sight of something so pure and good would stir encouragement and perhaps even happiness in a hollow society. The simple image could infuse a conquest for a better world, a world with no oppressive Nobles pushing us down into the artificial earth. It's incredible how something so simple could rally the entire Country against the Nobles. Simple, yet so powerful it is charged with imprisonment.

The moonlight glimmers above the mountain as I stare down onto the quaint town of Rente. It lies still and at peace, daydreaming in its own sugar-cane bubble. I am sure that even if I searched the entire Country far and wide, I would not find be a place as happy or as childlike as this little town. The hardships they endure are the same as everywhere else. But the kindness and lasting love that they have for each other, even their enemies, keeps their hearts as tender as new born lambs and as pure as tears.

I can see the little houses, illuminated by the full moon. The streetlights are dark and lifeless, meaning that the national curfew of ten pm is long gone. I imagine the people sleeping innocently in their beds. How many of them have experienced loss and pain at the hands of the Nobles? How many hearts are aching as they cry for their families and friends? But still, so many of them put their lives on the sharp edge of humanity each day by working with the Resistance, passionate about stopping what is happening to the Country, and preventing what might happen soon.

This small town, which I first thought was weak and naïve, is now a role model of bravery. Far from living in a fairy-tale, these rebels live in hope. Hope as strong as the full moon that shines above me, smiling down on the town.

I stand in the silence for a long time, breathing in the beauty and the peace around me, something I'm guessing I won't experience much more of.

I begin to look around, not frantic yet but suddenly urgent. Where now? To have come this far and not be able to go any further is something I can't let myself to do. If I was found here... I won't even think about it.

Slowly, I walk down the mountainside towards the village, only paying enough attention to stop myself from falling head over heels. Escaping the mountain had seemed so impossible that I hadn't thought beyond it. There's no way I could walk to the Big City. It is too far, and the memory of last time still burns painfully in my mind.

I stare at the town that looms closer and closer as I move towards it. The layout is strictly organised with the houses to the left ordered by size and wealth. A cheap and scruffy estate sits closest to the centre, surrounded by a thick barbed wire fence and a gate that is locked by night, like every impoverished habitat of the Country. The gate sits directly opposite the town square, where the screen stands, now seeming desolate and lonely.

I slink into the shadows, paranoid that I will be spotted and arrested for being out after curfew. But the town is silent, without so much as a lamppost breathing in the streets.

I jog through the town square, past empty shops and empty buildings that only seem to be there to fill the spaces. I have no idea where I'm going, racking my brain and scouring the surroundings for inspiration but coming up with nothing. I pass another shop and my eyes snag on something in the corner of the window.

At first, the sight of the gun makes me almost scream. But as I peek through the glass, I quickly confirm that no one is inside the building.

Taking deep, even breaths, I turn around, and start running towards the factory.

As I run, I remember that the guns from the factory are transported by government officials to the Big City. They don't go during the day, as they would attract too much attention and risk a riot. Instead, the workers leave the finished products in two large storehouses each evening and they are then taken to the Big City under the cover of darkness.

The fourth Noble, Hardnida Delvaaint, takes charge of weapons and destructive substances, and he co-ordinates the gun's safe passage to the Big City. Shivering, I can almost see his eagle shaped face looming in front of me, whispering his sarcastic motto; "To prevent and to protect" as I realise that whoever works beneath him and transports the weapons must have been fully born and bred in the Big City, or else they would run away.

I slow to a walk as the adrenaline from my escape wears off, my limbs are already weak and tired. It seems like hours before finally, the grey, stone walls of the factory loom ahead of me.

My heart beats faster, my stomach flips as new energy courses through my body, and I hug the walls, skirting the building until I reach two, huge storehouses. On the gravel path beside them sits a large block on wheels, which looks like some sort of train.

Dad used to tell me about trains when I was younger, whispering in his gentle, magician-like voice that in the Big

City there were massively long electric vehicles which could travel so quickly that if you blinked, you'd miss them.

I recognise the shining steel and streamlined body in the front of the 'train' however behind the long silver carriage there is a long line of metal carts. These are a lot shorter than the main carriage and an odd, upside down triangular shape with a single wheel at the tip, which in this case sits at the bottom of the cart. Each cart is attached to the others via a long metal bar, and even from this distance I recognise it as Cognofie; an extremely malleable however incredibly strong metal.

There are six carts in total, all lined up like convicts before a firing squad. Each cart is embroidered with the Noble's ruling crest that repels any intruders, and to me, is associated with memories that send shivers down my spine in irregular volts of electric shocks.

The lights flicker on in the second storehouse and I flinch back into the mess of shadows as voices emerge from the large metal door.

"How many have we got in here?" A rough, female voice asks.

"Seventy-two shotguns, fifty lasers and twenty bombs. One hundred and forty-two in total." A small, squeaky reply. Young and uncertain, and his tone suggest that he is far beneath the woman, desperate to earn her approval.

"That few? Leave a recording telling them to increase production or Hardnida Delvaaint will visit them in person."

"Yes Ma'am." Through the door to the storehouse, I hear shuffling footsteps and a grovelling murmur as the message is repeated into a tape recorder.

"Hurry up!" The woman barks, and her voice has a threatening undertone that I fear the squeaky voiced male knows only too well. "Stack the weapons in the carts!"

Chapter 25

From my shadowy hiding place, I see a small, bent boy emerge from one of the storehouses. The other, I now notice, is empty.

He is followed by the woman, who's tight bun and curled nose personifies her voice faultlessly. The boy, who can't be more than fourteen, carries a large pile of guns bundled in his arms, and as he struggles to open the metal doors to the first tram, he drops several weapons to the floor. The woman does not attempt to help the child, but instead stands mechanically vertical, every vertebra of her back articulated, as she stares down her jagged nose at her minion. Once the tram is finally open, the boy drops the guns into an already half-full container and returns to the warehouse.

Hearing them stumbling around inside, I take a deep breath and seize my opportunity. I run across the cobbles of the courtyard and clamber into the open tram that is now almost completely full, dragging the heavy doors closed behind me and diving into the sea of metal. Seconds later, I hear the woman chastising the boy as they approach the train. I hold my breath when they pass my cart, but neither of them seem to notice that the doors are now shut. I listen to the clatter of another pile of weapons crashing into the cart, and then what sounds like a painful blow to the child's face. A short whimper is quickly snuffled by a harsh word, and the boy's footsteps move towards the next cart in silence.

I lie still, frozen amongst the guns that seem to be taunting me as they press their cold metal into my bare flesh.

"What is it like here?" The young boy whispers to the woman, "living on the outside".

"How should I know? I've lived in the Big City all of my life, just like you have. But haven't you seen the cameras and the locked gates? The people here are just as enslaved as we are! Besides, we could never live out here, even if we wanted to."

"Why not?" The boy asks, seeming to have lost all his shy fear in the few seconds since he last spoke.

"When a slave is born into the Big City, they're implanted with a tracking device. If you even try to run, they'll catch you in minutes. And then...."

"And then?"

"Malintaret."

Even the sound of my mother's name turns the air stale and deathly. It's as if the word is a taboo, causing the winds to change and the skies to darken to a deeper shade of black.

"What happened to that little girl they arrested? Maple...her daughter?"

May? At the mention of my sister, my breath freezes in my lungs and my arms and legs tense.

"She's alive. The Emperor won't kill her yet. Not until he's got the other one." I hear the woman pass my cart and make her way towards the front of the train, her solid shoes clicking on the gravel with sharp, dicing clarity. "We should be going. The others might come after us if we're any later."

The conversation has been dropped and I hear the boy's dragging footsteps as the gravel clings to the grooves on his shoes. He quickly scrapes them clean before entering the main carriage. The door slams shut, and beneath me, I feel the silent rumble of an engine as the train lurches forwards.

My hand is resting on something rough and metallic. It doesn't feel like one of the guns, but is older with chips and cracks lining the surface of the metal. The tram doors and intrusive darkness, seeping through the cracks from the outside, blind my eyes, but I carefully run my fingers over the foreign, metal object that is attached to the base of the cart.

A strange whirring noise seems to be echoing from it, and it begins to heat up. My hand flinches away when I realise it is the engine.

The mechanism scares me. I don't know anything about motion technology; only that last summer there was a huge explosion on the outskirts of Rente when someone touched an engine.

The seventh Noble, Maninta Genzashu, has the responsibility of 'Handling Public Relations'. His job is to circle the towns and villages and infuse even more fear into the citizens of the Country.

I remember the day he came to Rente. We were marched from the factory to the town square, as we are each month for the Screening. But this time, when we arrived, they had built a large wooden stage. We were made to stand in age groups and the edges of the square were bordered with guards and guns, pushing themselves into the crowd if someone even breathed too loudly.

May was dragged away to stand with the other eleven-year olds, near the front of the crowd. We all stood and watched Maninta Genzashu as he made his long and threatening speech on how defying the Big City or disrespecting the Nobles, would lead to an endless whirlwind of pain. He told us that death was a mercy, and that they took special care to ensure children who dared to defy the law would continue living in the memory of pain and regret.

"Even the young ones." He said, and the seventh Noble snapped his fingers, as a guard dived into the crowd and seized a child in the front few rows. Everyone held their breath, stood on their toes and strained their eyes to find the poor victim, and my blood turned ice cold when I saw the two, frightened eyes of Maple.

Maninta seized her by her small neck, and her face contorted as his fingers found a pressure point in her back. A woman behind me screamed. I didn't dare to look back, I just heard the gunshot and felt the vibrations through the floor as the woman's limp body fell to the ground.

"What's your name?" Maninta released his grip on the child, not seeming to have noticed the murder at the back of the square. Silence screamed for a few moments. What if he recognised her? May's wide eyes scanned the crowd before they finally found mine, and I sent her a silent warning not to tell the truth.

"May...." She stuttered "zee." The syllable ran off her tongue quickly, like a waterfall flooding out of her mouth. "Mayzee Tille."

Maninta snarled. "Have you been good Mayzee Tille? Or are you a bad girl?" He breaths heavily and May closes her eyes. "Because you know what happens to bad girls!" He sneered, and threw her back into the crowd.

Later, when he was leaving the town, we were all ordered to stand on the hillside and wave him off, as if he were a celebrity that we all couldn't wait to see again. Seven cars full of bodyguards and servants, four of which preceded him, as the other three trailed behind, accompanied his indulgent limousine.

They were about half a mile away from the town when it happened, but we were all still standing there, watching. None of us had dared to move until he was completely out of sight.

The front car exploded first. I remember the loud bang, bouncing off the hills and reverberating like it would in one of the infamous cathedrals the Nobles loved to plaster across our screens in boastful pride. The vehicle went up in a cascade of orange flames that quickly spread to the next car, and then the next. Before the limousine itself was absorbed in the phoenix flourish, the small frame of the least valued Noble leapt from the bullet proof glass door onto the gravel road.

Many hours of intimidation followed, as the Noble and his five surviving henchmen held us all at gunpoint. But no one confessed to causing the explosion. Engineers from the Big City arrived whilst we were all forced to stand on the hill-bank for hours, afraid to breathe lest we be accused and arrested.

It was finally revealed that the explosion was caused by a guard accidentally brushing the delicate engine mechanism in the front car. None of the living guards confessed to it, and they stood like naughty children as they received a long lecture on the sensitivity of the newly discovered hyper-acid, and the dangers of even breathing on the complicated mechanics.

The five soldiers stared fixedly at the ground, and despite that the culprit had probably already been blown to bits in the explosion, they were all shot dead. 'Just to make sure.'

Chapter 26

I edge cautiously away from the motor, remembering once hearing someone say that the night trains are twice as powerful as the Noble's cars or limousines, to give them the speed to complete their rounds in time. It's roughly five hundred miles from Rente to the Big City, and these trains have to be inside the gates before dawn. My whole body lurches as I suddenly realise how fast I must be travelling and my heart begins to race as I become more acutely aware of the explosives around me crashing into each other with every jostle of the car.

I feel the train speed up as it twists and winds along the roads. All I can see is a terrible, never ending darkness that makes my heart feel as if it has dropped into my stomach the way that a stone quickly sinks to the bed of a river. Guns push into my arms and my legs, and I feel barrels and handles pressed against my back and chest. All it would take is one small movement to knock a trigger and blast my body to smithereens. I can't tell whether I'm sitting or lying amongst the weapons, but I don't move. Only absolute stillness will preserve my life.

I wonder which types of gun are facing me. Before we were relocated in Rente, Sokk gave us a fact file on what life was like there. We were told about the factory, and explicitly informed about the many different forms of guns that were made.

I carefully trace the nose of the gun beside my right hand to find a small star shape pressed into the metal that confirms what I fear. These are Ex-thermin guns that only workers over the age of thirty are even allowed to touch. Only made by those who are too crushed to consider their rebellious potential, people who have lost their youth and hope, and people who the Nobles wouldn't glance back at if the guns pushed them into their coffins.

They make these guns half a mile away from the main factory and explosions happen almost every month. The danger lurks in the poison released by the bullets, created by scientists - the underdogs of the fifth Noble, three years ago.

It kills by draining all of the fluid from its victim's body, tested in a cold November Screening when we were all crowded in the courtyard crunching a thin layer of frost under our toes as we tried to stamp out the cold.

The victim was a young boy, like the one now driving the train. The Nobles like to use children, not only because it is more torturous and painful for those watching, but also to kill the naive hope of young revolutionaries, and force them back into the Noble's submission.

The boy was shot with the bullet squarely in the stomach, but the poison began its lethal work in the child's eyes.

Whilst they began to dry into salty sockets that looked like miniature sculls, his hair grew wispy and dry.

The boy clutched at his head and screamed at the pain that was squeezing the juice from his brain, but then, the acid clipped his mouth and he couldn't make a sound. We watched in equal silence as the pigment in his skin faded to a greyish white and his body collapsed, folding in on itself as his nails fell off, one by one.

When he finally lay still on the ground, he looked more like an old man than a young boy.

I now stare fearfully at the gun as I wonder how long I will spend incarcerated in this cart with it. I feel like I should hold my hands up in surrender to the solemn faces of the dark weapons surrounding me. I try to plan for what lies ahead but I don't know how the Big City is laid out. Though the screens in the town squares and in our homes often show us public courtyards or grand buildings, the overall layout of the ostentatious city is kept hidden.

I rack my brains for anything Sokk might have told me, but after my breakdown over the Noble's fact files, he hasn't given me any more useful information.

The Resistance base outside the Big City is found by diving into a hollow tree. Trains transport goods from every town and village, and the last ones that travel from the small peninsular of the Country, will not reach the Big City until dawn. This would mean the gates open and close constantly throughout the night.

So, I'll rescue them, and we'll jump into the tree and the safety of the Resistance. Pictures of May flutter across my mind. Images of her and I being together, reunited at last. Her smile and gentle laugh as we climb mountains together and eat blackberries picked straight from the bushes. Her warm hands soothing my cold ones as we sit around the small fire telling funny stories and playing silly games.

Finally, I let myself think of my father. I remember him laughing and smiling, hugging May, holding my hand when we walked across the seafront, lifting me over puddles and pressing delicate shells that he said were made especially for me into my palm.

He's missed so much as I've grown up. I wonder if, even if my appearance hadn't been changed when I was relocated, he would recognise me now.

Did he recognise May? She's no longer the innocent seven-year-old he knew. The pain of losing him and learning of her past and legacy has aged her decades in years.

Who even is he now? Who has he become? Five years is such a long time. So many days and nights that he has spent in constant agony. Pain that I can't even think about. Infamous machines and contraptions; knives and bullets. Even imagining that someone I love so much could be undergoing so much torment makes my palms sweat.

May. I can hardly think of her without bursting into tears. It has been too long. For almost all of her life she's only known suffering that she doesn't deserve, and now she's alone and afraid, probably bleeding and weeping in a cold prison cell. I lost track of time when I was in the mountain, I couldn't even tell day from night. But I know that it must have been weeks, maybe even months that I spent cowardly trying to forget the world.

My mind whirls like a cyclone of fear and regret, and I silently beg the train to travel faster so I can reach the Big City soon and protect the people I love, who have suffered for far too long at the hands of the Nobles.

Guilt stirs inside me like a python, especially when I think of May. It should have been me that the Destructors took. Maple is too innocent. Too young and sweet. Who could hurt her? Who could be heartless enough to lay a finger on the very image of light and hope?

Once again, I hear her terrible scream that is trapped, forever echoing in my ears. My grandfather's sly words are tampered with and worsened by my imagination as they fester in the dark guilt inside me.

It should have been me. It's my fault she's in such pain. If I'd been there, I could have stopped them. I could have hidden May where they wouldn't find her.

I know in my heart that the Nobles would always find her, no matter where she hid, but I push this into a deep corner of my mind. They have radars that detect human life to the nearest inch, but maybe they were faulty. Maybe the technology would have more of a heart than the Destructors and let her go unseen.

I want to scream with an agony that should have done something to help her. However, my dark imaginings soon flee from my mind as I am thrust forward and the train purrs to a halt.

Chapter 27

I lie in tense silence, ready to leap out of the cart at a moment's notice if I need to. In the dramatic quiet, my breath echoes around the cart sounding harsh and loud. I hear the creaking of an electronic gate and the train starts to move once again.

When we pass through the gates, the entire atmosphere seems to change. Even though I can't see through the walls of the cart, I sense the very moment we enter the Big City.

It feels strange. The refresh of the outside world has vanished completely, and there is a jarred atmosphere of oppression and obedience. Though the silence is no more intense, it seems more solemn. Even the guns around me are less threatening, as if they have bowed down in submission to the harsh light seeping through the cracks below the cart's doors.

The train rolls onwards, more slowly this time, bringing me further into the depths of the Big City. I'm strangely excited as the aura of the city settles, so many rumours and myths have circulated the place, I feel almost privileged to be here.

"Wake up, you stupid boy." My thoughts are cut short by the razor-sharp words of the woman driving the train. "We're right outside the Quarters. Be back here after dawn to unload."

I here two sets of footsteps fade into the distance, one sharp, the other lethargic. I wait for what is at least another ten minutes before even daring to touch the side of the cart, but when I do manage to push the metal doors, I am forced to slam them shut by a loud red light glaring into my eyes.

More carefully this time, I push the doors open by an inch, and though again I am almost blinded, I struggle with the light until my eyes adjust. I realise that the strange redness seems to be coming from the thick smoke that clogs the air. Moments before it starts to seep through the small crack in the doors, I yank them closed as I realise what the smoke is.

DNA smoke. A chemical that will register, analyse, and report anything unknown, living or dead, that enters its biological composition.

Nervously, I open the doors again and look around, searching for a way out of the cart. The red smoke is billowing everywhere, lighting the night with its radar senses and baited thickness that is probably poisonous to intruders. As I prepare to dive and risk the fog, hoping to find some sort of emptiness beyond, I spot a small patch of blackness to my right that seems to have been avoided by the thick mist.

I glance around at the empty night and leap out of the cart, carefully landing crouched on the floor. Like a crab, I scuttle underneath the clouds of red fog with my jacket pulled up over my head, and all of my exposed skin facing the ground, as low as possible. I reach the clear patch with my nose pressed to the floor, and when no alarms seem to sound, I move around until I am sitting in what I can now make out as a small hole within the wall of a building. The air in the hole seems heavy, too heavy for the smoke and threatening to smoother me if I don't move soon.

I stare out at the fog, relying on its light to see how far it extends. To the left, it stretches for as far as I can see and destroys the eerie darkness, and below it a greyish road leads around the corner where the train has just carried me. I thought that I would be able to see the gates there; but I guess they are cloaked in the identity-betraying mist.

My stomach lurches as a wisp of fog almost strokes my bare hand. Not only would I come up as an intruder to the Big City, but they would be able to identify me easily. Though relocation has changed my physical features, there is still no discovered way to morph a person's DNA.

I look straight ahead to where the fog is slightly thinner, but still weighs heavily on the atmosphere. I glance upwards, and when I shuffle slightly sideways I can see a plaque on the wall of the building above me. There is a clear image of a man and woman dressed in rags and sleeping on rusty bunk beds. I assume I'm hiding in the wall of the servant's quarters.

The heavy pressure of the air around me is becoming too much as I look to my right, desperate to find another patch of safety. A long way off, the fog seems to thin and disappear, and I can almost see another building. Hugging the wall and kissing the ground, I prepare to edge towards the next haven where the smoke cannot scavenge for my identity or hunger for my flesh.

When I creep out of the hole, I suddenly feel light and dizzy, and have to stop for a moment before I shuffle along the wall, pinching my eyes shut against the morbid, prickling atmosphere. The fog seems to become thinner and thinner as I travel further towards the next building that looms with sharpening clarity. Finally, the air is completely clear, and I can stand up straight, slowly breathing in the, still thick and stale, but compared to the fog, refreshingly light, air.

I glance back and gasp at the way the fog gradually grows, the servant's quarters now completely hidden in the murky red distance. The road emerges from the mist, winding its way through a maze of trees that clump together and form a forest. I almost laugh at the way the forest has been mechanically put together. The artificial trees look too perfect, too immaculate to pass as real organisms, and they smell of burnt rubber and plastic. They sway gently, despite the lack of even a breath of wind in the air that resembles the stillness of one of the solid, antique statues which glare down onto the road from either side.

A mechanical whooshing pierces the silence and makes me jump. I swerve away from the trees, knowing that most people would dart into them for cover and to hide from any patrolling guards on the outside.

But I know the way the Nobles think, and though trees provide respite, they also conceal what might be lurking inside. Traps and alarms will be littered everywhere. The floor of the forest is artificial, and probably rigged with sensors that would either detect and betray me instantly, or blast me sky high before I can even open my mouth to scream.

To my right is a long, thick building imprinted with another plaque that tells me it houses more slaves. I press myself into the shadows and hope that the wall doesn't have detectors. As I slowly creep further away from the entrance to the Big City, and the fog, I can faintly hear sobs, whimpers, and the occasional snore coming from the other side of the wall, and I imagine the servants lying there, some with their families, others shivering alone, on this dark and dreary night. Would they be blamed when me and May escape? My heart lurches but I can't help but hope that they wouldn't mind being punished for her freedom. If they knew her, or had even seen her kind, loving face, I'm sure they would walk into furnaces of fire for her, just as I am now.

Chapter 28

The trees that surround the road gently curve to the left and I can imagine the Nobles travelling through them in their ostentatious limousines, completely oblivious to anything except their own indulgent bubble. They sit back and shut their eyes as they pass through the red fog and the servant's quarters, not humbling themselves to even think about the suffering men, women and children drowning in their own filth. I can see them entering the forest and smiling, perhaps remarking on the beautiful, artificial scenery, or the machine generated weather. The chauffeur stares straight ahead, silent in his duty and forcing himself to show the Nobles feigned respect for the sake of his family's lives.

The Servant's Quarter's reach an end and I have to dart across open tarmac to where I can just make out the end of the line of trees. The road brings itself out of the woods into an enormous parking area.

I stop and gawp at the mass of machinery, as my eyes find a small gap in a large circle made up of fourteen cars.

The vehicles are parked in seven pairs, and a golden number is painted on each bonnet. The same number is shared by each limousine car that travels on four solid wheels, and its accompanying glider. I stare at the gliders in awe. They rest about a foot above the paved tarmac and the space underneath them is slightly translucent.

Air cars, or gliders hover above the ground, using some kind of magnetic repellent to keep them afloat. They can rise up to more than twenty feet above the earth and travel at over six hundred miles per hour. However, the Nobles tend to use their limousines more often when they visit the Country because of their longer ranges. Therefore, to most of society, gliders are fables, starring in fairy tales and bedtime stories as the height of richness, instantly recognisable but never really believed to actually exist.

The cars are bathed in a golden glow that seems to hang above them like a mist. Each of the Nobles have two main carriages, and I'm almost certain there are dozens more in the large garages that lurk directly behind the ring of vehicles. As the Noble's rise in status, according to their number, so does the grandness of the cars. The body of the second Noble's limousine is bronze, and the glider is tinted with pale bronze windows and mirrors. The first Noble's car shines a bright, clear silver, making me jump when I see myself in the reflection on the bonnet.

Finally, I turn around to gaze into the centre of the circle.

A blaze of golden glory almost blinds me as I gawp at the Emperor's luxurious limousine. It looks as if it were made entirely out of gold, a metal made extinct years ago. It's pure glistening colour is magnificent, and I now realise that it is emitting the soft, sparkling glow that reflects off each of the other vehicles. The limousine is studded with jewels that create the word Emperor and draw the Noble's symbol on the grand doors. The windshield is tinted with a colour that is like the shine of the sun on blonde hair, and the windows hold elegant patterns that slip seamlessly amongst the curves of the limousine.

I then turn my attention to His glider, and I have to strain my neck to look up at the spectacle resting seven feet above the ground. Directly below it lies a pool of golden light that somehow sparkles, as if there were crystals floating in the air. It is a different shape to the other gliders, representing a kind of spacecraft with wings sticking out around the base, and a domed body, again bathed in a colour of pure glory.

I suddenly jump when I realise how long I have spent staring at the cars and hurry out of the circle, past the dozens of closed garages which I know must hold more treasures.

I shrink into the shadows, where my footstep's steady thud on the ground beats in time with the thrum of my heart and anticipation begins to eat me from the inside out.

I stop, gasping, when I see something I recognise. The sharp pebbles looming ahead make me cover my eyes, shielding them from the sight of the shallow courtyard. I can't look as I run past the spectacle that I witness every month, shrouded with loudness and jeering as each Screening unravels. Now its eerie silence makes it even more terrifying, and a mixture of memories and imaginings send shivers down my spine.

I pass buildings on either side that loom ostentatiously grand with no idea where I am going. All I know is that I have been running straight into the centre of the City, sure that I must be getting closer to the Noble's grand mansions.

Majestic palladiums and theatres stand like gargoyles all around me, alongside other buildings that I don't recognise, let alone understand the purpose of, though I'm sure there is some sick pleasure that the Nobles can leech from everything.

May wouldn't be in a prison on her own. She'd be guarded, and close to people who could torment her.

Just imagining where she might be tightens my chest and I have to stop for a moment and close my eyes to calm myself down.

The torture chambers are inside the Emperor's mansion. 'I don't even have to step outside for perfect entertainment.' He said once, during one of his long and abusive national speeches.

When I reopen my eyes, I see a large, golden number seven hovering in the darkness in front of me. I tip toe forward and can soon make out an enormous building that lurks in the distant gloom – a mansion. It is still quite a long way off, and I quietly crouch down behind a thick bush as I survey it.

The seventh Noble's Mansion is five stories tall. I can't make out any features of the house, but the illuminated number shows me that there are no lighted windows. A sigh of relief escapes me as I think about how awful it would be to be discovered here, so close to finding my sister yet still so far from escaping with her.

I glance around, and see two roads branching off to the left and right. Carefully removing one of my socks, I tie it to a twig in the hedge, so I'll know which path to take coming back with May, and dad, but as their names cross my mind my muscles tense. Shaking my head to stop my thoughts, I follow the hedge down the left-hand road, hoping that it will lead me to the other Noble's homes.

I realise that I am travelling in an arc, when I see the sixth Nobles' mansion, this one a lot grander than the seventh. A light shines in a window on the top floor and my breath catches when I notice a silhouetted figure standing against the glow. Thankful for the bush I am behind I rapidly scuttle onwards, not stopping until I am well clear of the house.

The arc becomes a circle and then turns into a spiral; I am crawling on all fours, with an uncanny sense of twirling into oblivion as I hide in-between two hedges that almost completely conceal me from view. Each mansion I come to is grander and more ostentatious than the last, but as pits drop in my stomach, I realise each mansion has increasingly more security. Front lawns the size of football pitches, and each littered with painfully obvious traps and alarms, as well as others that I'm sure lie cleverly hidden.

When I reach the second Noble's house I hear the sound of dogenai barking. I panic that the mutant creatures can smell me and quickly crawl on. The first Noble's house seems quieter than the others. But I know too well that silence can be more deadly than the loudest scream.

I stop for a while, acknowledging the place I spent the first five years of my life. A part of me hopes to feel something, some sign of recognition or understanding. But no memory hits me. The horrors of my life here have completely erased themselves from my mind, only reappearing in nightmares that are too painful to think about outside of sleep.

The spiral ends with a pinnacle of grandeur that I could never even have dreamed of. The parallel hedges finish their journey and I lift my head to see a palace that pierces the air like a knife as sharp as blood. The building itself seems to be emitting a strange, golden light that shines onto the front lawn and the spiked fence with a dangerous arrogance.

The mansion is circular. I count the widows to find nine floors. On top, there is a dome that hangs about twenty feet above the building, supported by a long, thin tube that is not wide enough to be one of the platform risers that lift the Nobles between floors, and so must be a staircase. The palace seems to be surrounding something, and rising out of the middle of what I guess is a courtyard at the centre of the mansion, is a tall, circular tower that looks darker and somehow more morose than the rest of the building.

The front lawn stretches over a mile and has a long, wide path leading to an old-fashioned moat with a drawbridge raised on the opposite side. I wonder if they have a full-time guard operating it, or whether it is automatic, but I push the idea of going into the building through the front door firmly out of my head, knowing that it would be impossible.

Directly in front of me, a nine-foot tall, spiked fence shivers with electricity. Beyond that, I can see a complex structure of alarms and traps that are ready to pounce on anyone, or anything trying to get in, or out of the mansion. A thick forest of trees begins on the outside of the gate, and finishes just below a window on the seventh story, its artificial leaves swaying softly in the non-existent wind.

I stare at the image, hoping, begging for there to be some way to enter the mansion. I can't have come this far only to be stopped so close to the end. Even from here, I can almost feel the screams echoing inside. Maybe not now this instant, but yesterday, and earlier today, and I can't allow them to escape tomorrow.

Chapter 29

I softly creep forwards to get a closer look at the alarm system.

The wrought iron gates stand between two menacing towers which I'm sure are manned with gunners ready to pounce on any sign of movement. The gates themselves are decorated with long, sliding patterns that slip between the metal bars like snakes, with ridges and dips on their bodies that look like they're laced with poison.

The tall, sly fence slithers around the mansion, smugly smiling in its refusal to allow anyone to pass. If I crane my neck upwards I can just about spot the glistening spikes on top of the fence reflecting the moonlight. Lying below it are a mob of dead leaves, twigs, and small animals; blackened and burned as if they have been fried before being finally laid to rest, contorted and almost unidentifiable.

I sit painfully still as I stare through the bars and onto the front lawn of the mansion. The luminescent green grass is littered with ornaments, fountains, statues and other luxuries that I haven't seen before. I feel sick as I think about how the Country is pushed down into poverty, barely surviving in a world where children starve and go without smiles for days, and here the Nobles choke on unnecessary wealth and never-ending riches.

A glistening path leads from the gate to the mansion and I gasp when I realise that it's made from ironed money. A silver, mechanical light shines through the translucent paper notes, one of the more obvious traps that I'm sure would either suck me into the ground, propel me into the sky, or just have me shot on the spot from one of the many towers which are decorated with guns and lasers.

These towers line the mansion, and are situated every twenty feet along each wall. They stand uncannily straight and loom blacker than the night, each menacingly angry with a luminous, golden spot painted on the front of each turret.

From the top of every tower glares a large, intense spotlight which concentrates itself on the lawns as it harshly rotates, following its set path like a soldier, with exaggerated vigour and purpose.

Guns, hyper-sensitive to movement, are embedded in the walls of the towers, positioned to reach every inch of the grounds with a bullet that either kills its victim instantly, or stuns and painfully tortures them.

The soft grass itself is ridden with traps and snares ready to massacre anyone who touches it uninvited.

As I take in every inch of the battlefield in front of me I slowly sink back into my heels, my hopes sparse and crumbled, and think about turning around, sneaking out when the last train comes in, and going home with my head held low and my tail between my legs.

The trees wave and taunt me as I admit defeat to the mansion's unbeatable security. The trunks on the inside of the fence glisten with traps, and the bed of artificial leaves below them cover empty holes in the forest floor, pushing intruders who might have hoped that the cover meant safety, into the Noble's firm grasp.

May is so close I'm sure that if I shouted her name she'd hear me, but she's still too far away for me to sing or even whisper words of comfort to her. I squeeze my eyes shut to the point where all I see is a fuzzy mess of colour, glaring with an intrusive stare as the mansion slowly fades away.

Even now, with the world shut behind my closed eyelids, all I can see is May. Her face, so young and beautiful. Her eyes reflecting the innocence of the whitest lily as it floats on top of a river. Her lips curling to form a perfect smile as she seems to grow younger with each passing second, holding my hand and transporting me back to a day at the beach nine years ago.

She had just turned five years old, I was seven. We were sitting with dad on the long stretch of sandy coastline that holds our only happy memories. It was the middle of July, and the sun beat down on us with a soft firmness as May and I played in the sand, creating a fortress out of the golden dust. Dad watched, gently amused as we built a moat and even carried water from the sea to protect us from whatever enemies would be small enough to be stopped by it.

May ran to search for decorations for the sand-mansion, and I lay down beside my father, turning my head and staring up into his wise old eyes.

"What would happen if I swam out to sea, and never stopped swimming?" I asked, glancing at the endless expanse in front of me. "If I kept going, forever?"

"You'd drown." He said bluntly, "or die of hunger or thirst."

"But if I didn't. If I just kept going and going and going."

"You'd end up on a beach on the opposite side of the Country."

"Is there nothing else out there?"

He didn't speak for a while, and the silence sounded like the thoughts of a man who had to decide whether to impart truth, or a myth that people must live believing. "No, nothing" he said eventually. "Only water and fish".

At that point, May came running up to us with fists filled with shells. Her face was beaming, full of joy and innocence and I grasped her hands and pulled her close to me and the three of us sat for a moment, simply bathing in each other's presence, a family together.

The picture freezes, and I want it to stay like that forever, but my mind mutates the blissful faces in my memory to ones of hatred and spite. The happy family crumbles, and our joyful features twist into the all too familiar image of my grandfather, his hair warped and styled into the shape of a knife, and his lips dyed the colour of blood.

His emotionless, deceptive voice echoes through me like a sword as I remember his speech on the vulgar screen in the Resistance base.

"So, will you come Willow? Your sister is waiting for you."

"Willow, your sister is waiting for you."

"Your sister is waiting for you."

"Waiting for you."

"Waiting."

The words slice through my heart, as May's scream vibrates so loudly I can hardly tell whether it is coming from my mind or the mansion in front of me. My eyes flash open and I pull myself into the shadows, glancing around like a frightened rabbit. The scream slowly begins to fade from my imagination until all that is left inside me is a raw determination to either save my sister or die trying.

All of a sudden, I feel a shadow standing over me and freeze.

Slowly turning around, I almost laugh out loud with relief when I realise it is only a tree - a part of the grand forest that leads to the wall of the mansion but begins outside of the gates. These trees don't have glistening traps or deceptive claws because they are outside of the fence, reaching over it as they clump together and lean into the darkness.

The trunks of the trees are completely bare, and the branches have been hacked off with an electric chainsaw to prevent climbers. However, they are made to replicate very old oaks and as I stand up I notice small holes in the bark that lead into a looming hollowness inside the trees. I follow the forest backwards, further away from the mansion as the holes in the trees grow larger and larger. When I reach the end of the forest, the holes are still quite small, but I am able to haul myself into one of them. I place one hand on each side of the trunk and push upwards against it, pulling away from the ground. Swinging my legs into the hole, I softly drop down inside the tree.

The opening is small, and it strains against my hips, but I force myself through and land panting on a layer of brown dirt that sends up a cloud of smoke, choking me in stale air. The earth beneath me smells rich and pure as I realize that it is real, not like the chemically and ergonomically buoyant soil I have been walking on. I reach down and take some in my hand, letting it run between my fingers and caking my palms in its familiarity. Nature has always promised me happiness and hope. Nature, and the earth was there long before the Nobles came and started their rule of hate, and it will be there long after the Nobles have ceased to control us. The fresh, pure earth is like an invader to the Big City. I feel like it resembles me in some ways, there in secret to undermine the Nobles with an ever-present hatred. The dirty ground gives me new hope and energy to go on as I lift myself onto one of the little shelves of bark on the inside of the hollow tree.

Chapter 30

Inside the tree, the roots twist and tangle along the raw bark, mimicking the knots in my stomach as they create intricate patterns and ladders that wind upwards into the grand heights of the proud sapling. I crane my neck as I watch the swirling designs dodge up the inside of the trunk that becomes gradually thinner as it rises to the top. A burst of white moonlight shines through the very tip of the tree where there is a hole that, from the bottom, seems small and closed in, almost like a brightly lit ceiling.

I clamber up onto one of the thicker roots, wincing as it bounces beneath my weight. I relax slightly when it remains intact but grip another root above my head when I begin to teeter over the edge and lose my balance. Nervously, I nudge my left foot up onto a ridge that is higher up the tree and more embedded in the trunk, narrower but stronger. Tensing my muscles, I grab hold of ridges, roots and knots in the tree to stop myself falling as I slowly climb the inside of the trunk.

Scrambling higher and higher, my body almost paralyses itself in panic the first time I glance down. From where I am standing, the light is partially blocked by roots, and the dark, earth floor has merged with the darkness of the night. It's as if there isn't a floor at all, only a deep black tunnel. Despite what I know, my imagination sends me snapshots of falling for an eternity into warped horror as I feel my knuckles turn white in an effort to cling to the harsh wood above me.

The tree trunk is now so narrow that I can reach across and touch both sides. But as I continue to scramble upwards, I lose my footing and almost slip into the darkness underneath me. Desperate, I scour for holdings and continue to drag myself up towards the tip of the tree, only hoping to escape the dungeon closing in around me, steadily squashing me in its claustrophobic, icy grasp.

As I finally come closer to the top, the light shines more brightly and I can clearly see the twisted organs of the tree, smelling of nature and old wisdom. Each raised root and knot looks like a swirling mist, decorated with spiralling patterns that remind me of the layout of the mansions in the Big City as I finally reach the top of the tree trunk.

The hole is larger than it looked from the bottom, and I easily slide through it. I push myself up and out of the gap, sitting on the edge for a moment and letting my feet dangle inside the tree whilst I squint through the thick, large leaves that lie between me and the Emperor's mansion.

The Big City seems different from up here. The dim moonlight is shades brighter as it reflects off the silver roof tiles of the mansion which now looks even more magnificent. The building's great height is somehow more poignant, with two foreboding storeys now above me and seven heart lurching levels lying below.

The trees reach much higher than the spiked fence, and though the lower branches are shaved to prevent people climbing them, a large cloud of leaves covers tough, strong branches at the top, stretching out in all directions.

Slowly, I pull my legs out of the hole and begin to edge along a thick branch pointing towards the mansion. It begins so wide I can crawl across however as it gradually becomes thinner, I realize that I'm going to have to stand up.

My feet twitch with fear and I'm sure I will fall as I gradually let go of the branch with my hands and find my feet. I glance down before squeezing my eyes tightly shut again. I am at the very top of the tree, and layers of leaves stretch out for another twelve feet beneath me.

Barely able to keep my balance, I take one small step and my knees buckle. I fall onto the narrow wood which I automatically wrap my arms around as I close my eyes and try to calm down.

Directly below there is another branch, like the one I'm clinging to now, and from there, I will still be able to hold onto this branch, and move further along the webbed forest.

Gradually, I lower myself into a position where I am almost hanging from the branch, now above me; and scrabble with my feet until they come into contact with the wood of the branch beneath.

Still clinging to the branch above my head, I walk slowly and deliberately along the branch beneath me, laying one foot gently in front of the other. I wince as splinters dig into my palms and the rough wood etches painful patterns in my skin, but keep my eyes fixed ahead of me on my destination: The mansion.

I finally reach the branch of the next tree but there is a gap between it and me, and that branch is slightly lower than the one I'm walking on. I take a deep breath, and first clutch the higher branch of the tree in front of me before I slowly step onto the lower one. It trembles as it takes my weight and I'm scared that if I stay too long the last sound I will ever hear will be a scraping crack of wood, and so I take more steps, steadily but quickly pushing through the leaves until I reach the trunk.

At the tree trunk, branches stick out of the mass of wood like spokes out of the centre of a wheel. Holding it to keep my balance, I hop around the tree, jumping from branch to branch until I find myself still alive on the opposite side, staring straight ahead at the mass of branches in front of me.

Becoming more confident walking through the treetops, I begin to look around. The leaves hide me from the cameras and the booby traps are disguised lower down in the trees. To my left and right I can see the pale rooftops of the other Noble's mansions and slow flashing red lights from their defence systems. Though I'm sure that the Nobles would never even dream of someone climbing this high, I try my best not to disturb the leaves, painfully aware of the sensitivity of the Noble's security.

On the next branch, I look down and see the wrought iron gates. The spikes that appeared thick and menacing when I stood in front of them are just as unnerving, but thinner and sharper, seeming boastful and proud. The snake like, scaling patterns are sly and vindictive, angled sideways but still terrifyingly menacing from above.

A light flickers on in the watch tower and I freeze, imagining the guards inside, looking out. Searching for any sign of an intruder. Any sign of me.

I hurry across the branches and reach the first tree over the gates. Remembering the traps on the base of the trunks, I tread slowly, pausing after every step with a sick fear that a dangerously bright spotlight will illuminate and expose me. Or a trap will fall on top of me and send me hurtling to the ground where I will be pinned there, helplessly hoping for death. Or maybe there will be a gun or a bomb, and the last thing I will know will be a bang and a numb sense of goodbye.

My pulse quickens as I get further and further away from the gates, I look down at the incredible front lawn, clearly able to see the traps and bomb shells hidden beneath the soil and gravel. The ground beneath the trees themselves looks clean and comfortable; however, I know that the illusion only masks the pits and traps that lurk beneath soft, chemical earth.

I pass through the mob of branches and leaves, feeling like the extinct panther that used to roam in the trees, unnoticed until it pounced on its prey. As I stare at the seventh story looming ahead of me, I am filled with a determination that can only be felt by someone who can see no solution, but will still walk through walls to achieve their mission.

The tall towers that line the mansion jut into the air like knives, but I quickly move past them and suppress my fear. I pause for a moment as I reach the trunk of the final tree and stare back at what I have just overcome. It looks ordinary. No sign of searching; no sign that anyone, no man nor creature, saw me move. I smile to myself as I imagine Sokk in his doubting, constant lectures on how I wouldn't make it anywhere near the Big City, let alone reach the Emperor's mansion. I grin into the darkness, itching to shout out loud, "I told you so!"

Chapter 31

I now realize what has provided the faint light that brought me across the lawn and the trees - The mansion is glowing, illuminating the area in front of it with a golden glimmer that reflects gently off the sickly green grass and plastic leaves.

Underneath the golden light I can see that the walls of the building are pure white and unnervingly smooth, boasting that the Nobles have never been attacked and that their rule is supreme.

Windows embedded in the walls betray golden fabric curtains and elegant trains of flowers bordering their shy frames. Balconies, made entirely from unbreakable glass, jut out from large transparent doors that lead to grand rooms boasting of wonderful emblems of wealth.

I suddenly slip when the branch beneath me gives way. I almost scream as the lurching feeling of falling pushes me downwards towards the ground and my death. Flailing my arms wildly, my hands scrape the white, oddly artificial fence of one of the glass balconies and I grab hold of it, now hanging, with the great mansion preserving my life. With shaking limbs, I haul myself up onto the glass surface of the balcony and lie there, face down, panting for a few seconds.

A loud crunch makes me spring me to my feet as I hear the branch hitting the ground. Footsteps and a dog's bark soon follows, and I clutch the door handle of the balcony.

I don't expect it to open but when I does I fall into the room, this time onto soft carpet. Quickly leaping to my feet again, I stop and stare for a moment at the ornate dining hall I have just stumbled into.

A grand table stands majestically in the centre of the room, giving an aura of arrogance and smugness. The table is high and made of the purest glass, the legs a rare and probably extinct wood, and the floor is covered in a plush red carpet that it feels like a crime to stand on. A crystal chandelier hangs from the high, arched ceiling with unlit candles and precious gems charged with electricity, ready to be lit with a simple click or clap.

At the sound of footsteps, I glance around like a rabbit caught in the wake of a predator, manically searching for a hiding place. The room is lined with elegant cupboards and wardrobes decorated with swirling patterns that make me dizzy if I stare at them for too long. Without thinking about what might be waiting inside, I dart into the nearest wardrobe and close the too-smooth door behind me.

In the darkness, I shiver, as all around me is painfully black. I stretch out my hand, almost expecting it to be bitten by a rabid animal, but to my side there is nothing, just the soft wood of the wardrobe's bare floor. As my hand carefully circles upwards, the surreal nothingness envelopes my fingers in air and makes my joints stiff and numb with anticipation. They shake as my arm rises and I can feel my blood pumping through them at a rate that should turn them glowing red.

As I reach up into the area above my head, my breath stops, and my body begins to shiver when I touch a cold, dry surface, with an eerie smoothness that clings to me like glue. My fingers slip into a hole in the surface. It's small and delicate, a round oval shape. As my fingers resurface they find another hole further on, identical to the first.

My other hand climbs the air and finds more of these sickly, circular shapes, almost like large balls but more oval shaped, with two large holes near the top, two smaller holes further down and closer together, and one, oddly shaped gap at the bottom.

Unable to cope anymore, I leap out of the wardrobe. The chandelier flickers into brilliant, bright light as the loud thud of my body when I land on the floor resembles the clap that usually instructs it.

Staring back at me from the wardrobe, swing a long line of human skulls hanging on thin pieces of silk string. The empty eye sockets glare with profound hollowness and wisdom, and the nose holes look twisted and abused. The mouth is stretched into an eerie toothless smile which only makes me wonder how and why and who?

I close my eyes and turn away from the cupboard, scuttling out of the room and determined to forget what I have just seen.

The ominous corridor is dark, but I don't dare try to turn on a light, or do anything else that might wake the household.

May.

Where would she be? Everywhere I look I see her smiling face, her delicate laugh and her youthful innocence, and my pace quickens. I stop suddenly as I almost trip on a downwards step. Peering in the absolute darkness I clamour for the banister with my hands and as I cling at it, I follow it around to the adjacent stairwell going upwards.

Up or down? I don't know where to go. Where will May, and dad be imprisoned? Down, in the cellars or up in a lonely attic cell?

I remember that in my nightmares, pain was always directed downwards. Whether that was the direction it travelled or the direction of my body as it crumbled to the floor, downwards was the direction of desolation.

My feet are aching, my body is crying with tiredness, and in the gloom, I make out the glowing button and the glass door of a Platform Riser. My painful legs pull me towards it, longing to step into the cube of perfectly pressurised glass that will take me to any of the nine floors in seconds. But I know it's a stupid idea. I wouldn't know how to work it, it might make a noise or trigger an alarm, or even be rigged with traps.

I glare at the stairs, which I know that neither the Emperor, nor his servants, would ever see as anything more than an ornament. My sore feet drag towards the descending staircase and my knees almost buckle as I stumble down further into the darkness. I'm blinking rapidly in the gloom, but I still can't see anything as the black becomes more intense and the steps more steep the lower I go.

I crash against a hard wall that smells of fresh paint as the staircase decides to curve to the right. I can hear my breath catching in sharp and ragged bursts, and my heart is pumping with a booming echo that is frightening to listen to. The final step sends me crashing to the ground, but I quickly jump back on to my feet, as if the fast recovery will erase the loud noise that I have just made.

The wall and floor seem to disappear to one side and so I realise that the second set of stairs veers off to my right. I tenderly creep towards them, but my steps become slower and smaller as my senses stand more alert than they were before.

I stop and hold my breath, only to hear the sound of breathing continue. A familiar inhale and exhale that has been with me since the top of the last staircase. I can't tell where it is coming from and my mind lurches into panic mode. I can only stop myself from screaming by clutching at what Sokk taught me when I was still living Rente.

In one of my physical training sessions, I was standing in the centre of a large, windowless room as he walked in circles around me, instructing me with his strict but somehow soft, firmness.

"If you sense that someone is watching you, or about to attack, the most important thing to do is to remain calm. Keep going, as if you hadn't noticed them."

Following his instructions in my mind, I walk down the first step.

"Be careful. Rely on your instincts. Trained soldiers can throw their voice, even their breath can appear to come from all over." I remember looking around in wonder as he turned off the lights and made his booming voice bounce first off one wall, then the other. "You can't rely on your ears alone, if it is dark, look for a change in the texture of the darkness. And feel. Feel the atmosphere around you. Humans radiate heat. Is one side of you slightly warmer? Can you feel a breeze as your attacker moves?"

I stare into the blackness and try to obey his instructions. Can I feel anything? Everything is still. Silent. In front of me the dark texture is constant.

"What can you smell? Can you smell their heat? Their breath? Their perfume? Rich food or alcohol? The soldiers in the Big City bathe in scented milk and flower oils. Can you smell their wealth?"

My nose pricks as I quickly inhale, and then stop. The staircase itself smells of grapes and fruits, but there is another smell that seems eerily familiar as it creeps into my nostrils. It's the smell of maple trees. Still strangely fruity, but unique. Different. I very slightly twist my head from side to side to determine where the smell is coming from before, without thinking, I sharply turn to my left.

I realise it was a mistake as soon as I feel the gust of air flow past me.

I scream and lash out with my hands before they are gripped by gloves as smooth and bony as the skulls in the wardrobe. I kick out but am wrestled to the floor as sharp pain cascades up the back of my knees. A hand grips my neck and pins me down as the black clad figure ties my wrists and ankles together. I can smell their perfume from here and wonder if everyone has been ordered to wear it, to taunt my sister and father more. The figure pushes my knees into my chest and, still pressing his silk glove around my neck, binds my body together with coarse rope.

The first shaft of dawn cascades through one of the windows, giving me a short, hate filled look at my attacker before they tie a blindfold around my eyes and sling me onto their back. She is lean, dressed in a tight cat-suit with defined feminine features. The woman stands, creating a malicious silhouette against the weak light which illuminates her uncanny smile, imminent even through the dark mask.

I shut my eyes and try to block out an inner eruption of self-hatred and failure. But I can't erase the image of May's smiling face, her melodic laugh, and her innocent happiness that I have failed to save.

'I'm sorry May.' I whisper in the gloom behind my eyes. 'I failed you May. I'm sorry.'

Chapter 32

I feel myself jolted from side to side and though I can't see anything through the folds of my blindfold, I hear the steady thump of my captor's footsteps, and then the sound of a door creaking open. My limp body is pounded onto the floor and my blindfold is pulled back.

It takes my eyes a while to adjust to the bright yellow glow, but I wish it had taken longer. Above me, demanding immediate fear, are the warped features of the Emperor Alastair Greatest.

He glares with eyes so piercing they could shoot a bullet right through my heart. His stare is shrouded in anger and hatred, but laced with fiendish enjoyment and arrogance. I cannot hold his gaze for long, and soon drop my eyes to his sharp, knife-like nose.

" Talemia."

The name goes through me. I recognise it as a word that described me once, a long time ago. When I was one of Them. But it is not my name. I am not one of Them. The title seems empty, like a fog that seeps into my skin and travels straight through my body as if I wasn't even there, leaving me cold, numb and expressionless.

"Willow."

I jump this time. That is my name. The name given to me with love and care, with a promise of hope and peace. Unlike the other word, this acts like a hooked stick which seizes my body and shakes it to attention. It's a name, a personality and a voice that calls me, as my mind jumps through my eyes to look up at my grandfather.

"Congratulations. I'm glad you arrived safely." His voice is monotonic and expressionless, like a dark tomb with no light other than the grey spots of the shadows. "Your sister will be so pleased to see you. Every day, through her screams we hear her shout 'my sister will come. She's going to save me. Oh Willow please come!' And now, at last, she has her wish."

"Where is she?" My voice comes out as a growl, throaty and hoarse with fear and suppressed tears.

"You'll see her soon. And him."

"Dad?"

"If you still want to call that embarrassing snide your father. He's a traitor to his Country and his family. He sits alone in his tower, silent, day after day, refusing to respond to the...the promptings we give him. My son is a stubborn ox who will watch his own children suffer before defending his bloodline."

"Alone?"

"You didn't think we'd detain them together did you? How then, could we stop them forming a conspiracy? We have to protect ourselves you know." The corners of his mouth twitch and he raises his eyebrows slightly. "Obviously they can see each other. They can share long, reproachful looks, but with no words, no hope passing between them." He steps back, and I notice the long, silver whip strapped to his left leg. "And of course, they spend a great deal of time together in the chambers, though again, no words."

"STOP!" I can't take it anymore. Despite the ropes tying my body together, I fling myself across the room, barely gaining a meter before two soldiers seize me and pin back me down to the floor.

"Spirit." He laughs. "Your sister's like that. Well, she was."

"No. Please. Stop!" I scream as I fight against the two men who are each at least triple my size and strength.

"Take her away." He commands dismissively "To her own kind."

The men lift me into the air and carry me out of the room. They untie the chord strapping my knees to my chest, so I can stand, but fasten another rope around my neck and yank on it to speed up my laboured pace as I am forced to shuffle along the corridor.

With one guard in front of me and the other behind, I am dragged into a clear glass platform riser. I watch in dread as one of the guards gives a spoken order for the 'top floor'. We reach it in seconds and I am once again dragged along long, ominous corridors.

The fiery, red-orange sunrise glow filters through the windows and illuminates the hundreds of doors that line the walls either side. I stare at each one in turn, wondering which is to be my prison, however the guards push me on, pulling me past the rows of doors and down another corridor, through another labyrinth of walls that are bare, grey and windowless.

The guard in front of me yanks my neck sharply upwards as I stub my toe on the first step of a cold, stone staircase. It starts to spiral as we climb, and the steps are so steep I can hardly reach the next one without using my bound hands to pull me up. My stomach twists and turns like the stairs that swirl upwards as if they are a portal to another world.

When I reach the top there is one, foreboding door on the right-hand side of a tiny landing where a series of metal locks and complex passkeys are released and punched in by the guard in front of me. The guard behind me draws a sharp, dangerous looking knife from his belt and slashes my ropes, not caring when the blade cuts into the bare flesh on my wrist, as the ties fall off and the door swings open.

I hear the crash of metal closing behind me as my eyes adjust to the light of the room. The dim sunrise filters in from a window sitting about a meter up one wall, and the roof of the cell is shaped like a dome, higher in the middle, though there is still barely enough room to stand. The rest of the room is barren. The grey emptiness only interrupted by a heap of rags near the window and small chamber pot in the corner.

Directly in front of me, shivering in the gloom, large blue eyes stare through deathly pale sockets, as a small figure has scars covering her face and bones jutting out of her skin.

"May?" I whisper. I run to her and put my arms around the tiny frame that I am scared will shatter at any moment. "May?" I ask again, nuzzling her thin, weak hair.

"Willow" Her voice is flat, full of air, and has no tone.

"Oh May. I'm so sorry" I weep, my tears smothering her limp figure.

"No." Her fierceness surprises me. "Don't cry. They'll only beat you more. You can't cry. For every tear they...."

More surprised than anything else I stop crying and follow my sisters thin finger as she points to a small camera in the corner of the room. It blinks twice before I hear a hollow laugh echoing from within it.

I turn back to stare at my sister's damaged face.

"Oh Maple, what have they done to you?"

"What did you expect?" She says bluntly. "But what will they do to you?"

"It doesn't matter. I deserve it. I'm sorry May" I repeat. "I failed you."

"You tried" She clasps my hand "That's all you could have done." A short pause breathes in the cell. "Thank you."

I watch her pale blue lips that I remember once smiling so peacefully. Her eyes now full of fear that once only new love and hope. And I hold her hand, now covered with cold scars, that before only knew comfort and to help.

She didn't deserve this. She shouldn't have been through any of this.

Still clutching her bony hand, I take May to the heap of rags in the corner of the cell and cradle her as she falls asleep in my arms. But I can't close my eyes, I stare into the greyness of the cell around me, becoming more and more absorbed in self-hatred, hopelessness and most of all, fear.

Chapter 33

"Up! Out!"

The words come booming from behind the door as I jolt from my fitful sleep and look around in a panic. May has already stood up and holds out her hand to me. I take it numbingly as she pulls me up off the hard floor.

The door swings open on hinges which creak louder than the bellowing voices of the guards beyond it. May silently leads me through the door and into the midst of six guards who block my view of anything beyond their dark cloaks.

My little sister's step is so much steadier than mine. Her sallow eyes stare straight ahead, brave and strong, as mine scurry around in fear, holding back tears. It is almost as if she is the older one, leading me through the shadows and comforting me in the pain.

We walk down the steep, spiral staircase that I can now see is stained with hopeless, angry blood.

When we reach the floor below, instead of continuing along the rich corridor that I passed through this morning, we are pushed through a small, shabby door. I stumble and fall to my knees on the top step of another steep staircase.

May pulls me up with her spindly arms, and one of the soldiers behind us snarls before ordering us to walk faster. We stumble down another set of stairs that seem to go on for so long, I am surprised when I catch a glimpse of a small window depicting the outside of the mansion only just reaching ground level. Thirty steps further down, May squeezes my hand, signalling for me to stop.

The smell of stale blood stains my nostrils as we enter a long, shabby corridor with foreboding, dark doors looming on either side. I grip May's hand as we are hurried past dull plaster walls where, though I cannot hear anything now, I can imagine screams emerging from in painful frenzies.

Finally, we come to a halt outside a large, more door at the very end of the corridor.

I can feel May's fearful recognition as she presses herself into me. I put my arm around her and hold her close, promising myself that despite the horrors I have failed to save her from in the past, I will protect her now.

The doors pull open with a heart lurching grind of metal scraping against the concrete floor and we are pushed into a small cubical. One of the soldiers throws a long, grey tunic at me, ordering me to change. They leave, and the doors slam shut.

"Do as they say." May's voice is soft but firm.

Shaking, I pull off my old cloths which are ripped to shreds and caked in mud and filth, and pull the tunic over my head. It reaches almost to my ankles, massive on me with sleeves that fall six inches beyond my fingertips and a waistline that sits on the top of my thighs. But it's warmer and dryer than my borrowed T-shirt and ragged jeans that now lie in a heap on the floor. I smile weakly at May, but as I do a threatening announcement booms across the cubicle, seeming to echo from every angle.

"Welcome, children." Snarls the patronizing voice of Alistair Greatest. "You must be so happy. At long, long last you have found each other! Just one more addition and you'll be a family once again!"

To my left I hear a panting scream. One with no hope and no solace. But it's a voice I knew. A voice I recognise.

"Dad!" I yell, running towards the thick, grey wall on my left, but May pulls me back before I can reach him.

"Don't touch it. It's a trap!" She shouts.

"No. NO!" I break free of her grasp and pound on the wall, only to be thrown back with singeing pain exploding in my arms and fists.

The booming voice laughs as I look at my hands to find great, ugly burns already forming and beginning to decorate my flesh in dark red and sickly yellow.

"Isn't this fun?" Says the voice and I can almost see his snarling smile as I hear a loud click and the right wall of the cubical lifts upwards, into the air, revealing a man crumpled on the floor with an electric whip beating down on him.

"Dad?" This time May doesn't hold me back and I run towards him. He looks up at me and our eyes lock for a moment.

I step back, afraid and almost confused at the blankness in his face.

I haven't seen him for over five years. Not since I was ten years old.

There is no love in his eyes. Only fear and pain.

What have they done to him?

Five years is a long time. Have they broken him? Changed him? Moulded him into someone he's never been before? Or someone he might have been once but shouldn't be any more?

Before I can reach out and touch him a wall falls in front of me and separates us. I turn back to May but another barrier crashes down between us and I'm alone. I slowly crumple onto the floor as the booming voice returns.

"And then there were three! I hope you are enjoying this as much as I am! Though do remember, there is much more of the games to come! But for now..."

I hear the high-pitched, painful scream of my sister, and the ground begins to rock beneath me. Sharp knives and daggers jut out from the floor and walls and pierce my sides, and I let out a painful, severing shriek, before I hear another, hollowing yell from dad. Our three screams echo all around, changing in intensity and pitch with nothing but pain between us, before the knives finally retreat and I collapse, panting in the sudden silence.

"Happy families!"

At the Emperor's words, the two walls either side of me lift into the air and we run into each other. The three of us hold together, one solid mass of broken bodies in the centre of the large chamber.

May's body is covered with blood and dad's bare legs are punctured with small holes but as we cling to each other, none of us seem to feel our pain.

"Willow." Dad whispers into my hair. "My Willow. I'm sorry." I cling closer to him. "I love you." His breath is warm against my scalp and I almost let tears escape my frightened eyes. Trying to hold my heart in place, I murmur the only words I can think of to say to a father who I haven't seen for five years.

"I love you too dad."

Maple clings closer as she whispers. "I love you three!" The childish expression makes us both smile and for a moment we are together. We are strong. We are a family.

"How much do you know?" Dad asks to me through the folds of my matted hair.

"Everything."

"No. You know nothing." He says, his voice melancholy. "It's easier that way."

Understanding, I nod as I feel the ground move beneath me and the small part of the floor that we are standing on pushes itself away and begins to move. I glance around me - it's as if we are floating in a sea of hard concrete and looking at it makes me feel sick and dizzy. May and dad have their eyes closed. Pulling closer to them, I do the same, and imagine a time when there was no pain. When the worst thing that ever happened was a scratched elbow or a grazed knee. When May and I would argue over nothing before one of us apologized to the other and in petty tears and we became best friends again.

I remember watching the Screenings, but not being affected by them. Dad always told us they were re-enactments. No-one was ever really hurt. It was only a game. Of course, I'd learnt the truth about them in time. Dad had told me one day at the beach. But it was me who had to break the news to May. She was sad, yet her sweet, innocent heart immediately told me. "I'm going to rescue them. When I'm grown up they won't be dying anymore."

Chapter 34

I open my eyes only when I feel someone sharply tugging on my arm. As I squint in the dim light, I watch as both my father and my sister are dragged away by two solemn guards.

I glance up, expecting to see another guard looming above me, but instead a woman with cold, plastic features clasps my wrists and stares right into my soul.

Malintaret. My mother, has eyes the same shade of piercing blue as mine, but hers are bordered with ridiculous layers of paint, and are filled with a thirst for blood. As I meet her gaze, her nostrils flare and she violently drags me by my hair across the chamber, her elegant fingers and painted nails as sharp as daggers as they dig into my scalp.

Malintaret's long, flowing dress is the colour of concentrated blood, decorated with deathly flowers which are dark grey, like lost hope. Her high heels click on the stone floor as she drags me to a box made entirely out of glass in the centre of the room. I am held by my shoulders and forced to stare straight into the transparent cubicle and at the silver operating table that lies within it, with pointed light reflecting off the pristine surface.

"Welcome, darling daughter." Whispers a voice as sharp as the implements hanging from the table. "Time for you to tell us your secrets.'"

I am pushed through an almost invisible door in the side of the box, and immediately two guards take my arms and haul me onto the silver operating table. They tie me down, and as they loom over me, the crests on the shoulders of their cloaks make my heart stop. These aren't ordinary soldiers. These are the Destructors.

I hear a click, and the table begins to move. It tilts upwards and rises towards the ceiling until I am almost vertical, but still slanted slightly backwards so that my neck is exposed, and my body pushed down uncomfortably into harsh metal cuffs that cut at my wrists, waist, and ankles.

Through the glass, I can see the hollow, stone room which looks as if it's part of another world. The greyness that dominates out there and the piercing white in here seems to epitomize how much sharper and clearer fear and pain are inside this glass box, and how much more unbearable what is about to happen will be.

In the centre of the grey chamber, detained by two Destructors who hold his head up to stare into the cubicle, is dad. He is kneeling on the ground. His mouth is set in a detached line, bracing himself to stay silent. But his eyes brim with words and emotion, as if they are mouths and tongues in themselves. 'Be strong' they says to me. 'I love you. So be strong and I will be too'. May pushes herself into his side, with her eyes stolen shut.

For both of them, I vow I will try. The secrets of the Resistance will remain hidden. They will know nothing. If words must come, they will be the lies of truth. The bad fruit of a longing for good. The emotionless apathy of love.

My mother comes and stands directly before me. Tall and grotesque, with her hands clasped behind her back, she blocks my view of father and May, and theirs of me.

"Hello Talemia. It's lovely to see you again. I've missed my eldest daughter these past ten years." Her use of my

Noble name seems to objectify me. The word suggests that I am one of them. That I am on their side.

"I may be your daughter, but you will never be my mother." My voice echoes around the glass chamber and I fear it has been transmitted beyond it when I hear a sharp thud outside of the glass box. I strain my head to try and glimpse dad and May, but Malintaret steps in front of me, her hands still neatly behind her back, obstructing my view once again.

"Of course. You're quite right. You're not deserving of my blood flowing through your veins. Shall I help you relieve yourself of it?"

She produces a knife from behind her back and slashes at my arm. Pain seers through me as blood stains the metal cuff around my wrist.

"So, tell me," Her voice is soft and sly as she walks in a large circle around the operating table. "What do you know about this notorious little army hiding in the countryside? The Resistance?"

"Nothing." I grit my teeth through the pain.

"You must know something. How else did you arrive in Rente? With a different name? A different story?" She is now standing directly behind me, her knife tracing my throat as her breath tickles my neck.

"We....we.... we ran away and found ourselves there. Then a kind old lady took us in and helped us."

"Kind old lady? Oh yes. Dothelle. Your sister called her grandma Dothy. Isn't that sweet? I think you know what we did to her."

I can now clearly see dad and May. They have guards standing above them and I know they can hear every word we are saying. I shake my head, telling them that they can't betray anything. That I'm strong enough. That I'll cope.

"But really, are you saying that you and your sister, both so young at the time, walked over two hundred miles alone, knowing full well that you could easily be found and arrested, killed even for being so far from home without a guardian?" She pauses for a moment, pursing her lips. "How did you get your papers?"

"We forged them."

A long, metal hook grapples my neck and yanks it backwards, threatening my throat with a chain of sharp spikes as blood streams down both sides of my collarbone and stains the grey tunic I'm wearing.

But Malintaret is practiced. The hook does not disrupt my breathing, nor does it stop me from speaking. It only sends a torrent searing pain that explodes in my neck and fills my mind with thoughts of betrayal, making me want to tell her everything and anything to make the pain go away.

"How did you forge your new identity?"

When I stay silent Malintaret signals for something. She removes the clawing hook from my neck and stands in front of me once again, holding what looks like a small remote control in the palm of her left hand.

I hear a beep as her fingers gently tap it, and the metal straps around my wrists and ankles pull apart. Two Destructors grab me and pin me against a wall as the operating table sinks into the floor. Up rises a square, metallic frame. My wrists and ankles are immediately bound to the four corners as Malintaret presses another button on the keypad in her hand.

I start to spin. Faster and faster until the world seems to be everywhere and the ground seems to be no-where.

Everything around me is like a blur of colour. Faces and objects merge into seas of dull shapes. Blood rushes from my heart and pounds in my head, my hands, my feet and I feel like I'm about to be sick. Pain explodes in my head and cascades down my limbs as it ripples through each joint like a sea of poison.

The four corners begin to stretch. They are pulled further and further apart as my joints are yanked out of their sockets and my skin starts to tear. Every gulp of air is stolen from me by a scream that tries to release the searing agony coursing through my bones like fire. My shoulders and hips burn, as if they are mourning for the loss of my arms and legs which are almost numb, except for the white and yellow throbbing that envelopes them, drumming constantly and vibrating through me like extra heartbeats.

I can't see anything through the blinding colours of agony. But I feel the Destructors crowd around me. Leaping on me with knives and rib-crackers that attack my body as if I'm a wild beast. They ripple through my skin, into my blood and then penetrate my organs, spreading pain and suffering at each stage, until there is nothing else left.

Nothing but pain. It's like a collage behind my eyes. But the colours are un-definable. Too cruel to look at for long enough, yet consuming every part of my mind and my body.

I have to make it stop.

I begin weakly to jerk my head, and try to put it in direct contact with one of the bludgeons, so it will knock me unconscious.

"STOP" Malintaret yells, guessing my plan. The spinning and the stretching grind to a halt as her sharp words come back into focus.

All around me, the glass box is drenched in blood and decorated with dead skin. Malintaret however, is still pristine. If there were a drop of blood that dared go near her, it's warmth would fear her icy fingertip.

"Are you ready to tell us what you know?" I close my eyes and focus on the fading colours, trying to ignore her and pretend that she hasn't just given me a way to escape the pain. "No? Well maybe your father is? If the little one couldn't break him, perhaps you will."

Dad is pushed into the room, where he collapses on the floor, helplessly adding to the carnage.

"Will you answer my questions now? Or do you really hate your daughters this much?"

I can see that he is breaking. Feverishly, I shake my head at him. He can't. He won't.

"You don't know anything Malintaret." Dad stares straight into her piercing blue eyes, not even blinking to give himself relief from her harsh stare. "I do not stay silent because I hate my children. I stay silent because I love them. And I want them to know right from wrong. To know what is evil so they don't do evil to others. I want them to be strong and fearless. It is my responsibility to set them an example to follow. So that they can someday be free. And be happy."

As the Destructors crowd around my father, I suddenly understand how much he loves me. So much that he could watch me being tortured and stand still, say nothing. Because he values happiness, not as the opposite to pain, but rather something that can conquer it, something so much more than it.

I now see how much power he has. How he holds the one thing she doesn't. The one emotion she will never feel and can only define from a dictionary. Love. Something that will live through the never-ending darkness of pain and tears, and still shine the strongest.

Chapter 35

Dad is taken away. I watch his beaten body submissively follow three guards out of the glass cubicle. I sit, beaten and exhausted on the floor of the bloodstained box with only one Destructor holding me down. Looking around at the grey, concrete cavern outside, I suddenly realise that I can't see May anywhere, but even my fear for her cannot draw me out of this terrible exhaustion that pushes my carcass into a dull, half sleep.

"She's like her father." I hear Malintaret squall above me. "Iron boned. Stubborn. She doesn't care for her own pain. Though I'd like to see how she responds under other's."

"All in good time." I glance feverishly upwards to see The Emperor standing next to his daughter. "How did her father respond?"

"We got a few scraps. That's one of the only reasons we stopped. But there's no way to verify what he said. He could have just given us rubbish, like the kid."

What did he say? Did he really give them information to stop my torture? No. He couldn't have. He wouldn't have. He's stronger than that.

"What exactly was it that your dear husband had to offer?" The Emperor's words are sly and manipulative, but his gentle mocking makes Malintaret look at him with eyes like daggers.

"I would rather kill myself than remember the time I was married to that scum."

"My apologies. What did he say?"

"He told us that the Resistance was led by a man named Koss Grawn."

Koss? Whose Koss? I rack my brains but draw a blank. Koss, or Kos? I try to spell the name in my mind. Kkos. Sokk. They must be talking about Sokk. So dad did lie, but only a little.

Why did he just betray his best friend? Is he angry at Sokk? Angry for letting May and I be captured? Or angry that he has taken his place as our father for the last five years?

"Have you tracked his files?"

"He doesn't live in society. He is in permeant hiding, not even registered as a citizen."

Was that true? I realise that I've never actually seen Sokk out in the real world. Only ever in a Resistance base, or a private home.

"We will scour every corner of this Country for him. Now go. I need some time alone with my granddaughter."

I hear Malintaret's sharp heels click against the glass floor as she leaves the chamber, and the Emperor kneels at my side.

"Hello dear." He whispers. "You don't happen to know anything about this Koss fellow, do you?"

"No." I feel his rancid breath on my neck and as he speaks he spits in my ear. But I stare straight ahead, into the grey room outside of the glass box, not trusting myself to look into his eyes.

"Really? Well that's a shame. Are you sure your father never mentioned him? You're certain he didn't help you to escape and, what did she call it, Relocate yourself?"

"She?" My eyes flick to his for a moment, but quickly dart away when I see red sparks dancing in his pupils.

"Your sister of course. On her first day here, she told us that a kind man had helped you to Relocate to another area with a new identity, but she wouldn't give us his name. Was that man Koss?"

I suddenly remember my fugitive denial of having had help earlier. Are they punishing her for it now? No. They can't be. Doesn't this just make it more obvious that I was the one lying, not her.

"She's a child, she doesn't know what she's saying."

"You didn't answer my question."

"Where is she?"

"She's alone. For now."

"There was a kind man. He didn't tell us his name. He had seen you take dad away and so took us to Grandma...to Dothelle Nillon's house. Then he left." I shut my eyes, remembering that I was once told your pupils dilate when you lie. "We never saw him again."

"Did he tell you who you were? Did he explain why we arrested your father?"

"Yes." I answer carefully. "He was clever, and worked it out."

. "He can't have got it all right though, could he have?"

"No. He knew dad was a Noble and we were his daughters. He knew you were searching for us, and he knew that we were in danger. But he was just a kind person who wanted to help. Not involved in a Resistance scheme or anything like it."

"Congratulations! I declare you a natural liar." My grandfather stands up and finds another way to brake me. "You could speak on the Screens to the nation with your ability to outwit the public." He stops, turns, and stares at me, smiling. "You've been wickedly efficacious all your life. I know you'd like to think that you're all honest and virtuous, but never forget that you spent years working in a gun factory creating murder weapons; you deceived everyone around you by withholding who you really were; and you broke into a high security City in order to defy your lawful guardians. I would bet my life that in a heartbeat you would steal, cheat, or even kill if you needed to.

"Our blood still runs in your veins Talemia Antario. You are a cold-hearted Noble. Your ancestors were handpicked for their merciless character. Your mother is a torturous beast and your father a stubborn runaway. You've got no hope."

I barely breathe as he speaks, his words destroying me with every syllable as I have no power to deny them. Am I really one of them? Maybe I'm not now, but what if they do break me and I become something as vile as they are? Could I really turn against my own family and take pleasure in their pain? Could I ever actually kill? I know I would feel no remorse over the Noble's death, but could I hold a gun to their heads myself? These people, whom I have hated all of my life, are my ancestors. That I am one of them.

"Take her away." Orders the Emperor resignedly, "We'll continue this induction tomorrow."

With no energy left in my bones to fight, I am marched up the stairs that seem even longer than they did this morning. My eyes drop to the grey stone beneath my feet, and it seems as if my mind and soul are no longer a part of my body, but I am looking at myself from a distance, knowing about my own pain and exhaustion, but not fully feeling it. The cell door is opened, and I walk obediently inside. No fighting. No rebellion. Only submission.

As the doors close behind me, May jumps on top of me, enveloping me in love and comfort that I so sorely need.

She holds me tight and whispers in my ear. "I'm covering the camera. Get it all out now while they can't see."

Understanding, I start to cry. Tears of the pain that plagues my aching body. Tears of failure and self-hatred. I weep for being a part of a family that kills for pleasure. But most of all, I sob for all the heartache, all of the physical and emotional pain that I, my sister and my father have suffered, and all the damage that is still to come.

Silently. I draw back, murmuring a small 'thank you' to May. She smiles and walks behind me, gently taking my long, thick hair and beginning to untie it from the plait that has now become ragged and heavy with blood.

"What are you doing?" I ask her as my hair drops limply down my back.

"Cutting it." She replies, fiddling with the thin band that I used to fasten the plait. "This metal part is sharp. I can use it to cut your hair."

She takes one of my matted locks and begins to twist it through her fingers. Then, she uses the serrated edge of the metal, treating it as if it were a chain saw and quickly travelling it back and forth until the curl unravels and falls to the floor.

We sit there for a long while in silence, each of us lost in our own mind, thinking, maybe too much, about the world that surrounds us. As my hair drops to the floor, so do my hopes. Freedom, happiness, rebellion. They are all being chiselled away by the Nobles, to collapse, in a lifeless heap on the dirty floor.

Chapter 36

"It was bad today." May whispers, almost to herself, as she slices my hair. "Mother was wild."

I wince painfully when she says mother. She notices.

"She makes me call her that. It helps sometimes. It makes me seem younger, more innocent. It saved me a couple of beatings. You should try it."

"I will never call that woman my mother. No matter how much she tortures me."

May smiles, as if I'm a naive and stubborn child. "They don't usually use as much physical violence. After the first day I mean. Today was just to assess how easily you'd break, and how much they could get out of dad."

I think about my father, my painful memories of him always seemed decorated with some sort of pretend happiness. But It's strange. A part of me feels as if I hardly know him.

"How easily did he break?" My voice trembles as my heart rises into my throat.

"Not too much. You heard about Koss?" A small smile plays around the corners of her mouth, and for a moment, there's a glimmer of light in her eyes. But it lasts for such a short time that I might have imagined it.

"Yes." I pause. "But they knew I was lying."

Silence lies between us like a shroud that tries to suffocate even the sounds of our breathing. "What happens now?" I say.

"For you? The rest of your induction." She finishes cutting my hair and picks up my arm, carefully stroking her fingers across each of my scars, removing the top layer of blood and grime. Pain shoots through me as she touches them, but I look away, so she doesn't see the wince darting across my face. "The next step is deprivation. No sleep. No food. No water. You lose sight of everything beyond surviving the next thirty seconds. After days like that, you'll eagerly trade your life secrets for a tomato."

"I don't like tomatoes." I smile.

The light darts through her eyes again, so small that I can barely recognise it, yet still proof that some of the joy I remember remains in her. "You can have the blankets tonight. You need all of the sleep you can get." She nods towards the pile of rags in the corner of the room. "Deprivation is one of the most effective ways of extracting information, but you have to stay strong. They will show you videos, of me and dad, but you can't pay any attention to them. Focus on yourself. We don't matter. Just stay silent." She puts a hand either side of my head, so I am looking straight into her eyes. They're pushed deep into her skull, and darker than I remember. Older and sadder with more pain and more knowledge overflowing from them.

"They haven't quite developed mind reading equipment, but what they've got is pretty close. It captures images, the pictures that your mind creates, and analyses them to form information. You can't think about anything that they want to know."

"What can I think about?"

"Nothing. Lies. Create stories in your mind. That worked for me. Imagine things, but not food, water, nor sleep."

"Imagine?"

"They didn't keep me too long, it was easy to see that I knew nothing. They only really used me to get to dad and to lure you in. I'm pretty much worthless otherwise. I guess they'll get rid of me soon."

My eyes suddenly drop, and I wrap my arms around her as I realise what she's saying. "No. Don't say that May. My May. They won't. I won't let them. They can take me instead. But they won't hurt you. I will do anything to keep you alive."

I hold her close to me and remember to turn my back to the camera, for it is she who is crying now. She's so young, so gentle, and I promise myself that I will protect her at all costs. Even if I do tell them my secrets, even if I betray the whole Resistance it will be worth it, for her.

"No." May almost shouts, reading my thoughts. "You won't. Not for me. I won't let you jeopardise everything for me. Not one word. Not one scrap of information will you give them because of me."

"All right." I take a step back, surprised at her attack.

"Promise me. Look into my eyes and promise me that if it comes to it, you will stay silent and let me die."

I stare deeply into the wells of her large blue eyes. The baby flickers of light are completely gone now, replaced by an adult, iron core of resilience. "I promise." I say, the oath sealed on my heart.

"You have to be strong." May walks over to the window. She's so small she can only just see out of it. "Like dad."

I go to join her and put my arm around her scrawny shoulders. Out of the window, the skies are artificially blue and the sun glints like a golden plate. We're staring into the inner courtyard of the mansion where, at the centre, a long grey tower rises upwards, looking bleak and miserable against the bright sky. The top of the tower is like a hat, pointed and sharp but opening out into a wide brim, as one, small window directly faces us. A forlorn figure leans against the window frame, gazing across the wide gap between us as if he longs to jump over it like a leopard.

My father's weary eyes find mine, and we exchange a meaningful look. Love, hope, sadness and regret fill him and me simultaneously as we try to convey what can't be spoken.

"He says, stay strong." Whispers May.

"What...?" Did his lips move? How did she know? How could she hear what his heart was saying?

"We've watched each other across this courtyard so many times that we can almost read each other's thoughts. Well, emotions at least."

Empathy. Another thing we have, but the Noble's don't.

"Tell him...tell him to stay strong, that I'm all right and that we're together, a family again. That's all that matters."

May doesn't move. She doesn't sign with her hands or her head, she only looks at him, different emotions crossing her face.

"Does he have the whole tower?" I ask, thinking about how lonely he must be.

"Only the top floor. Below there are live-in guards and a personal... chamber."

A loud clatter suddenly surprises me as I whip round to stare at the door. A small hatch has opened and a silver container about the size of my forearm is pushed through. May turns around more slowly and goes to fetch it. She opens it and retrieves two small sticks of bread and a long vile of water.

"You have all of it." She says, passing me both sticks of bread. "You're going to deprivation tomorrow, you need all the nourishment you can get."

I whisper a weak thank you and begin to eat the bread.

"Eat slowly. It's more filling that way."

Obeying May's instructions, I nibble on the food, though it still doesn't last for long. May takes a small sip of the water and gives the rest to me. "I'll be fine, if it rains tonight I can catch some more."

I devour the water in a few short sips as May place the small container on the windowsill, wedged at an angle between the bars so that any falling rainwater will dribble into it. She sits down on the cold ground as I lie on the rags, and once again I am reminded of her lost childhood, and how she has had to grow up far too quickly.

Chapter 37

The grey ceiling above me refocuses as I wake up, and for a moment I don't know where I am. Then, a shudder ripples through my body, bathing me in the aching pain of memory from head to toe.

I sit up, the disks in my spine faintly clicking, and see May leaning against the window. Her body stands practically motionless, apart from the slow expansion of her visible ribcage. As if she can sense I'm awake, she turns and gives me an encouraging smile, the kind of smile an adult gives a child before they are about to go through something terrible.

"Deprivation" I murmur, my voice oddly hoarse, "What else happens?"

"It depends on your weaknesses." May says flatly. "You should meet the rest of the Nobles. You might return with a few more bruises. But it's mainly about the sleep. When you've had no sleep, you can't tell the difference between left and right, let alone what's a secret and what's not." She looks towards the window. Towards dad. "It exaggerates everything. And then they'll tempt you. But with what depends on your weaknesses."

I sit in solemn silence. My weaknesses? My weakness is my sister, my father. How can I sit under their pain and not do anything to stop it?

"I guess they'll use us. But you can't say anything." May says, her bony hands touching my shoulders. "Dad's been here for over five years. I've been here three months. You can't destroy our silence on your second day. Even if you do see pictures, or videos of me and dad, ignore them. Block us out and focus on something else. We can look after ourselves."

A loud crash echoes behind me as I feel the guards ripping open each bolt, thirsty for blood. Just as they enter the room and tear me from my sister's grasp, she says something strange. A command that I wouldn't expect her to even dream of giving, let alone order in front of armed soldiers.

"Fight." The word is barely a whisper, but her voice could be heard miles away. "Show them that you're not theirs."

There is a moment of shrill silence, where nothing happens but everything takes place. Thoughts stop in their tracks and my mind is full of emptiness before finally, the guards pull me into their midst.

All fourteen of them have the same crooked nose and bent glint in their eye. Eerie dread seeps into the marrow of my bones when I realise that they are not ordinary guards.

These are the Destructors. Rumoured about, threatened with, and full of nothing but stone-cold hatred. Will it soon be my time to meet their leader?

Revicartus.

Revicartus Antario.

Revicartus Antario my grandfather.

With fourteen men who kill for pleasure standing around me, I know that if I fight I won't escape. But it will still show the Nobles that I am not, and will never be, one of Them. It will show them how much I hate every part of their smug life; their horrid riches and their lifeless mansions; their murderous weapons and their inhumane tortures.

I push myself against the soldiers to my side, battering at their hard bodies with my fists and screaming into their hollow chests. But without flinching, or even turning his head to look at me, a Destructor throws me back into the centre of the circle where I don't find my balance quickly enough for the men behind, who push forwards as if there is nothing but air where I stand. I run again at the other side of the circle, trying to provoke a reaction, but nothing retaliates, except a hard push and a constant march that drums through me like an unresponsive heartbeat.

"You're all evil." I yell, longing for my words to affect them. "Evil, sadistic, beasts." They continue to march. "Do you even have hearts?" I grab the unsuspecting arm of one of the Destructors in front of me, twisting it behind his back and attempting to wrench his fingers into unnatural positions whilst punching my sharp nails through the black cloth of his glove and into his exposed flesh. I draw blood. "Cowards" I whisper at their inactivity. "Cowards!" I shout loudly and boldly into the black sea of their cloaks.

This finally gets their attention as all fourteen Destructors turn inwards to face me. I cling on to the fingers of the Destructor in front of me, despite his strength and my incapability to hurt him. He seizes my hand and unclasps it from his, but now he's the one who doesn't let go.

Pain surges through my fingers as he squeezes my hand in his clenched fist. I can feel my hand turning purple, and then blue with agony, but I don't let the pain show in my eyes, meeting his snarl with a long, defiant stare. He releases me, steps back, and sneers, looking as if he is struggling to contain his delight.

I am pushed down, sprawling on the stairs where I refuse to look away from the line of identical faces. I keep my expression tempting as I focus my eyes individually on each of the fourteen masks, willing their facade of discipline to break.

I snort, mockingly at the third Destructor in the line. He looks younger than the others, more susceptible. I watch the glass protection on his face slowly braking with each of my well positioned looks of contempt that form my attack.

He steps forward. His fist draws back swiftly as I resist the urge to close my eyes and bow my head, facing the attack full on. I goad him, smile as his iron arm swings backwards like a pendulum. As a heavy thrust brings it forward, I concentrate on glaring into his eyes, and despite the sharp pain that whizzes through my jaw, I don't allow the force of the blow to push me backwards.

My cheek throbs as much as my fist now, but I'm determined not to let it show on my face. That would be a sign of weakness, and I will not be seen as weak by these men. The Destructor draws back to his position, not a hint of emotion in his dark eyes.

A Destructor behind me pulls me to my feet, tying my wrists behind my back with what feels like iron-studded rope. He harshly scrapes my bruised hand and knots the rope so tightly that pain sears from my wrist, all the way up to my shoulder. The sting is hot and intense, but I grit my teeth and show nothing but a self-righteous snarl. I won't give them the satisfaction of seeing me hurt.

The Destructor tugs at the end of the rope and sends another shock of pain into my injured hand. This time I can't hide a gasp, and I think I hear the Destructor laugh before we continue to march.

We finally stop on a small ledge near the bottom of the second flight of stairs. I jolt, crashing into the Destructors in front of me, but they remain rooted in their machine-like, vulgar discipline, barely noticing as one of them opens the dial pad on the wall. A small hatch, barely higher than my knee, opens and I am pushed in front of the Destructors. They press down on my shoulders, and I am forced to kneel on the floor where another Destructor practically kicks me through the hole. I have no other choice but to claw my way into what can only be more pain and fear.

I find myself crawling onto a ramp that leads to the back of a vehicle, realising with dread that it is the Destructor's van, the same one that carried both my father, and my sister away from me.

I don't move, wondering what will happen if I refuse to enter the lorry, and instead just stay where I am. But I soon find out when the ramp begins to lift. It rises towards the van, and I slide off the steepening slope it creates, tumbling into the darkness as the ramp forms the rear wall behind me, its tall barriers slotting inside the van and clicking into place with a growl meant to terrify me into submission and obedience; but instead provoking a shattering scream of defiance and rebellion.

I hear the slow thud of the Destructor's footsteps as they take deliberate steps towards the front of the vehicle. There is a prolonged squeak of the opening door and a slight bounce as they clamber onto the soft, elegantly padded cushions that I'm sure line the front seats. It goes without saying that for every pain I endure they gain a luxury.

Chapter 38

I barely hear the electric engine start purring beneath me, but I feel the lorry jerk forward as I am thrown against the front wall. I slide down into the corner of the van and hug my knees to my chest, closing my eyes as we start to move.

Crouching in the semi darkness, a cold slither begins to envelope me, starting at the top of my head and plastering my face as it works its way down my body. I glance upwards and my heart yelps when I see a layer of dark sludge dripping onto me, moulding around whatever it hits first and setting into a hard cast that threatens to paralyse my body. I pull my head forward with a hard tug that sends a searing shot of pain through my scalp and triggers a loud crack as the gel snaps. I roll away from the wall, clutching my head in my hands as the sludge starts to soften, and becomes easier to remove now that it has been cut off from its life source.

Thankful that it did not touch any other part of my body, I quickly scramble to my feet and run to the other side of the lorry, the farthest point from the gel.

I lean against the wall, panting loudly, though I'm not sure why. Maybe the sound of my breathing subconsciously comforts me.

I press my face to the small, plastic window in the back of the door and try to picture my sister and father doing the same when they were captured, as though this small action will connect me with them, and bring me their comfort.

Out of the window, I can see the Big City soaring upwards on either side. It looks so different now in the day, I can almost believe that the venomous dark horror I passed through only a few nights ago was just a dream. A nightmare, like the ones I have become so accustomed to, where I no longer try to resist the fear that sweeps over me and chokes my chest.

Looking through the small square of glass, I see the same, ominous mansions that loom several stories high, but in the sunlight, they shine white, silver and bronze, and the foreboding aroma that was so potent in the darkness, seems more subtle and natural. I almost think that if I didn't know who lurked inside of their walls, nor about the blood that forms their foundations, I could admire the craftsmanship in the buildings' architecture.

A pea-green park glints in the artificial sunlight as we turn a corner, with a sparkling blue fountain, as tall as the surrounding trees, in the centre. A young boy is running on the glistening turf, clinging to the hand of a wide-eyed little girl. They are laughing, with a light in their eyes that is only ever present in the youthful and innocent. One wears teal, and the other a pale blue, indicating that they belong to the families of the fifth and the sixth Noble; undoubtedly already arranged in marriage to each other despite that they are no more than four or five years old. I don't recognise them, but I usually let my mind distract me during the 'Family Viewings' that we are forced to watch.

Between them, they hold what looks like a small doll. I almost smile. Their innocent childishness has not yet been corrupted. They kneel on the floor, playing with the doll as children should, happy and blissful, genuinely excited, and for the moment, unaware of who they will grow up to be.

Suddenly a sound wafts over the meadows, though I cannot hear it, and their young heads pull upwards in unison and turn to their right. Grins are chiming on their faces, and the same innocent glimmer in their eyes brings them to their feet, running eagerly towards the prize that they have been promised, the doll now forgotten.

They leave it on the ground, and as they dart away, my eyes are drawn to it for a small second before the van carries me away, out of its sight. But what I see has me gasping for breath and stepping away from the window with bile rising in my throat. I close my eyes, but the image is imprinted on my mind.

The doll, which had seemed like a symbol of their goodness, was maimed. Blood - I don't know if it was real, I hope it was fake - dripped from the corner of the plastic smile. One eye was smudged with something dark purple to represent a smoky bruise, and the other was just an empty socket. The nose bent crookedly and had been painted dark red whilst the doll's short blonde hair was pulled out, leaving painful bald patches and exposing raw squares of scalp. The tilted head revealed a long scar lining the exposed neck, and the shoulder was twisted at an awkward angle, pushing the arm behind the back of the doll where blood oozed from the wrist that hung from a single thread of what must be plastic, but from where I stood, looked like a small slither of bone.

Pressing my back against the cold wall of the van, I collapse with my arms wrapped around my bent knees, staring into the whirlpool of grey floor beneath me, and pushing out the thoughts that pound across my mind.

I don't know why it disturbs me so much, I've always known what the Nobles do. But they were so young. I was five years old when dad escaped the Big City with May and I.

Was I like that? Innocent of anything good? Naive of peace? Knowing only blood thirst? I think about the wound in the fingers of the Destructor that I scrammed. The feeling of achievement I gained from it. Am I still like that?

But then, I remember dad, Sokk, Grandma Dothy, all of the Resistance workers who are prepared to give their lives for the smallest chance of peace. To give their lives for me. I realise that I can't be like my ancestors, not for my own sake, but for theirs.

I vow that even if that means killing the part of me that longs for my enemies to feel pain, becoming utterly selfless like the people in Rente, I will do it. If not for the quest of peace then for them, so none of their work will have been in vain.

The electric engine purrs to a halt and I squeeze my eyes tightly shut. When I reopen them, the door to the back of the van has been released and sunlight filters in, half blocked by the fourteen Destructors ready to catch me and beat me if I fight. But I don't resist them physically, as I walk out of the door and allow them to flank me. I am calm, but that doesn't mean I am beaten. My head held high in pride, I stare straight ahead, preparing myself for what I am about to experience, but not allowing them to see the uncertainty that breathes inside of me. To fight back is to show that I have fear. That is something I cannot do. To show fear is to boast of weakness and that is something I will not confirm. My hands shake and my breath trembles, but I stay strong in my decision. I am willing to die silent. I would rather die than become like the torturers who call themselves my family.

All around me are thick bodies covered in black armour. I cannot see anything beyond the Destructors and even if I crane my neck to look up, my eyes squint at the artificial sun that pours down onto me like a spotlight.

I wonder what I am walking through. Under my feet there is hard tarmac, but could there be grass, or even dirt or sand beyond it? Are there other people around? Watching me with hawk-like eyes and sneering, maybe laughing at me. Who are these people? My aunts, uncles, cousins?

Even before I knew who I was, it was always only dad, May and me. Whenever I'd asked about our family, he'd told me that all of our relatives, including our mother, had died in a soldier training exercise, and we had moved away to the small, seaside village when both May and I were very young.

My whole past has been a lie. My entire world a sham, and the family that was warm, loving and generous in my imagination, is harsh and bitter in reality.

After I found out who I really was, I began to dream even more desperately of a heritage who didn't kill for pleasure, and I was ashamed to see my relatives' faces blaring across the Screens every day.

Though of course I have been disowned by them, it means nothing. I decide that I will relish it when their knives pour out my blood, for it means that there is less of them in me and that therefore I am less like them.

We stop suddenly, and I trip, falling against the Destructor in front of me. He doesn't react as I bounce off him, landing in a heap on the ground. I quickly jump to my feet, scowling and hissing through my teeth as I am marched through a set of thick double doors. I tread onto a metal floor, and my bare feet sting with its cold bite. I hear the crash of closing doors behind me, and get an uneasy feeling that they will not open again for a long time.

There are more noises. Sliding. Scraping. Bolts slotting into place. Then a harsh twisting sound. A key turning in the final lock.

The Destructors in front of me step to either side, revealing a grand hallway made entirely of silver. The harshness of the metal is absorbed into the floors, walls and ceilings that seem heavy and imposing. It is as if they are looking on me with the same contempt and hatred that the Nobles do.

Another door dominates the wall in front of me. I stare at it for a brief moment before the cold, electric lights pulse into darkness, and I hear the sound of the door crashing open. A gloved hand on my back pushes me forwards before I hear a slam, and not so much see but feel a stare shivering into my body through the blackness.

Chapter 39

Lights gradually grow around me, and the dark void becomes like a dim, black and white photograph. I glance around the room, my legs trembling slightly beneath my weight.

There is someone else in here. Someone with such a strong presence of menace that they could be detected a mile away. My head twists to the left as if pulled by some invisible force, as a figure steps into view.

He is large and broad, taking deliberate steps that cause the tiles to light up under his feet He stands erect, straight and cruel, the stance of a soldier but also of a king. His arms, hanging readily by his sides, twitch with anticipation and excitement, his hands relaxed though prepared to clench into fists at a moment's notice.

His hair shines jet-black, dyed at the roots where it must glimmer grey underneath. Despite his age, he has undergone extravagant plastic surgery and looks no more than thirty, with a forehead so smooth it's as if it has never seen creases or worry. His eyebrows are crow-like, sharp and defined, and his eyes gleam with a dark intensity that bores into my soul with a powerful anchor that does not let me look away. His nose, finely chiselled by spite and arrogance, pulls his face forward, making it narrow and cruel, as his mouth, pursed with disgust, starts to move.

"Willow" He snarls. "I've heard so much about you." I stare at the floor, bile rising in my throat. Stealing one look at him, the hatred inside of me boils, and my lips curl into something resembling a sneer. It's a small movement, but his pugnacious eyes notice it immediately and his sharp anger flares. "Is that the way to greet your grandfather after almost eleven years? You should be bowing to a man of my importance."

He suddenly smiles, a smile that rises high up his cheekbones and brings dark fireworks darting into the corners of his eyes. "That's right Willow. Bow. Bow!" Abruptly, a great clamp drops from the ceiling above me and grips my shoulder, pushing me to the floor and pinning me down in submission to the first Noble.

Now towering above, me, Rebato Antario marches around my collapsed body, his footsteps making the tiles glow a brilliant white beneath his black boots as he steps on them. I force myself to stare at the floor, not trusting myself to look up and meet his gaze.

"You are so gifted at contempt. So ergonomically evil. You could have been great you know Talemia." I wince at the sound of my regal name and I can feel his pleasure in my discomfort vibrating through the gleaming floor tiles. "You could have married the Emperor's first son, Alomandre Greatest. You would have become the Empress, Talemia, governing the Country from your throne on high, living a life bathed in gold and riches. Aren't you jealous of Leannette?" I think of Leannette Antario, daughter of dad's younger brother, who I now realise is my cousin. Last August she was betrothed to Alomandre Greatest, a miniature replica of his father. "You could have been her Talemia" His words reach out with tiny arms and grip my attention with an iron fist. "You could have been the Empress."

"I would rather die."

"Well I'm afraid your fate lies in our hands, not yours. Death is far too kind for a traitor like you."

I scowl at the floor, not hiding the anger that screams through my face. The clamp pushes me further down, my nose pressing into the cold floor as I feel his beady eyes staring fixedly at my back.

"Your father, my son, always speaks very highly of you. He tells me that you're good and true, innocent even. But those are not the qualities I'd want in a granddaughter. No. My descendants should be brave. Strong. Ruthless."

The clamp loosens slightly, and I can finally lift up my eyes to stare at my father's father. My grandfather. The first Noble. Forcibly praised and adored by all.

I wonder what it was like for dad to grow up under the command of this man. This man who was feared by anyone who'd ever dared to take a breath on this planet. Renowned for being a man who would kill for pleasure. Who even now is preparing the spectacular destruction of his own grandchild. I feel sorry for dad. Not because of the fear that surrounded his upbringing, but because he had nothing to look up to but a selfish coward.

"You are not brave." My voice comes out as barely a whisper. "You will never be brave. And I am not your granddaughter."

"Ah. You and I share the same dream my dear." His voice is patronising and sickly sweet. "Indeed, it would be one less shame to tarnish my reputation." He spits out the word 'shame' as if it itches his tongue. "But look." Rebato crouches down to me, clutches at my hair and wrenches back my neck. A knife in his closed fist slices at the skin above my collar bone, oozing dark red blood onto the fabric of my clothes. He releases me, and brings the knife to his own palm, cutting deeply into his skin, yet not even flinching as he presses his bloody wound onto mine. "We are the same, you and I. The same crimson blood flows through our veins, and the same genes are passed down through our generations. So, you see, child, you are my descendent. Therefore, I am your ancestor, to be respected and obeyed." The clamp on my shoulder is released, and he pulls me to my feet.

"That doesn't stop you though, does it?" I hiss. "That doesn't stop you torturing your own grandchild. Your own son."

"Why should it?" His seems genuinely confused. "You're my defendant. That gives me power over you. You are my disobedient descendant. That gives me a reason to punish you. Being someone's relation does not mandate that you must be kind. Kindness is a waste of time and emotion. I feel the same hatred towards you as I do to every man, woman and child who tries to undermine this Country. The fact that you're my granddaughter only gives me more power over you, more access to your emotions, your fears. You're a tool. I can use you. I can use you to increase my power. Power is what I want. Power where no one will resist me. Nobody will question me. Everyone will live in submission to me."

He walks to the opposite side of the room where an opening suddenly materialises in the wall. He marches through the doorway and the wall reforms behind him. I run after him, battering at the hard plaster with both of my fists, but it's as if he was never even there.

Panting in frustration and hopelessness, I collapse against the wall just before a huge gust of wind hurls me back into the centre of the room. I sit, hugging my knees and waiting in fear that doesn't even let me breathe, for what I don't want to come.

"Welcome to Deprivation." The voice of my grandfather echoes around the room, booming and flooding through the air. "As a part of your initiation as a captive of the Big City, we administer a time period where you do not eat, you do not drink, and most importantly, you do not sleep."

"Why?" I choke on the question as it churns in my stomach. I think I already know the answer.

"Tell us anything about the Resistance, their plans to undermine our government or any information regarding their secret bases and membership, and you may receive a small reprieve, depending on the validity of your account."

"How long?" The question is almost silent, addressed more to myself, but he hears, and laughs.

"You will be held here until we receive sufficient information."

If I die? I don't voice this question, but he answers it.

"There is enough moisture in the air to keep you alive, but barely. You will be existing on the threshold of life and death, where everything is grey, but pain is still vivid, and your blurry concentration morphs the shadows into your worst nightmares, or your most remote dreams." A delicate cackle vibrates through the room. "If you get hungry, you can always suck your own flesh."

From the floor, rise four manacles which slither towards me and attach themselves to my wrists and ankles. They pull me up, so I am sitting like a rag doll, yanking me a foot to the left as a large metal rod falls from the sky, one side of it cradling a small syringe full of a green liquid. It takes aim, and plunges itself into my neck.

"It stops you sleeping." Rebato answers my unasked question. Another metal arm falls from the roof, this one holding a steel helmet. It clips itself to my head and compresses itself so tightly that I wouldn't be able to pull it off even if my hands weren't shackled. I can almost feel it probing into my mind as I remember Mays warning.

Don't think. Don't think about anything.

Then, the questions begin.

Chapter 40

"When did you join the Resistance?"

I must not think. Must not think!

"How did the Resistance workers learn to read and write?"

The know the answer to that! They must do. They're just testing me. I imagine dad, his picture delicately embodying my mind.

"Thank you."

I start, and scowl, is nothing my own anymore? Not even my thoughts? The voice continues, and I realise how careful I have to be.

"Where is the headquarters for the Resistance?"

No image. Think of something else. A distraction.

"Who coordinates the Resistance?

Think of something else. May. Think of May. She cares about me. She cares about me very much. A large picture of her beaming face fills my head.

"How old were you when you joined the Resistance?"

Think of May. May is very young. Not old at all.

"How long will it be until the Resistance launch an attack on the Big City?"

May. Imagine her smile, her laugh. Her laugh makes me smile.

"Why is it that the bombs and guns from Rente never work properly?"

I didn't know that.

"Do you tamper with them?"
No!
"How many people work for the Resistance?"
I can't think. Mustn't think!
"How do the Resistance communicate?"
It goes on and on. Different voices sometimes. Some male, some female. Some soft and deceptive, some harsh and demanding. Sometimes with an undercurrent of pity, but more often an overtone of threat. The same questions over and over, rephrased, asked in different ways by different people. I can feel the helmet buzzing, sending shivers of painful electricity through my skull.

"Enough!" The voice of my father's father echoes in the silence that follows his booming command.

The release of pressure as the helmet stops pumping energy into my head, pushes me backwards. But the relief lasts only seconds before the walls around me turn into screens that tauntingly flicker to life. My heart leaps into my mouth and begins to choke me as a small, enclosed room blares all around.

All I have to see is the large wooden block in the centre of the room, and the tall menacing woman standing before it, relishing a whip, to guess what is to come. The chains still hold me down, strapping my arms and legs tightly to the floor, and forcing me to watch a small, limp figure being lead to the block. I try to look to the floor, but even the glowing tiles have transformed into a screen, displaying May now tied to the wood with coarse brown rope. The block is covered in small silver blades poking out from it and piercing her neck.

I shut my eyes but a pain stabs through my head so blindingly and sharp that I am forced to push them open again. I remember the syringe containing the green liquid to stop my sleep, and snarl under my breath. Nothing, not even an eyelid, will keep me from witnessing my sister's pain.

The camera zooms in and focuses on the torn dress that clings to her shaking frame. She is pushed to her knees in front of the wooden block, where chains snake around her ankles and fasten her calves to the floor. Her wrists are manacled and small trickles of blood seep from underneath the harsh chains, colouring her hands a pale, unhealthy red.

It happens slowly. Painfully slowly. As if time has manipulated each passing second to last an eternity. Malintaret. Her mother. My mother. Stares straight at the camera. Boring into me with eyes that seem to reflect a sickly myriad of colours.

"Willow" She says bluntly and tonelessly. "Good morning. I hope you're enjoying Deprivation." Her mouth smiles wryly, but her eyes remain solemn and cruel. "As you can see, I'm spending some quality time with your precious little sister, who I'm sure you'd hate to see hurt." She slashes the whip so it lands on the block, less than an inch away from May's face. "So maybe it's time you co-operated with us." She returns the whip to her side. "It's simple. You tell us what we want to know, and the little Maple tree only gets her daily quota, nothing more." She pushes my sister forwards so that she is leant over the block, her pale back exposed and visible through the tunic's thin fabric. Still holding the scruff of May's neck, so she can't move, Malintaret brings the whip up high above her head. "If not..." The whip falls, slashing through the delicate material and penetrating my sister's vulnerable flesh beneath.

I gasp, straining against my chains to reach her. But it's no use, the scream of May's pain echoes through the room, youth and innocence shattering like a glass vase as it falls onto the floor and breaks into a million tiny pieces.

"How do the Resistance intercept our information?"

The voice surprises me, though I don't know why. I stare at the image of May, now zoomed in on her scarred back, as every inch of the walls, ceiling and floor is splattered with her agony. I try to keep my mind blank as my heart tears itself apart.

He thinks I won't answer and his voice comes again, though this time directed into the torture chamber where my sister still writhes in pain, her face pulled taught.

"Be creative."

Malintaret jerks her head upwards, and a moment later she smiles. Her hand still clutching May's neck, she drags the small, helpless figure to her feet. The camera follows them to a metal desk that looks like a surgeons operating table. May fights and tries to resist her mother, as she is forced to lie on the long shelf, and a barbed wire, metal circle is pushed onto her head, cutting into her scalp and drawing blood. A wire, charged with pulsing electricity is attached to one side of the crown, as the other end is slowly being lowered towards a battery, by a delicate, pointed hand, to complete the circuit.

"STOP!"

An order that I don't hear is given, and Malintaret stops preparing to fry my sister in sizzling electricity, a look of disappointment lining her face.

May looks relieved for a moment, but then fear darts across the intensity of her bright blue eyes as she realises why she is not currently screaming in cruel pain.

"How do the Resistance intercept our information?" My grandfather repeats.

"Let her go." I slowly instruct, keeping my mind clear.

He chuckles. "I don't think that you're in the position to be making bargains with us."

"Let her go and I will tell you."

I hear a sigh, and two guards appear on the right-hand side of the screens. They reach May, marching at the pace of snails, and take her from the bed. As she is paraded from the room she looks straight at the camera. Straight at me. I close my eyes, fighting against the searing pain that it causes, not bearing to look at her disappointment, to acknowledge that I have failed.

But how? How could I watch you drowning in so much pain when I was able to prevent it? My eyes spring open, watering with the effort it cost to keep them closed, and May has vanished from the room.

"She's gone." Says the voice in a way that should sound harsh and coarse, but now everything seems to have a distant quality, like I'm watching from outside of my body. "But we can always bring her back." My mind remains blank and I remain silent.

""How do the Resistance intercept our information?"

I can feel his anger fusing.

"They have computers. Super computers that they have built themselves. These intercept the radio waves that you send and decode the messages, using the information to stop you murdering innocent people." My voice sounds monotonic and distant, with no emphasis and no passion, as if it isn't my own. If it was my own, would I be ashamed of it? Of what I have said?

"How do they decode the messages?" There's no praise. No reprieve because I answered the first question.

"I don't know!" The sounds and the colours around me suddenly become louder and more vibrant, as if I am returning to my body after having been apart from it for a long time. "I don't know anything! Just let me go!"

He laughs and then the room becomes silent.

Chapter 41

I sit in the solemn, empty chasm, unable to even blink without sharp pain sizzling through me. The darkness is too gloomy for me to spend the endless minutes studying the walls, yet light enough to cast uncanny shadows into the room, patterning it with strange and unnerving shapes, designed by the Nobles.

My hands and feet are still manacled to the floor and the helmet is clamped to my head, where sometimes I feel it vibrate, reminding me that my thoughts are not my own. After tireless hours of staring into nothingness, my mind wanders back to May.

Where is she now? Is she safe? Or at least out of the room with the operating table? My heart quickens and my pulse pounds in every part of my body as I remember her writhing in pain. I remember my promise to her, that no matter what, I would remain silent, but feel no regret for breaking it. Maybe my priorities are wrong. But she's my sister. I've always taken care of her, always been by her side with my arms wrapped around her, at a moment's notice. I am her sister, we share a bond of alliance that I have never held with anyone else.

But I am also someone else to her, a figure that neither of us have ever had. In so many ways over the past five years, I've been like her mother.

Could a mother, a true mother, not someone like Malintaret, ever watch her own child undergo so much pain?

The answer to me is obvious. In my mind, I apologize to those I've betrayed, aware of the helmet and conscious not to think of their names nor conjure their faces. But I still don't wish that I hadn't given in. Anything else, anything, and I would stand by and defend them, join them in doing whatever I could to defeat the Nobles. But she is too precious. My sister is worth far more than the Resistance's victory.

Maybe I'm selfish, but what else can I do? What else can I feel? Again, I imagine her tormented face, looking at me, begging me to promise her I would stay silent. I failed her.

I failed her.

I suddenly realise that this is not the first time I've thought those words. I've failed her in so many ways, so many times.

My mind feels like it's quivering; and the helmet trembles, as if it pities me.

I have thought too much. I let go. My brain surrenders and falls into a murky darkness the same texture as the room around me.

I don't know how long I've been sitting in the same position, with my feet and arms manacled to the floor. I feel like a dog tied to a post, unable to do anything but sit, and stare, and sit. I could have been here for hours or even days. Time doesn't seem to be relevant; a year, a minute; what's the difference? When I'm here with no purpose other than to suffer? What does it matter?

The thirst comes first, slowly climbing through my body. I roll saliva on my tongue, savouring each drop in my mouth before I finally swallow. He told me I wouldn't die. There was enough moisture in the air to keep me alive. Barely. My mouth runs completely dry and feels like a piece of parchment, endlessly begging my brain to find liquid. My parched lips stick together. It's painful to pull them apart so I just leave them there, glued to each other.

Cramp seers through my leg, but I fear that any movement will make me perspire, losing even more precious hydration. My throat burns, and it feels like the helmet tightens and grows heavier, causing my head to pound.

Then, the hunger. Beginning with sharp but suppressible pangs in the pit of my gut, developing into unusual noises that I have never heard before, and then becoming an agonizing pain that seems to be wrenching my stomach inside out.

Images of fresh bread, and large pails of water hover just out of reach in my imagination. Hallucinations of fresh, juicy apples, like the ones that May and I used to pick from the gardens, when dad would lift us up to reach the tallest tree's, dance in front of my eyes, the colours becoming uncomfortably vivid and bold, as if they are part of a cartoon.

I concentrate on breathing deeply, through my nose so I don't have to separate my dry lips. The scent of fresh bread and warm soup fills my nostrils. I must be imagining again, and I try to banish any thoughts or cravings for food. But the smell remains, and I realize that it's not just a faint dream lurking in the back of my mind, but is actually there, in the room, lingering in the air around me. I twist my head with a scowl plastering my face, my thoughts forming vile images demonstrating my hatred of the Nobles, picked up by the buzzing helmet and transmitted to them. Taking meticulous detail over a limp and powerless image of my grandfather, I wonder if they will react.

They do. The smell becomes stronger and more intense. If my mouth wasn't so dry, it would be watering as the aromas make me shiver with pangs of what cannot be described as mere hunger anymore. More like starvation, or the wrath of a dragon inside me that has nothing left to tear at but my own flesh.

I try to hold my breath, sealing my airways until I feel like my lungs are going to burst. Then another short, deep breath. But as I inhale the fumes reach my organs and torture me, unable to escape. I exhale, releasing the toxic perfume, trying to close down my lungs, though they are already depleted and empty.

Panting, and almost screaming, I blurt. "Stop! Please. Stop!"

At first, I think that no one will answer me.

"Where is the central base-camp for the Resistance?" The voice is cold, with no room for compromise.

"I won't tell you." I say, before I am invaded once more by the smell of gorgeous bread and pastries, cakes with warm icing and raspberry sauce. I can envision each scent, each element of the rich tapestry that the food creates.

The screens flicker to life around me, displaying a spring of flowing water, fresh and glimmering in the yellow sunshine. My throat burns with a parch that slowly travels down through my organs, intermingling with the hunger so that my body turns on itself to torment the bare emptiness inside of me.

I try to clamp my eyes shut against the vile images of the water that runs so freely on the screens, nourished by the grassy meadows and the glimmering sunlight; but agonizing pain forces them to flash open again.

Every sense is threatened. My sight by the water, looking so close and wet, I can almost touch it; my ears by the sounds of the trickling spring, and my smell and taste by the intensifying bakery of scents that are so vivid I can envision their sources lingering in front of me, but still not real enough for the food to materialize in my mouth.

"I'd rather die." My defiance whispers through every self-preserving bone in my body.

And so, the whirlwind of suffering and temptation, goes on and on, like a hurricane that will never be satisfied with the havoc it wreaks.

Then, everything seems to disappear. The smells, the sounds, the pictures. The hunger and thirst still rage inside of me, but it's no longer violent, as if my body has simply accepted it as a natural physical procedure.

I must have been here for days. Sometimes it feels like longer and I can't remember anything else. Sometimes it feels shorter and the past lies only just out of my reach. The hunger is still there, burning away in a cold agony, and the thirst still splits my head and tears my throat apart, but now it's superseded by an exhaustion that grips my eyelids and pulls them closed, only to meet with a pain so shattering. I scream and slump, panting on the cold floor, trying to recover my breath for minutes, maybe even hours, afterwards.

The fatigue grips me with a tiredness that shoots everything out of proportion. My head feels like lead and my knees throb at the awkward angle they're bent at. My ankles are manacled so tightly to the floor that I can't move them, and my wrists are chained in front of me in a twisted and painful position that makes my back bend over and every muscle ache. I can almost feel the sleepless green serum poisoning my veins, turning my cells against each other and waging battles within me that I don't have the energy to fight.

Chapter 42

Where am I?
How long have I been here?
Why am I so dizzy?
I've been awake for so long, why aren't I asleep?
Sleep is good. Sleep is kind. I close my eyes.

Pain, blind and white with tinges of green skimming the surface and probing into my mind, vibrates through me, so shrill and sharp my eyes flash open and are forced to face the sharp exhaustion.

The walls around me turn into murals, painted in bright colours that are slightly hazy around the edges.

The wall in front of me is smiling.

Why is the wall smiling? Walls don't smile. The walls eyes are closed, it's asleep. I'm jealous. Why aren't I asleep?

Words labouring around my mind mix into a blur of black and white, merging the two colours into a grey that doesn't know right from wrong, good from bad. Sounds seem to rise out of the walls, but I'm so far away from my own consciousness that I don't recognise the piercing voice. That I don't realize what's coming next.

"Where do the Resistance get medical equipment?"

I'm so tired. I wish he'd stop talking and let me sleep.

"Where is the central base for the Resistance?"

It's just a little information. A little secret can't hurt.

I blink. Pain dashes through me, awakening my senses as I realise in horror what I was about to do. No. Even through this sleep deprived haze, I will not ruin everything that the Resistance has worked for. My mind feels like grey, unwashed wool, but at least it's blank. My jaw is locked, and my heart and my secrets remain shielded from my interrogator.

"When do the Resistance plan to attack the Big City?"

Distract yourself Willow. Think of something else, anything. Just not sleep. Not food. Not drink. Not the pain that writhes inside of me like a dragon battling for escape. Not the parch that pulls itself through me as if it were an electric current rattling through the desert.

Think of a time before this. A better time. A happier time. I reach into the past, but those memories are too distant and overused, I have turned to them so many times in my suffering that they have become mutated, and now only reflect the pain that has built itself around them. My imagination wonders, something I've never allowed it to do before, turning to a future, or perhaps it's the present in another place. A place that will never actually exist. It's probably damaging to even let myself think about it - I might just believe it. But anything, any damage is better than this. It has to be.

My eyes are still open, but they blur, no longer the focus of my brain power. Instead my thoughts create an image. I don't initiate it. I'm not aware of my mind filling up with my own ideals, but I feel as if my skull is relaxing, the tenseness of discomfort slowly beginning to evaporate. I feel empty. No pain. No joy. No past. No future. It's too much effort now even to conjure up the present.

Everything is gone, everything except this lonely image, a picture from a storybook, a life that's far away but still within the confines of my mind.

One of the first things I notice is the warm sun suspended in a soft blue sky. It's a myriad of colours; orange, yellow, pink and gold. In my imagination, I hold out my arm and feel it gently beating down on me, my skin delicately reflecting the hazy glow. But it is not my arm. It's darker, and stronger, lined with delicate muscles that hang like crystals on a chandelier. Glancing down I realize that I am further from my feet, taller, and my fingers are longer and thinner. I touch my hair. It's thicker and more course, and I tug at dark brown extensions the colour of coffee.

Who am I? Why do I look like this?

But then, what do I expect myself to look like? When I was born, I was a Noble, with their distinctive pointed nose and snarling lips. When dad escaped with us, I became a rosy little girl with bony elbows and blonde hair. After that, we were relocated again, and my hair took the colour of chestnuts, with more flesh lining my bones and paler, more care-worn skin. I wonder for a moment what will happen to the artificial fat underneath my skin now. It won't erode with lack of food like it should - it's not natural. I'm not natural. Every time I look in the mirror a different person stares back at me. Why should it surprise me that I'm different again within my own imagination?

A long dress reaches almost to my knees, deep blue with emerald birds flying across my collarbone and waistline. It's not a regal dress, nothing that the Nobles would wear, but it would never be seen on a civilian in the Country either. It doesn't fit into a social class, into the mould that we must conform to. The dress is neither rich nor poor, happy nor sad, good nor bad.

Grass is spread below my bare feet, fresh and gently green. I wonder why my feet are bare, but I get the feeling that I have chosen not to wear shoes. The lawn is interspersed with rows of flowers that glow like angels in the sunlight, but I couldn't name them, they don't exist. One variety boasts of each petal in a different shade of purple, another seems to be sprinkled with every colour, but subtly, a gentle rainbow that grows softly from one leaf to another.

A tiny creature darts into the flowers, with a small, thin body clipping together a pair of wings that span the length of my little finger and are elaborately decorated with colourful swirls. I feel as if I should know the animal, but it's not something I have ever seen before.

Trees line the edges of the grass, tall and majestic as they climb into the air. One side of the lawn is bordered with willows. I was always told that their hunched stance was one of grief and weeping, but now they seem as if they are bowing, in awe of some majesty.

I turn to the other side of the clearing, and see row upon row of maple trees, their branches delicate and feminine like the graceful arms and legs of a dancer. Their leaves are as red as a furnace, the sunset reflecting off them, and making them even more vibrant.

Moss covers a rock that rests in the centre of the clearing in front of me, exuberant and fresh; relaxed and contented.

I'm standing within a representation of my family, a symbol of everything that is dear to me, everything in my life that is good and true.

A tall woman walks out from between the trees. Her hair drapes behind her back, lose and free, hanging to her waist in gentle brown waves. Her face looks as if it has been sketched by the hand of an artist renowned for perfection, her eyes wide and bright, and her lips parted and curved upwards. She wears a dress that is similar to mine, but hers is deep lilac and embroidered with white flowers. I feel as if I should be afraid of her, but instead I find her smile filled with comfort and hope.

"Hello Willow." She says as her bare feet come to stand before mine. Her voice is soft and melodic. "Do you like it here?"

I try to reply, but no words come.

"They call it the Pain Haven. It's the place where those who are strong enough, escape to when there is nothing else, when all they can feel is hurt and heartache." She pauses, waiting for me to reply. I don't. "You can't stay here for long, and you only ever visit the garden once. Make the most of it." She twirls, her dress billowing out at her sides. "Keep going Willow. You're doing well."

"Is this?" I stutter. "Is this real?"

"Keep going Willow." She doesn't answer my question. "We're all so proud of you." The conviction in her voice has her turning and walking away, through the trees and into whatever lies beyond.

"Wait! Where are you going?" I want to chase after her, but I can't move. Instead, I stare at the place where she was standing, at the aura of hope and beauty that she left behind.

An animal that has only ever existed in my mind, never in my world, sits on the ground, his feathers so white that they absorb the setting sun and glimmer almost gold. His beak is pale orange and his eyes a shade of black that goes beyond the realms of darkness and into the beauty of light. Out of his mouth pokes a green leaf, and as he lifts his wings, he takes off from the ground with feet that are both strong and delicate. His tail fans out behind him like a river that forks into little white streams, and his wings stretch out magnificently, stroking my cheek.

Overcome by awe, I gaze at the dove. The very symbolism of truth, peace and love. I remember the little wooden carvings that dad used to make. They were beautiful, but nothing compared to this. I stare at the majesty of the bird as the scene around me starts to disintegrate, the willow trees, the maples and the moss slowly crumbling into the vanishing horizon.

The dove is the last thing to disappear.

I hear loud crash and my eyes refocus on the sight of debris flying across the darkened space as the helmet on top of my head explodes. Electrical wires and metal casings litter the room that is now suddenly flashing crazily bright colours from the screens on the walls and floor as my head bursts with a high pitched, painful ringing. The energy from the helmet's explosion has been transferred through my skull and I can almost feel it coursing through my brain, wreaking an agonising havoc that blinds and deafens both physically and mentally.

I pant, lying on the floor as I subconsciously realize that my chains have loosened and slip off my wrists and ankles.

I blink to try to distract myself from the agony in my skull with another pain, but there is nothing. The shock must have deactivated the green serum.

Glancing around, I see a door opening and the Destructors marching through it, followed by my grandfather who is wearing a deathly, paralysing expression. They haul me to my feet and push me into their midst where Roberto grips my shoulders. He pours a large bucket of water over my head. I catch as much of it as I can in my mouth, relishing the sweet taste. A dry chunk of burnt bread is thrown in my direction, which I grab and gratefully bring to my lips.

I stare at Roberto, confused but not trusting myself to make an audible sound, in case it betrays my fear.

"You broke the helmet." My grandfather says bluntly. "You overloaded it with power and shorted the entire City of electricity."

I let out a silent gasp, rooted to the spot in shock until he drags me forward again. We march through the doors, into the corridor, and finally out into the cold, icy night where the moon shivers in the dark sky above me.

Did I really do that? Were my thoughts, my daydreams, that strong? That powerful? That they could break the Big City's electricity?

But a tiny burst of contempt rises up in me. I'm glad. It's a small price to pay for the pain of the many who have suffered at the feet of the Nobles.

Chapter 43

May!" I gasp as Roberto finally releases his grip on me, and pushes me into the dark cell. The door slams shut behind me and the bolts slide across with a rushed and panicked rhythm, as if the Destructors are afraid of me.

"Willow." Maple catches me as I almost collapse onto the stony floor, and half carries me to the pile of rags where I struggle to find the energy even to breathe.

She lets me drop onto the bed as she scurries to the windowsill, almost immediately beside me again with a small vile filled with water that she gently tips down my throat.

"It rained today," She whispers, trying to sound reassuring, her thin face almost smiling. "And Malintaret gave me this." Her hand clamps around mine where she presses a round circle of bread about the size of my palm. I bring it to my lips and relish every tingle as it darts across my tongue. I can feel it slithering down my throat and into my stomach where it spreads and fills me up as if it was the largest meal that I had ever eaten.

"Thank you." I whisper, my voice barely audible.

"You need it. You were there for eleven days, Willow."

I stare at her, shocked. That can't be right, I couldn't have survived that long without... without anything. "No…" I say, almost to myself. "I would have died."

"The moisture in the air keeps you alive, but a few minutes away from there without water and you'd be gone."

I remember the bucket of water that was thrown over my head before I left the Deprivation chamber. "May," I murmur, "What happened?"

"You tell me!" She almost laughs. Almost. "I was sitting on the windowsill, looking out through the bars, at the moon." Her face is suddenly serene. She is not looking directly at me, but instead at a distant spot on the wall behind me. "Then the lights went out. It was instant, no flickering, no warning, we just dropped into this terrible darkness. I didn't know what was happening. I heard shouts and cries from the courtyard, and then Malintaret burst into the room. She was furious." May bit her lip, finally turning her gaze onto me, with intense sadness lining her face. "She beat me first, then afterwards told me that you had shorted all of the electric cables that supply the Big City. You'd left them vulnerable for attack, she said. She seemed to think it was a part of a plan to undermine and destroy the Nobles. The beginning of a battle. She told me that you were somehow communicating with the Resistance, mentally, and had deliberately sent so much power into the helmet that it exploded and cut of all of their electricity to weaken them, before an attack." She looks at me sadly while I stare back in confusion and fear.

"But, I didn't do anything! Not deliberately! I don't even know what happened. It just... just exploded!"

"Don't worry. I don't believe them, since when could anyone talk telepathically! But whatever image that was in your mind and was projected into the helmet was too powerful for it, and they're not going to let you rest until they know why and how it happened." Her eyes close, and then open again filled with a mixture of anguish and love. "Sleep now." She orders suddenly. "When the electricity comes back, they'll take you to Punishment."

The pale light from the moon streams into the dark cell, bringing a softness to May's face, and for a moment, it's almost as if all the pain and sorrow has vanished from it. Comforting myself with this picture, my eyes close and I sleep for the first time in eleven days.

I dream, deeply and strangely about a meadow with a laughing brook that giggles like a child. I follow the brook through a valley where shadows are suddenly cast over me and the only light radiates from the small trail of water. Then, the valley vanishes, and morphs into a garden with lush grass that is more golden than green, decorated with a large vegetable patch growing leaves that look like feathers. There is a small pond in the corner of the garden, elegantly getting larger as my feet move towards it. I reach the water, but I don't feel it flowing over my ankles. I'm not wet, but am now standing on a heap of leaves in the middle of a forest.

The forest seems to be made up of two different types of trees, and living in two contrasting seasons of the year. The maple trees are red and gold, secreting an autumnal promise of warmth beside a roaring fire and an old man telling an ancient tale from times gone by. But there are willow trees too, living in a springtime filled with hope and new life as birdsong filters through the thick leaves that cast majestic shadows on the ground. As the forest establishes itself, I notice a woman wondering between the trees, a beautiful woman with long hair and laughing eyes.

"Wait!" I call, chasing after her, needing to reach her for a reason that I don't yet know but must be important because of the intensifying urgency I feel, that makes me run harder and faster towards her. But just before I can reach out my hand to touch the woman, her feet leave the ground.

She transforms into a dove, elegant and heroic, circling the trees that slowly start to fade, until finally, all that is left of the vision is the graceful, pure bird silhouetted against the hazy sky.

Suddenly, the dream has vanished, and a loud clang makes me leap up from the pile of rags on the floor. Maple turns from where she is standing beside the window and runs towards me, another small water vile clutched in her hand.

"The power came back about twenty minutes ago." Her mouth smiles reassuringly but her eyes burn with fear that is far too visible in the mechanical light bathing the room. "Drink." She hands me the vile. "Quickly!"

In a narrow moment I swallow the water, press the vile back into my sisters shaking hand, and turn to face the door as three soldiers march through keeping rapid time with my heart beat. May is looking out of the window, refusing to make eye contact with me or the soldiers as they tie a rope around my waist and drag me through the door.

I am pulled down the long, spiral staircase and out into the hallway, where instead of going towards the torture chambers, I am dragged through a grand corridor and onto the mansion's central landing.

A platform riser looms ahead of me. It looks somehow too clean and unused, as if it has a specific destination that is only visited on special occasions. The glass cylinder opens, and I am pushed inside, the end of the rope thrown in behind me. I can feel my heartbeat pumping in my fingertips as the doors close and outside, a soldier presses a large, red button. I scream and pound my fists on the glass, but the soldiers walk away, and as they do, I swear I can see glimpses of identical smirks on their expressionless faces.

The cylinder begins to descend as my heartbeat slows in tempo, but becomes louder in anticipation. I can feel it thrumming everywhere except in my chest. My head, my fingers, and my feet all pulse with drumming terror as my muscles tense and my breath catches sharply. I watch as I sink through dozens of floors, empty of people but each one gloating of ignorant grandeur. My hands fiddle with the folds of the grey tunic that is now stained with blood and tears as the platform riser finally finishes its journey.

The doors open out onto a large arena with a viewing gallery hanging from the wall directly ahead of me. In the glass gallery sit row upon row of spectators. The seven Nobles perch on miniature golden thrones to the right of it. As my eyes meet Roberto's he smirks, his eyebrows lifting ironically. In the left section of the gallery sit the women, the wives of the seven Nobles, and sitting behind them are the unmarried members of the family.

I notice a high-backed chair, empty and foreboding, where Malintaret should sit, in the centre of the gallery, behind a line of miniature plush stools, from which Noble children jeer and shout at me. Just the sight of the cruelty on their faces makes me shiver, hating them and pitying them at the same time. Somehow, I feel almost responsible for their heartlessness. Maybe because I was once one of them.

Beside them, in a separate box that is suspended from the ceiling, the Emperor sits in front of a large control board that glows with the hatred filling the air. He is smiling, a smile that tells me that he will soon bring the music of my screams to his ears and relish in the sound.

Several other boxes are dangling from the ceiling around the arena, but these are empty, unoccupied glass cubes that stare at me with lifeless eyes.

I turn to the centre of the room. The floor emits a faint red light, colouring everything around it in dark shades of blood. A wooden block, a metal chair, and a series of other instruments that I have never seen before take precedence in the centre of the room, and a long metal chain with three shackles hangs from the ceiling, facing two manacles which sprout up from the floor.

A loud hush envelopes the room as Malintaret walks towards me, teetering on her high heels that click loudly on the hard, marble floor. She wears a long dress that reaches to her ankles, and is decorated with black and red spots, gold and silver embroidery lining the collarbone and waistline. Her hair, dyed a royal plum, is ostentatiously styled to stick out of her head at all angles, looking like a purple porcupine held back by a red bandana. Her face is heavily made up with long black eyelashes and bright red cheeks, and as she opens her mouth to sneer at me, her red painted lips highlight her artificially whitened teeth that resemble fangs.

I shake my head as the silence grows into a roaring hiss, and let the growling fear squirming inside of me take control.

Chapter 44

Malintaret and I stare at each other across the room for a long time, neither of us daring to move. Once, I would have tried to run, but that time has passed. Rebellion now seems childish, as if I really thought that I could escape the monsters that ruled the earth. And if I did escape, it would cost me too dearly. The lives and the hopes of May, of dad, are worth much more than my own. I understand this now.

Malintaret reaches for my arm. She is tentative at first, nervous as if I might hurt her despite my weak, barely alive state. Like a cat reaching for a low flying bird, she almost grabs me, but then retreats, as if my skin is electrified and she doesn't know whether it's safe to touch.

I lift my gaze to meet hers, the cold, black pits where her eyes should be, which would once have forced me to look away. But now her callous stare is met with my own, so full of anger and disgust, surprise flashes across her sombre expression for the briefest of seconds. Hatred fills my body with the angry energy I physically lack, and gives me confidence that will not achieve anything, but is something that I will never regret.

"Coward." I murmur. My words create a strict silence where a pin dropping to the floor would be louder than a piercing scream. "You're too afraid to even touch me." My voice growls, growing in volume until it is loud and strong, but most of all, alive. "At your feet lie thousands of dead bodies, yet you're afraid of me." I can feel the reactions of the Nobles witnessing us from the gallery, but I don't take my eyes away from Malintaret. Surprise contorts her face, and the astonishment that freezes her expression gives me a window of opportunity. "Cowards. All of you! You kill and torture and dictate. You destroy the lives of the people in your Country, the innocent people who hate you because you force them to watch your evil games! You corrupt the happiness of your own children for the sake of power. For the sake of your own selfish ambition!" I'm shouting now, screaming at the rows of faces on the balcony. Some expressions are pulled tight, with lips sealed in indignation, others blaze in anger with their jaws pushed forward and their noses breathing fire. Most however, sit in shock, mouths slightly open, their angry façade lost in a moment that forgets appearances; eyes wide and confused as if, for the first time, they see the damage that they have caused.

The world seems to stop, trapped in this silent moment where everything is hanging upside down. The prisoner has the power and all the oppressors can do is watch, ensnared in the chains of my words.

All of a sudden, the room springs into action. Shouts, screams and insults are hurled at me, but I don't hear any of them. Instead, I refocus my eyes on my mother as her face begins to warp, changing into something dark and deadly, with an expression of hatred that I had never seen before. In fury she grabs my wrists and pulls me with strength fuelled by the anger brimming from her eyes.

The long chains in the centre of the room pull towards me as if I am a magnet. The larger manacle fastens itself around my neck whilst the two smaller shackles grip my wrists as the restraints that rise from the floor wrap themselves around my ankles so tightly that the cold metal makes the areas around them turn white.

A hush falls across the room. I glance upwards to see rows of Noble faces that now mirror each other in a putrid hatred.

Malintaret takes slow, carefully calculated steps towards me. She stares for a while, considering me as if I were an artefact on the shelf of a shop. I see her smile and she slowly nods, but not at me.

A sudden jerk and the shackles have pulled me upwards, the chains attached to my feet lengthening as I rise into the air. My head is pulled back and my pale neck is exposed to the knife that is gripped in Malintaret's right hand.

"You think that we're the cowards." Malintaret circles me, so close that I can feel her breath stroking my skin. "You, who bleats with terror at the sight of pain that isn't even yours. You, who would sacrifice your most treasured secrets for the life of a child. Love is cowardice." She spits the words. "Love. My own daughter. Such a downfall of your character." She runs the knife along my exposed neck, so lightly it doesn't pierce the skin, but leaves a trailing shiver that threatens what I know is to come.

Her voice is now lower, malicious with a hint of excitement decorating the last syllable of each word. "Last night, you were responsible for undermining the security of this City, cutting off our power and leaving us vulnerable to attack. You left us in a darkness where even the sky was ruined, and we lost all of the data that is mandatory to our existence." A small bead of blood trickles down my throat. "You were a part of a plan, weren't you? Whilst we were weak, you plotted with the Resistance to undermine us. We haven't found anything contaminated so far, but we're still searching for the breach we know that you are responsible for." The knife slices across the back of my neck. I close my eyes and suppress the sharp pain that darts down my spine. "What did you do?"

"Nothing." I hold my breath.

"Which part of the City was infiltrated last night?" The knife creeps down my jawbone, towards my neck.

"None of it." Blood dribbles from the corner of my mouth, pale and weak, revealing how I feel inside.

"You're strong. Stronger than your sister. Stronger, even, than your father. But you'll break. We'll break you."

I feel sick. Blood is rushing through, and out of my body and I can feel it swirling around in my mouth, my nose, and my ears. My heartbeat radiates to my fingertips in fast, heavy thuds that makes every nerve shiver and every muscle flex with each pulse.

"You caused the temporary deactivation of the Big City. For this, you will pay." My head is pulled back by the shackle, so I am looking directly into the viewing gallery where the Nobles sit, arrogant and scorning. Their cold eyes gaze through me as if I am a character in some sort of fictional entertainment. "Seven Nobles". Malintaret chants. "Seven lives that you robbed of hours that you did not have the right to take. Seven lives that are each more valuable than seven of your own."

But they ruined my life. Doesn't that matter?

"Seven Nobles" She repeats, "Seven punishments to be delivered. Each one customised to the taste and for the particular enjoyment of the perpetrator." She turns towards me, snarls, and spits. "Scum. My father, the Emperor, your Emperor was in the cavern beneath the courtyard in the centre of the City, recording invaluable information on the computers there. When you cut our power, he was left trapped in the darkness, sealed in the underground tomb for the entire twelve hours that it took us to regain the electricity. He had no food and no water, he couldn't even sleep because of the fear that you had brought on him."

"Deprivation." I whisper. She strikes the knife against my cheek where it slashes my pale flesh thirstily, coming away covered in blood.

"His punishment will be the most severe. No expense will be spared for you, my child." She is standing behind me now and I cannot see what she is doing, only hear her sickly voice. "A team of fifty of our technical experts spent twelve hours re-establishing the power to find another hidden sabotage." I hear a click and the chains jolt, making my body rattle in the air. "Every file, every scrap of information stored on our computers is gone. Vanished. All of our back up files are blank and the information vital to the survival of this Country is now non-existent.

"Every record of every man, woman and child in this nation, has been lost forever. Do you know what you've done?" Suddenly, the chains release me, and I fall onto the floor, my body collapsing directly over the wooden block. "Do you realise how much danger you've inflicted on us?" The first slash of the whip hits with no sense of precision, fuelled only by rage. "We could be attacked, and we wouldn't even know who by. The cameras around the Country have only just begun to relay information again, but the people running wild in the streets are unidentifiable, their data is unrecorded." The strikes are harder now, my blood sprays onto my skin either side of the wounds where it splatters cold in comparison to the white-hot pain coursing through my body. "We cannot control the population. No culls, no captures, and no personal reminders of our supremacy." I can hardly hear what she's saying as blood roars in my ears, deafening me. "It will take at least a week to restore the current charges and activities, but past information, so carefully stored and collected over generations of Noble intelligence, is gone forever."

The pain stops. My body crumples for a few moments before I am dragged to my feet and forced to stare once again at the viewing gallery, and the rows of morbid faces.

"Seven Nobles. One Emperor." She repeats, her voice haunting and foreboding, like a lion preparing to pounce on a lamb. "Eight lives each worth more than eighty of your own. Eight punishments and eight perpetrators. The final worse than all the ones before it."

A chair on my right sits painfully empty as I realise that the seventh Noble, Maninta Genzashu, has left the gallery. I hear the doors of the platform riser open behind me and close my eyes.

'Whatever you do.' I almost say out loud. 'Don't cry.'

Chapter 45

Maninta Genzashu's footsteps echo around the room, slow and stately like an arrogant buffalo preparing to pounce. Malintaret smiles in contempt over my shoulder as her icy grasp holds my shoulder and a silver voice echoes in my ear.

"Do you remember the time I came to Rente? When I plucked your sister from the crowd?" His sharp features seem to cut into my skin. "I recognised her immediately." He snarls, as if he is a lion and I am his prey. "Her neck. The vein that runs down the back of her neck, the un-concealable vein that is only visible in the Nobles." I feel the cold, familiar blade of a knife follow the vein down my own neck. "I longed to kill her there and then, to find you in the crowd and be done with it. But our attack had to be planned carefully. We didn't know how many Resistance workers hid in the midst of the mob, and we wanted to observe you for a while, watch your movements in an attempt to extract information about the rebellion."

His burlesque hand clutches my shoulder, and with Malintaret commanding my other, they push me backwards onto a flat, metal board.

"Tie her down." He orders, as the Destructors surround me. "You once saved several children from drowning." I notice a large jug cradled in his hands. "Have you ever wondered what it feels like? To drown?"

A black cloth is thrown on me, covering my entire face. Almost instinctively my eyes shut, as if within my own head, the darkness is acceptable.

Firstly, I feel a small trickle of water falling onto my forehead, surprising me but hardly hurting me. More water is poured onto the cloth, this time further down, covering my nose so I can't breathe. It becomes more intense, now falling on the cloth covering my mouth so that any hope of drawing oxygen into my lungs is lost and I start to struggle, and gasp for air.

Torrents of water cascade onto the cloth, drowning my mouth and nose as my head starts to spin. The water is heavy and cold, pressing into me relentlessly as it seeps through the material and runs through my body that is screaming for oxygen. I want to cough but haven't got enough air to. My lungs burn and pound as they fill up with the pressurising liquid that is pushing me further and further downwards into oblivion. As the water chases everything else out of my body, I can feel my mind start to warp inwards and reel in confusion. Colours merge into each other and are decorated with irrational thoughts that I don't understand. I think I'm screaming but my mouth is filled with fluid pouring down into my organs. A loud rushing noise echoes in my ears, like the sound the mermaids call inside a seashell.

I try to fight, pushing against the chains on my hands and feet, but more water seeps into my nose and mouth as pain rips through my struggling limbs like a hurricane. Over the pounding in my eardrums, I hear a laugh, hollow and menacing. More cackles join in, and even some claps as the water smothers all of the energy in my body which slowly begins to collapse.

When I feel like there can only be a few more moments left before I die of suffocation, the cloth is removed, my bonds are untied, and my body is jerked upwards. I gasp, and quickly gulp the air deeply as oxygen rushes like an excited wind into my lungs and my brain. I want to crumple and have at least a minute of calm before whatever happens next. Just a few moments to breathe and absorb the cold and nourishing atmosphere around me. But I know this won't happen.

I look up to see Genzashu smiling, fiendish delight radiating from his pink face. "You are responsible for the destruction of this City. You left us vulnerable to attack and for that, the punishment is severe."

He turns and walks towards the platform riser, towards the viewing gallery where I know he will watch in pleasure as the other Nobles take their turn.

Out of the platform riser bursts a tired and ragged figure, he limps hurriedly towards the centre of the room, worried that at any moment his entitlement to stand on the blood red floor will be removed. I watch dad pull himself to his full height, facing Malintaret with a bravery that can only be grounded in love.

"Let her go." He orders, coldly and calmly. "Let *our* daughter go back to her cell. Now."

"*Our* daughter" She snarls at her old husband "Is responsible for the undermining of this City. She alone disarmed our security systems and deleted every piece of intelligence that it has taken centuries to collect."

"She's a child." He's almost shouting now. "She doesn't know the first thing about your technologies. How can she have done any of it deliberately?"

"How could she have not done it deliberately? No other power on earth could equal what she projected into that helmet. She has been trained by the Resistance, to be used for this purpose, at this moment in time."

What? Is that true? Have I really been trained? Am I just a pawn for the Resistance?

"How can you do this to her?" Dad's voice becomes desperate. "Your own child?"

"She is guilty of the highest treason." Malintaret's voice is harsh and final. "I may be her mother, but I have no feelings towards her other than hatred. She's young, but not young enough to escape punishment. If I had any sympathy for her I would have killed her a long time ago." She turns her back to him, facing me but speaking to two soldiers standing beside the platform riser. "Take him to a box. Make him watch."

As he is dragged away, he brushes past me. "Dad?" I whisper, gently touching his hand. "I'm OK." I bite my lip and hate myself for lying.

He smiles, but it wavers. His face is lined with apology and fear. "Don't cry." He says, but I'm not sure whether he is talking to me or to himself. The platform riser doors open laboriously, then close again as he is lifted up by the small glass circle and disappears, soon re-emerging above me in one of the glass boxes hanging from the ceiling. He kneels on the floor with his hands pressed against the glass, pain and regret staining his face.

Malintaret looks at me, her eyes deep and her brow furrowed, in careful thought. She smiles. "You're not a child." For a moment her voice seems gentle and soft. "On the day that you were born I knew you would never be a child. You're a Noble, Willow. You could have been so great, remembered forever for your ruthless leadership. You chose this, Willow. This is all your own doing. You could have been great."

Out of the platform riser behind me, steps not Trentaku Frinalle, the sixth Noble, but his son, Derone. He has not yet been exposed too much of the Country. He is still a boy. Sixteen, the same age as me. As his steps come closer, I realise that I have already become accustomed to the sound of the hollow click of the platform riser, and the change in timbre of the shoes as they step onto the floor. He smiles weakly. I don't. I am pushed into the cold metal chair and strapped into it by ropes pulled across my arms, my legs and my waist.

I chose this.

He doesn't speak. No introduction, no verbal torment. It's as if he wants to finish his punishment quickly. Maybe he won't relish in my pain the way the other Nobles will. Wires find my skin as I start to imagine what is to come, as if anticipating the torture will make it less severe.

I chose this.

Derone takes a few steps backwards, his expression solemn. He looks into my eyes without hatred, but only an empty sadness that makes me almost pity him. A small control panel is clutched in his shaking palm, boasting of one, large red button.

The atmosphere is as numbing as alcohol and as sharp as a thousand daggers. "Just do it!" I want to shout.

Instead, I stare at the boy and slowly nod. He closes his eyes as if it is him that will soon be screaming in agony, and not me. I look away and await the storm.

The chair begins to shake, electricity rushing through it and into my body. The shock penetrates my skin and vibrates through me, beginning in my arms and legs before travelling into my torso, making my muscles burn with the electricity pulsing into them. I smell the stench of my flesh sizzling before I fully register the agony rippling through my body. It's white hot as it courses through my veins like a rabid animal that will never be distracted from its mission of devouring me. I can't describe it. I can't rationalise it. Only feel, see, smell, hear and taste my body as it disintegrates.

I don't fight it. I let it wash over me, knowing that if I rebel against the pain I will only suffer more. That there is nothing I can do that will make it any better. I chose this.

It doesn't last long. When the punishment has fully wrecked is havoc, my eyes flash open. Derone stands before me, but now his expression is hard, reflecting the hatred in the other Noble's solemn stares.

"We used to play together as children." He says, feebly.

I briefly wonder how he remembers me, as a Noble child. What games we played together? Or did we spend our time maiming and destroying plastic dolls?

Chapter 46

I do not see the stout figure of Rengini Egnigina, head of intelligence and information, but I hear his voice as it booms over the loudspeaker, and immediately fresh fear rushes through me. He was in charge of securing the information that I destroyed. The past twenty-four hours have humiliated him, ruined his soul purpose in life. And he blames me.

"Everything I have worked for over my entire life was destroyed by you." The voice echoes around the chamber, "For this, you will face a punishment beyond the realms of pain, but in the world of fear, for fear is far worse than pain."

The room is suddenly black and empty. As my eyes adjust, I am in a forest with trees so thick that they block out any hint of light. I reach out and touch one of them. It feels strange and inconsistent, as if it isn't actually there. I smack my palm against the trunk of another tree, but it bounces back, now splitting with pain, electric pain. My hand glows blue for a moment as I tentatively place one finger against a branch. It feels strangely smooth and artificial, but yet there's somehow an impression of it not really existing, as if it were air, or a magnetic field repelling in the direction of my hand so strongly that it seems solid. An invisible force centred in one spot.

I remember the layers of security fields around the Big City, almost like invisible gates with enough charge in them to send electricity coursing through your blood for a lifetime.

This is a column of an electric field, encased within a hologram of a tree.

A harsh sound makes me glance upwards, towards the blanket like, holographic leaves as something wet, red and all too real drips onto my shoulder. The foul stench of blood fills the air as more drops quickly start to fall, landing heavily on my head and shoulders.

I start to run, weaving through the trees and trying to escape the growing storm behind me. An ear-piercing scream fills the air, followed by a howl of triumph. I run faster as the growling gets louder, nearer; winding through the whirlwind of trees that don't seem to end. I come to a heap of rocks, in a panic I clamber onto them, realising as my hands stroke their smooth texture, that they too are strong magnetic fields shrouded in a hologram. Standing against the force is slippery, but I keep climbing, higher and higher as the sounds behind me grow closer and more intense.

When I can't go any further, I turn around, facing the howl that grows into a pack of rabid dogs, their open jaws dripping with saliva. The flesh below their stomach sags as if they haven't eaten for months and their stench tells me that, though the trees and rocks are all a part of a simulation, these creatures are real. They circle the pile of rocks I am perched on, giving me no escape.

Slowly, a paw settles on the first ledge.

My heart beats in my fingertips, fear rips through me like a whirlwind, sharper and far worse than the physical pain I will soon meet. The first dog catches me. He slashes at my arm, drawing blood and inciting physical agony that runs parallel to the fear.

I fall, crashing to the floor that is quickly beginning to gleam a polished red as the rocks disappear. The trees vanish, and I am back in the arena, the dogs are pulled off me by the Destructors as I lie panting on the floor, and the fear slowly begins to subside.

Hardnida Delvaaint stands above me, the fourth Noble, in charge of weaponry. He says nothing but holds a gun pointing towards my feet.

As he pushes the trigger, a blue beam shoots into my toes, making them scream with agony. The beam travels upwards through my body, torturing every limb as I throb with a pain that pushes everything else away. As it climbs into my neck, I hold my breath. My eyes start to sting, and I try to curl into a ball to expose as little surface area as possible to the weapon. But my body doesn't move. As if it has been taken from my control. As if it is not my own.

"Punishment will resume tomorrow" A distant voice I assume is Malintaret's calls from somewhere in the gloom beyond my pain.

I am vaguely aware of thick arms carting my limp body back to the cell. I feel rather than see May leaning over me, worry lining the contours of her face. I try to speak, but the words in my mind die before they reach my lips. 'Don't worry' I want to say; 'it's only me. I'm not that important'.

When I wake up the following morning, my body has finally begun to jerk back to life. I move each of my limbs in turn, nervously, as if they are fragile and likely to snap like twigs under the slightest pressure.

Glancing around the cell, I can't see May and my heart leaps into my mouth as my body starts to shake violently and uncontrollably. But before I can even acknowledge the fear growling in my stomach, the Destructors crash through the doors and drag me back to the arena.

I pack my sister into a small box in the corner of my heart as the platform riser slowly descends. Only four more punishments. Three Nobles. And the Emperor.

The arena has been cleaned of the smears of blood and flakes of skin and sweat that littered it yesterday, and now the red marble floor sparkles more intimidating than ever. The Nobles sit in the viewing gallery like statues. Today, there is no light in their eyes, no excitement at my arrival, only a dull sense of expectation, as if they are bored of me already.

The Emperor takes his prime position in the hanging box, in front of the complicated desk of controls, and next to him, in another, smaller box that hasn't been cleaned and is still smudged with the efforts of grimy fingers, Maple and dad kneel on the floor, clinging to each other with hopeless fear lying subdued in their eyes.

The centre of the room boasts of the same equipment as yesterday; the block, the chair, the chains, and the board, all now sparkling clean and blood-free. Yepole Carrinte, the third Noble, drums his fingers against the back of the chair and Malintaret stands a few metres behind him. Carrinte snarls as his army of Grangers pull me towards them, violently pushing me into the chair and strapping me down.

"The world inside your head is often far more vivid than reality." Carrinte chants. "Mentally, you are a fortress, but I feel that the time is right for me to break down some of your walls."

He pulls my head towards him so that it smacks the metal back of the chair, and pushes a syringe filled with blue liquid into my neck.

My eyes are pulled shut by some invisible force and my imagination drags me into a large field. The grass is withered, brown, dead and harsh against my bare feet. The endless wasteland stretches for miles all around, and impulsively, an awful feeling of foreshadowing wells within me.

There are several seconds of nothing. Silence that is so ominous I can almost see tumbleweed dancing across the horizon.

Then. A scream: Young and painful. My head twists to the right.

Miles away from me, in the empty distance, I see May gasping, tied to a stake with small curls of fire lapping at her toes. I run towards her, preparing myself to leap into the furnace and pull her out. But as I watch the flames growing stronger and fuller I realise that I am getting no closer.

I keep running, but the nearer I should be to reaching her, the further away she becomes. I have run more than twice the distance between her and me already, but still endless ground stretches out between us. It is as if for every meter I gain, she is pushed two meters further away. The flames start to engulf her, as her screams penetrate the air. But they are much softer than they were, suppressed by the thickening smoke.

"Willow!" May screams "Help me! Please! Save me!"

Then a low grunt echoes from behind me. A cry of fear from someone who is too strong to show it. I spin around and see dad tied to a stake in the centre of a large pond, water lapping at his ankles and rising quickly.

I start to run towards him, but the water is rising quickly, already stroking his neck. Then May lets out a long and guttural scream behind me. I stop and turn; meeting her eyes, half obscured by the flames. I look from May to dad, both infinite distances away from me, knowing that I can't even save one of them. Wheezing, I collapse and crumple to the floor, the bird like screams of my sister and anguishing groans of my father echoing across the never-ending guilt and self-loathing both inside, and outside of my mind. I dig my nails into my wrists and swear that I would rather die myself than have to live with the memory of their deaths.

Sweat is pouring down my face as my eyes flash open, and it's only the chains binding me to the chair that stop me lurching forward. Laughter echoes all around me, as behind me there is a projection blaring the final image of me weeping on the floor with dad and May captured miles away on either side, burning and drowning, as all three of us sink into death.

My eyes find dad and May suspended in their glass prison above me. May has her face buried in dad's bony shoulder and he clings to her so tightly his knuckles are white. Dad's eyes are open and vacant until they meet mine and we share a long, meaningful look filled with too much apology and emotion.

The chains are unlocked, and I am immediately lead to a large box by the second Noble, Jerapo Bellona, head of security. But I still don't break eye contact with dad, not until I am pushed inside of the box and the lid is closed on top of me.

Bellona, the second Noble is head of security in the Big City, the security that I undermined when I arrived here and then disarmed when the helmet exploded. He says noting - or if he does I don't hear it. The box around me gleams silver, metallic and heartless, much like him. Silent. Cold. Deadly.

Suddenly, without any noise or warning, the box begins to shrink around me. I pull my knees to my chest and bury my head between them as it constricts, pushing me into myself from all angles so that I can't move and can hardly breathe. The metal sides press into me, crushing my shoulder blades as my muscles tense, my body fighting to resist it, although my heart and my will has already surrendered.

As I stare into the darkness beneath me, I try to forget the familiar pain that courses through me. I try to think of a good time. A happy time. A smile. May's smile as she gave that elegant locket to dad on his birthday, long ago. Dad's pride as he fingered the delicate drawings on the wooden tray. The happiness that decorated the room as we ate the first chocolate we'd had in months, maybe even years. May spilling it down her clothes and licking it off with her finger, mischief alive in her eyes as dad shook his head, laughing, probably for one of the last times.

I realise that I have been holding my breath as the box collapses around me. I exhale, look up, and laugh, thinking about chocolate cake.

Chapter 47

Two more. Only two more punishments to go. Only my two grandfathers are left to deliver their tortures.
I wonder what they will do. I wonder what they can do. Pain hardly hurts me anymore. Emotional pain is worse than physical. But both are now at least tolerable.
The Emperor. His will be the worst. His will be the most severe, the most painful, the most creative.
But they won't see my reaction. I won't give them the satisfaction of seeing fruit of their labours. I stand straight as my father's father steps out before me, towering over me. I'm not afraid of him. I should be. But I'm not.
"How well do you remember your childhood, Willow?" He asks. My mouth is clamped shut, my dry lips forming a seal that I will never break. "You were an 'Example Child.' Do you remember that?" I don't move, but stare fixedly at the wall behind him, concentrating on the elegant designs on the stone, just one grey shade lighter than the black around them as the long stripes curve downwards and gently stroke the floor, following the path that a feather falls. "I am going to remind you of an event which took place three months before you abandoned your duties with your father and sister. You were five years old, and your face was plastered across every screen in the Country. Not only your face, in fact, but your wrist."
He grabs my arm, and his bony fingers press on the long scar that leaks downwards from my elbow to my wrist,

following a similar path to the decorations on the wall. I struggle now, but his grip is too strong.

A poker that gleams black, white, red and orange all at the same time touches my arm, fitting perfectly into the contours of the scar. Heat presses into me, alongside an overwhelming pain that makes me want to howl through my tightly closed lips.

I suddenly remember Sokk telling us why dad had escaped the Big City when he did. "A white-hot poker was strapped to your arm".

A white-hot poker that left the scar this instrument is now reinstating.

The fire spreads down, and through my skin, but I don't scream like I would have done a few days ago. I understand now that my silence is more painful to them, than this roaring agony is for me. My eyes stay open, focussed on the falling feather carvings on the wall, but they still don't distract me from the agonising hurricane that spreads much further than my body and demands to be felt.

I don't know how long it lasts. It's as if, slowly, I become detached from my body, disconnected from the whirlwind of anguish; as if I am not myself, but a spectator to my own pain, an observing feather falling through the patterns on the wall.

I am only a member of the audience, empathising to the point where I feel the pain, but it's not real, not my pain.

I do not whimper, or yell, or scream, or cry. My face is a mask. It shows them nothing. No sadness. No happiness. No anger. No hatred. I feel nothing. No pain. No regret. No longing and no hope. I am strong. I am empty. Like a bottomless pit with no emotion and no feeling. Like a Noble.

But I'm not a Noble. I never will be. Every time they hurt me, every millilitre of blood that spills from my wounds, makes me less like them. I am strong, but not because I can hurt people. I am strong because I can withstand being hurt. I am empty of the desire to kill and destroy, but full of longings to love and protect. They say that I am one of them. But how could I be more different?

The pain vanishes, causing a sharp stab of intensity before an incredible relief. I hardly notice.

I refocus on the room, bringing myself to stare at his face, into his eyes.

"You're screaming inside." He says distantly, disappointed at my lack of reaction. "You will never truly hide your pain. Not from us."

As he leaves, I want to collapse, fold in on myself and beg for this all to stop. But I don't. I stand there, unrestrained, but incapable of moving. My arm still throbs. The burn is raw, and so delicate that the softest stroke of a feather would immediately ignite an explosion of blood and agony.

Finally, the air bristles, as each Noble creeps to the edge of their seat. Malintaret respectfully bows her head as her father, the Emperor, takes one loud, booming step after another into the large room. He does not look at me, but addresses the rest of the Nobles, standing directly in front of me, so that I cannot see his face.

"The final punishment is notoriously the worst." His voice is laced with commandment and authority, and infected by arrogance, but also the smallest suggestion of regret, as if he wishes that this was not his decision to make. "This is to be no exception." His head twists sideways, I cannot see his eyes, but he seems to be looking towards the box where Maple and dad kneel on the floor. May clutches dad's hand with both of her own, and her eyes are wide with fear. "For the undermining of the Big City; for the obliteration of our intelligence; I hereby punish my granddaughter, Talemia Greatest, by sentencing the execution of her sister Amerina, to be the subject of the next Screening."

I don't hear what he has said for several seconds.

May.

No.

No.

NO!

May.

He can't. How can he?

How?

I run at him, jumping on him and grabbing his shoulders, pushing him to the ground. "No! NO!" I scream. He only smiles and raises his right hand to stop the Destructors dragging me away.

"Please. No!" I pound my fists on his chest. He keeps smiling. "Kill me. Kill me. Please just kill me! Let her live. Please. Please!"

I collapse, sobbing onto the floor, my heart wrestling with my tears as all of the previous pain I have endured fades away into insignificance. Memories of May invade my mind. Pictures from long ago when life was sweet and innocent. I remember her smile as she ran across the beach, the cold sea tickling her delicate feet that dad could hold in the palm of his hand. The myriad of colours which shone bright and careless on her favourite dress as she wore it with so much pride on her seventh birthday. The glitter of joy and hope in her eyes when she spent a Sunday afternoon drawing and painting beautiful murals of the lush nature around us.

Slowly, my body stops shaking, and the world around me returns. My lungs absorb rattling oxygen as my palm touches the side of a cold glass box surrounding me, clear and confining. As, and as I exhale, my breath condenses on its smooth surface like a purposeless cloud.

The galleries above me are empty, the hanging cage where dad and Maple once crouched now desolate and lonely. I jolt, as my own glass box lifts, and as I look upwards, I realise that the box is tied to the ceiling with a long, thin rope, swinging me from side to side as the torture room sways below.

What's going on?

What punishment could they possibly now exact that would cause more damage than they have already done?

A long table, moulded from molten glass, lies beneath me with eight chairs settled elegantly around it, all of them occupied.

I feel silence fall, though I was never aware of any noise, and a screen lying flat on the table illuminates a bright list of words I can't quite make out.

"How?" The Emperor asks. "We have the victim. Now we need the method."

His eyes are cold and hard, more resolute than usual, as if it is an effort for him to hide a flame of sympathy for his granddaughter beneath his plastic facade.

"Fast or slow?" Malintaret smiles, no guilt in her inhumane eyes.

"Fast." Utters the Emperor quickly, as Rebato menacingly says. "Slow."

The disagreement heralds silence, as each member of the council sits tensely upright.

"Fast for the victim, slow for the spectators."

The victim! Is this what she has become? Losing all of her identity, even her gender? *The victim.*

A nod of agreement travels like a wave around the table, quickly, afraid of any more arguments.

The symbols on the screen change, as images echo the various options. A noose; a spider; a bucket filled to the rim with water; and a wooden stake burning so vibrantly on the screen that I expect the bottom right hand corner to turn black from the burn; flash blindingly upwards.

"How do you think she should die, Willow?" Malintaret's cold, unforgiving eyes flash up at me. If there wasn't a layer of glass between us, the intensity in her stare would have me screaming in pain.

"Alive." My voice is low and cold. "With me in her place."

My mother laughs. A soft, detestable laugh filled with mocking pleasure. "But you see, your sister is of no use to us. You, on the other hand, withhold valuable information. Besides, we would not give you the privilege of death, it is too high an honour for a prisoner of your position, and Amerina's execution is the final, most integral part of your punishment." Her laughing eyes drop to the screen as I slump against the wall of the box, hugging my knees, like I did in Deprivation, the last time my lifelines were yanked away.

"Hanging?" Someone suggests. I do not look down to see who, they are all clones of the same deadly murderer to me.

"Too quick" Says another, and the noose vanishes from the screen.

"Poison has been used too recently." The Emperor sighs as the spider vanishes and leaves only two options remaining on the screen, drowning or burning.

Yepole Carrinte, who injected me with the simulation of my father and my sister's death, shares a long and sustained look with his fellow Nobles. The bucket of water vanishes, and the screen is filled with the image of a wooden stake, tied to it, a screaming child.

"To take place, tomorrow." Concludes the Emperor, as bile begins to rise in my throat and my head whirls in a dizzy rage of fear.

My breath is short, as tears full of the water my body should be preserving, roll down my cheeks. My fists punch the glass as I scream even louder than the simulation on the screen, even louder than the mute excitement of the Nobles beneath me.

The glass shatters and I fall through the bristled air and land, still screaming, on the glass table where the screen smashes into tiny shards of electrical evil. I fight through the shocked Nobles and run to the Platform Riser, pushing buttons at random before a Destructor materialises in front of me. The leather glove cloaking his hard fist scrapes against my face, as a sudden numbness swamps me and I collapse to the floor.

Chapter 48

I wake up in the cell, my head resting on the pile of dirty rags. I sit up and lean against the wall, exhausted as my thoughts spin around my head in a frenzied whirl of confusion and loss. May sits cross legged on the floor opposite me, her eyes closed and her hands resting on her knees. A peaceful expression settles on her face, calmness and beauty alighting every feature, colouring her dry, pale skin in a soft light.

"What are you doing?" My voice sounds harsh and unkind. "Sorry." I mutter quickly, hating myself for wasting the precious moments that she has left.

"It's alright." Her voice is still calm and sweet, almost musical. "I'm forgiving them."

"What?" Anger mixes with confusion as my words choke my throat. "Why? How?"

May pauses for a moment, then her wise eyes settle onto mine, her gaze intense and strong. "Do you remember the people in Rente? Their beliefs and morals?" She smiles. "They would forgive someone for murdering their own child - and though they hated the actions of the Nobles, they didn't consider them enemies." She does not move; her body is oddly still and far too serious. "I never had the opportunity to become a full Resistance member. But in this way, by forgiving them, I am as close to them as I can be." She looks at my puzzled face and continues.

"Willow, the Resistance don't want the Noble's to die because they hate them. They love them in the same way that they love everyone. But after centuries of oppression, their death is the only way to end the misery of thousands. So many people have suffered at the hands of the Nobles; there isn't another option. But if I was going to be there when it happens, I wouldn't rejoice at the Noble's defeat, but be sad at the loss of their lives."

I hug my brave, strong little sister. "I'll try to forgive them too." I whisper into her course hair. "For you."

Forgiveness is strange. It does not happen instantly and it's not easy. I close my eyes and imagine Malintaret, but all that I can feel is hatred. Then, my eyes open and all I feel is a surge of love for May. I once told myself that I would go to any length for her happiness, I'd never have thought it before, but maybe forgiving her killers is the greatest sacrifice that I could make for her.

Instead of remembering how Malintaret has murdered and tortured people, I imagine her sparing a life, giving May extra food and reducing her lashes. Though now, she is cold and emotionless there must have been a time when she was young and, if not kind, then humane. She was once a mother after all.

"In Rente" May says, encouragingly. "They used to say that to hate another person was to see yourself as perfect."

I remember all of the times that I have failed people, May, Sokk, dad, myself. I remember being a little girl and walking by the roadside to hear a guttural cry for help, but ignoring it with a selfish desire to get home sooner. I imagine Malintaret again and now I feel nothing, still no love, but at least this time, no hatred.

"I still hate what she has done." I whisper.

"That's alright, I do too. But now that you have forgiven her you can be forgiven too."

I don't quite understand what she means. Who am I forgiven by? What does it even mean to be forgiven? But a weight seems to have been lifted from my chest, and a calmness cools the spaces where guilt once was. I laugh, I don't know why but somehow there is joy in my heart. May smiles and laughs with me, her childish giggles turning the cold, gloomy cell into a room of innocence and excitement. Almost like a home.

"I'm content to die." May says, looking at her hands. "I don't see why people are afraid of death. It's got to be better than this, right?"

I almost weep at my baby sister's peace. "Right." I blink the tears from my eyes and smile. "Anything is better than this."

She walks to the window, slowly and deliberately, as if each step is committed to absorbing every sense that rises up from the ground and touches her bare feet. Staring into the courtyard beneath us, where the Screening platform and cameras are already being set up, Maple seems to grow taller, more confident than she ever has been before, as she gazes upon her fate.

"When?" She does not face me, but stares out of the window towards the place where her execution awaits.

"Tomorrow." I can't look at her. I've turned her into a time bomb, where her destruction is inevitable, and I am the one revealing the position of the clock hands as they tick closer towards the end.

"How?"

"Burning." I say too quickly, afraid to tell her but knowing that an empty silence would betray her even more.

"Like the punishment." I can almost hear a wry smile of irony in her voice, however when she looks at me her face is expressionless, like a corpse; as if practising for the time when blankness will be the only emotion she can show.

"You can't die." My voice cracks as I grab her shoulders, "I won't let you."

"There's nothing you can do." May closes her eyes, as if in resignation, accepting her end.

"I don't want you to die." My heart aches as May leads me to the rags that now feel like a splintering raft in a cruel ocean threatening to drown us.

"Do you want me to live?" The question surprises me, but as I think about the pain that we have both endured, and how often I have longed for death myself, I can almost believe that May's execution isn't necessarily bad.

"The Emperor wanted you to die quickly." I say. "It was as if he cared for you."

"They're not all evil." May's gift for seeing the goodness in others shocks me again. "They are only afraid. Like us. They're scared Willow, so they defend themselves the only way they know how."

I want to argue with her, but I won't waste May's final hours by rivalling her rose-tinted perception of the world. I close my eyes and whisper softly into her hair that somehow smells of lavender.

"Do you remember the day we built that massive sand mansion at the beach?" She leans into me, and it is like it was when we were younger, the times after father's arrest when we would wake in the middle of the night and hold each other, distracting ourselves with silver-lined memories that became bedtime stories. "You were five, and I was seven and we collected sand from all four corners of the beach, so that the mansion could be inclusive and accepting of everyone."

"It was taller than you were, with turrets that gleamed like the Emperor's gold in the sun. We carried buckets of water from the sea and dug a moat for protection, 'flowing with milk and honey'. Do you remember?

"We took one of dad's wooden doves and he told us that we could only use it if the mansion was to be peaceful, so we called it the 'Harmonious Home of Happiness' because of course, only peaceful homes can be happy. When dad was teaching us writing that evening, we wrote a story about the lives of the people who lived there, they spent their days helping each other and they shared everything. Dad said that they should hold feasts where each guest was given the same amount of food and nobody would sit at the head of the table, so everyone was equal. Each worker in the mansion played a valuable role, and the cleaner who made the room look so beautiful was just as important as the doctor who saved people's lives."

May lies slumped in my arms, her eyes closed in innocent sleep and a smile that may be her last, dancing delicately on her lips. I hold her close to me, enjoying the sound of her steady breath as it draws cleanly in and out of her lungs.

I slowly become aware of my own breathing, and the sickening privilege that I have to breath after May cannot. Silently, as darkness blankets the room, I vow that every breath I have that she hasn't, I will use to honour her, in my thoughts, my words, and my actions.

Chapter 49

I wake with a start. My heart freezes when I realise that May isn't lying on the rags beside me.

It's still dark outside. All I can see are outstretch shadows cast by the dim, artificial lamp on the ceiling.

Have they taken her already?

No. Please, no. Let me say goodbye. Just let me say goodbye!

I turn my head towards the window and almost scream as the fear drains out of me, leaving a hollow mixture of relief and dread. She stands with her back to me, staring out towards the sky.

"There's a dove!" She says, sensing that I am awake without either of us needing to move.

"Don't be silly." I get up and walk to her, "They've been extinct for centuries. It's probably just an Evod." I suddenly hate myself for my pessimism, but there is no room in the silence that follows to apologise.

"It's a dove. A real, living dove. Like the one's dad used to carve. Look!" Her voice is more adamant as she points to the sharp tip at the top of dad's tower in the centre of the courtyard. The roof of the tower is made up of long, uneven slabs; dark, but not quite black; dull and neglected as all prisons must be.

A silhouette dances across the tiles, flying and spiralling around the tower's peak. I can't see any colour in the creature, the false light does not reach it, but it is small and light, similar to the Evods that I used to watch every day circling the factory in Rente. But unlike the Evod, this figure's movement is fluid and dance-like, its shape is elegant and natural as it seems to be filled with a sense of beauty and a life which no human hand could ever recreate.

"It's a dove." I let out a dream-like, disbelieving laugh. "How? Why?"

"Do you remember the lullaby we used to sing?"

"And the dove will signal the revolution." I hum, under my breath.

"With feathers, as white as snow." Sunrise begins to peek through the courtyard.

"He will sing his song and restore our freedom." May presses into my side, lost in the music, more peaceful and contented than she has ever been, or ever will be.

"His love and peace we all shall know!" As the sunrise summons a dawn painted with vibrant reds, oranges and yellows, the dove flies into the sky, shining almost golden in the light, though underneath, the bird's pure white feathers beam through, smiling like a toddler's grin revealing a pearly set of milky teeth.

"I'm happy to die, now that I have seen this."

A loud crash suddenly echoes around the room as the door is pushed open. The seven Destructors turn the tranquillity into an aura of fear and violence. Roberto Antario, my grandfather, heads their loathsome triangular shape which has haunted my nightmares for so long.

I push May behind me and stand in front of the window, protecting both her and the dove, another gem of beauty and innocence that they might destroy.

"Willow, it's all right." Murmurs May, stepping out from behind me. "I'm ready."

"I'm not." I say without looking at her. "I'm not ready to lose you."

The Destructors don't move, Roberto smiles, knowing that the longer this moment lasts, the more painful it will be for both of us.

"Shush," May wipes the tears from my eyes, "I'm only going away. Just for a little while."

Why am I crying? She's the child. She's the one who's been sentenced to death. I should be comforting her. I'm older, why am I not stronger?

"I don't want you to die. Not on your own." She smiles at me, and there's no sign of fear or sorrow in her eyes, no self-pity and no anger or hatred. "I'm coming with you." I say. "I'll find a way."

"No!" May's tone is stern, her eyes still young and innocent, but now solemn. "You can't. You have to stay alive. For dad if nothing else. Live for him, he can't lose both of us."

I nod, a promise that I know I must keep despite the pain that it will cause. May wriggles free from the hand that I hadn't realised I was holding, and walks towards her grandfather. Her head is bowed as she is pushed to the right of Roberto's, where two Destructors plant gloves on her shoulders and turn towards the door.

May glances up, looking into my eyes as she whispers. "Goodbye." I hardly hear her over the roaring in my ears and the crackling of my heart as it breaks in two. Can I offer her one of the broken pieces to beat in her?

As the door closes behind my sister, I collapse to the floor, sobbing floods of tears that I can't hold back any longer. My sister, my beautiful, innocent sister. My sister who once cried at the sight of a dead wasp on the roadside, now walks to her own funeral without a shred of sorrow.

She's strong. So much stronger than me. So much stronger than anyone I know. She has the strength to forgive her murderers and the power to be contented in her death. I've always thought that she wasn't made for this life, for this world, but created to live in another, more beautiful time and place. But perhaps she is…was here for us. To show and to teach everyone else how we are supposed to walk this world. To tell us that life isn't forever. That death isn't the end and that forgiveness is the key to peace.

I stand shakily and walk to the window. The dove has vanished, as if it were only ever to be there for a moment to tease us into hope. A figure rests against the window in the tower, and I smile feebly at my father. His cheeks are stained with tears and his eyes burn with pain.

I'm sorry. My eyes tell him. It's my fault. I shouldn't have let her go. I shouldn't have imagined the beautiful garden in Deprivation. I should have let the pain, the hunger, thirst and lack of sleep consume me. I should have surrendered to the Noble's and let the pain win. I should have forced them to kill me instead of her.

As if he can see through my eyes into my thoughts, dad shakes his head. It's not your fault. I can almost hear his soft, pleading voice. You couldn't have done anything to stop it. I love you Willow.

I don't hear him speak, but in his eyes, and his expression, love is etched with the deepest of understandings, and with forgiveness that says there is nothing to forgive. The words he needs to say dance in his eyes and pass straight into my heart.

Down in the courtyard below us, men and women run like ants, carrying microphones and cameras in preparation for the screening.

I wonder if any of our friends in Rente will recognise the scrawny figure on the execution stand. Will they have been told who we are? The Emperor is bound to give a long and torturous speech on May's true identity. Do they hate us for it? Will they now grimace every time they think about the two little girls who came to live with their grandmother in Rente?

The centre of the courtyard, where the death will take place, presents a low wooden plinth backed by a long pole. Long sticks, and thick branches of wood surround it, with yellow specks peeking through, which might be clumps of dry leaves, but are much more likely to be small cases of dynamite.

I look at the sky and wish that the heavy clouds would drop rain, though I know that the Big City's force field wouldn't allow it to even spot the pavement on this dreadful day

Will we be taken to watch? My eyes meet dad's as, as if in answer to my question, the heavy door opens behind me.

Chapter 50

I stare at my feet as I am lead by three soldiers down a new flight of stairs, to a side door which collapses open like a singer taking a deep, monotonous breath before they carry on once again with the same, repetitive tune.

The air hits me with a stale onslaught of freshness as the breeze gently slaps my face. If it wasn't the saddest day of my life, I might have enjoyed the privilege of simply being outside for the first time in what feels like forever.

But this thought rapidly flees my mind when I see the courtyard lying before me like a plate of food, prepared with misguided care by a chef seeking his master's approval. It's a scene I am far too familiar with – but from the town square, the monthly Screening seems so distant. A young and imaginative heart can pretend that it's only a game, staged so that the threat seems real, but no one is really harmed.

But this is real. More real that the breath in my lungs and the tears on my cheeks.

A mess of technology surrounds the courtyard; cameras and microphones, radio receivers and men and women shouting to each other across the jungle of black wires and cables connected to battery packs and charged with electricity so strong that you can see it glimmering unnaturally blue through the wires. A line of thick tape creates a square five feet away from the first level of the courtyard, outlining the 'performance space'.

The beige cobbles scream at the clouds, cruel cracks running through them which have been meticulously and artistically placed where science confirms they will strike the most fear in their audience.

The top shelf of the courtyard awaits the Nobles to come and take their places and snarl at the cameras; and the second is still covered with a flurry of fussing workmen. I cannot see the lowest shelf of the courtyard basin - perhaps it is for my own benefit that I'm hidden from its hideous design- but the large pole in the centre of it rises harshly upwards, ropes loosely hanging around it, preparing to hug my sister in their deathly grasp.

A figure swishes towards me, dressed in red and black, with sharply styled hair and makeup which makes her look like a doll. A knife glints through her red fingernails as she grabs my arm.

"You didn't get to die, so you can bleed instead." Malintaret whispers in my ear as she drags me towards the inner levels of the basin.

When we reach the second shelf, she yanks my arm so that it stretches out in front of me and the knife slips through my papery skin. Blood oozes onto the cobbles as Malintaret shakes me over the eerily smooth pave-stones. She drags me across the courtyard, her firm grasp cascading blood all over the basin's three levels, letting it land randomly in sprinkles, the way a farmer sows his seeds. It should hurt. I should be screaming right now as pain rips through my arm. But instead, I feel nothing. My heart is numb. My mind has lost the motivation to feel pain. To feel anything.

Finally, Malintaret drags me to a small cove of soldiers, just behind the cameras. As she finally releases my arm she bends down and whispers in my ear.

"I wish it was you."

I stare at her, into her black eyes that gleam with something that might have once been love. Not for me, never for me, but perhaps for May. Finally, it seems that we agree on something.

"I wish it was me too."

She turns and walks back towards the courtyard, showing no sign that she even heard me as the soldiers pull me into their midst.

Another figure kneels on the ground within our cavern of guards. I throw my arms around my father, not caring if the Nobles see my affection, not caring if they jeer at my weakness, he's all that I have left.

"I'm sorry." I whisper into his shoulder that is already wet with tears. "It should be me dying. I'm sorry."

"No. Don't say that." Dad says, his expression blank, almost as if being here for so long has robbed him of his emotions. "You've done nothing wrong. It was going to happen anyway. She wasn't useful to them."

I collapse beside him and he puts his arms around me, holding me close as we watch the throng of workmen running around, fussing over every little detail to ensure that everything is ready for the Screening.

So much attention decorates May's death. Why do they need to do this? It only makes every twinge of pain aggressively more intense.

This isn't a punishment for May, it is a punishment for dad and I. Her pain will soon be over; but ours is just beginning. Death only lasts a moment, but grief lingers forever. I suddenly realise that I don't want to die in her place because I want her to live, but as selfish as I am – it is because I want to die.

"Did you see the dove this morning?" Dad tries to smile. I nod, unable to find any words.

"There's hope."

It's all he says. I almost reproach him for being so optimistic at a time where we shouldn't even observe the concept of light. But then, I feel that same hope faintly flickering in an unreachable corner of my own heart. It's all he has. It's all I have. A hope that someday life might become more like the happily ever after of a fairy-tale, or a lullaby.

The crowd starts to hush as they retreat into their allocated, audience positions to watch the line of Nobles walk ritualistically out of the tall, imposing door to the Emperor's Mansion, each dressed in their most formal attire. A part of me wants to believe that the heartless expressions on their faces are masks, rehearsed facades hiding what might be remorse, or even pity, for the child who was once one of their dearest relatives, now preparing to face the flames of death.

The Destructors march into the courtyard, concealing May in their midst so that I can't see her. They walk down the steps, through the patter of my blood, to the platform. The wood surrounding it is piled so high that they must lift her over it, dropping her bare feet onto the splinters. As they draw back and reveal her,   I scream.

May's hair has been yanked out, now so thin that you can see her scalp glowing red beneath the wispy straws. Her face is pale and gaunt, big purple bruises decorating her cheeks, and her lips are dry and cracked. Her arms are wound behind her back, tied to the tall pole, and her shaking legs are manacled to the platform.

She's wearing a different dress. Not the tattered grey tunic, but one that is white, simplistic and innocent, like the dove. Her bright blue eyes shine wide, not in fear, but in confidence and hope. A martyr,

I run forward, fighting through the guards to set her free and hold her in my arms where she will be safe, forever.

"May!"

My thin legs leap over the line of tape and onto the first level of the basin before a pair of strong arms tighten around me, throwing me back into the scene behind the camera and pushing me down onto the cobbles beside dad.

The soldier tugs my hands behind my back and ties them together, keeping a firm hold on the rope as if I were a dog on a leash.

"No! May!" I scream, fighting against his grasp as he pushes a gag into my mouth.

I can neither move nor speak as May's eyes bore into mine. Hers are calm, but mine are frantic. She slowly shakes her head and somehow tells me that she is ready for this, and that I am as well.

I hear a distant shout as the national anthem begins to play, and the central camera beeps three times, to announce to the Country that this month's Screening has just begun.

Chapter 51

The Emperor laughs as several cameras absorb his face. "Welcome to yet another monthly Screening." He begins.

I cannot listen to his long trawl of the origins and reasons behind the event. The words enter my head but make no sense, all broken and disjointed, like the sound is coming through a faulty megaphone, miles away.

I close my eyes and pretend. Pretend that this is a good day, a happy day. I imagine the quivering audience inside the courtyard relaxed and joyful, with everyone, from the lowest to the highest, laughing and dancing across the cobbles, not for any particular reason, but just in sheer pleasure! An air of acceptance and togetherness colours the skies a naturally light blue, filling the atmosphere with a fragrance of happiness and hope. This place that is now a death trap, in my mind becomes a haven of life and acceptance.

The painting of oppression on the floor of the basin is replaced by a mural of flowers- some designs works of masterful artistry, others a mess of children's scribbles - but all coloured in vibrant reds, greens and yellows. In my imagination I smile, May runs to me, inside my mind, still young and naive, her eyes bright and beautiful like the sun glittering on a summer's day. She presses a flower into my hands. It's not a variety that I've seen before, but it is beautiful, white and pure, like a dove, or a martyr. Behind her, walks dad, his smile so energetic, it's as if he doesn't know the meaning of pain. His arm is draped around the shoulder of a young woman. A young woman whom I recognise, from a dream long ago when my suffering was selfish.

She smiles at me, and I suddenly remember the garden with the willows, maples and moss, when I was in the midst of Deprivation. Everyone else in my imagination fades away. Only May, dad, the woman from the garden, and I, standing alone in the courtyard that is now warm and welcoming, as if it doesn't even remember the pain it once accommodated.

"Mama." May says as she grabs the ladies hand. "My mama."

Mama, May and dad stand in a line opposite me. A family, like one I have never known before. I've never had a mother, I always associated the title with Malintaret, and her heartlessness.

"I love you Willow." The woman takes a step towards me, her hand outstretched.

I take her hand, and cling to it so tightly my knuckles turn white. As I do, the gaping hole in my heart slowly starts to seal.

I want to laugh. I want to cry. But all I can do is smile.

"Today's victim is an old friend of mine." As the Emperor speaks, the world seems to jolt, and reality becomes painfully focussed. "I'm sure you will remember the unforgivable desertion of my son in law, Revicartus Antario with his two daughters, ten years ago. Well, I hope you will share in my rejoicing at the arrest and successful punishment of all three." He stares at dad and I, and I notice a camera flashing at us out of the corner of my eye. I think about the image of our beaten bodies, Screened to the nation. "Today, to pay the ultimate price of betrayal, we have the youngest daughter, only three years old when she last attended a

Screening. Though then, she was a spectator, today Amerina is the victim."

May stares straight ahead, not looking at anything as the wood looms, stacked in piles around her, ready to be set alight. Her expression betrays no fear nor malice, her eyes are brave, her mouth strong, and her pale and beater skin resilient.

"This is how we treat those who dare to betray their birth right and commit treason. Those who plot to overthrow their own family. Goodbye child." He looks at her, and a shadow of remorse almost colours his face. "Farewell my granddaughter."

He stands back, in front of the line of snarling Nobles, as the Destructors march into the courtyard, each carrying a burning torch.

No! No, they won't! They can't! They can't actually do it! I fight against my chains and scream into my gag before a soldier yanks my head back and runs a knife down my neck.

"Kill me." I whisper to him through the material. " I'm not afraid of death."

He pushes me back down to the ground and places his foot on my back so that I can't move. I look to my right and see dad trying to run into the basin where the flames are already tickling May's knees. Soldiers pull him back before he is even past the line of cameras, and he is tied down and gagged.

One arm still free, he reaches for my hand and clutches it desperately, the reflection of his youngest child's death, trembling in his eyes.

The flames climb higher and higher, engulfing May up to her hips so that all you can see of her legs is a silhouette. A silhouette in a white dress. She smiles at the camera, content, almost happy. Dying without fear. Like a martyr.

The flames rise higher, catching her dress that explodes in a deep orange all around her. I see her gasp as the fire climbs up past her shoulders and smoke conceals her face.

Through the fog, her lips are pressed tightly together. She is holding her breath. Why? Surely, she knows that the smoke will kill her first. It will poison her lungs quickly and efficiently. It would be far less painful for her to swallow the thick cloud and let it destroy her respiratory system, rather than have the flames lick her till the heat burns so strongly, and her wounds are so severe, that her heart slowly and painfully ceases to beat.

But she has chosen the more difficult way to die. The method that keeps blood flowing through her veins for longer. She is strong. And her final moments of life must show this in every breath of poisonous smoke she chooses not to take.

Through the smoke and the flames, I can hardly see her. But her eyes are still open, gleaming blue through the furnace; wide, defiant, and forgiving, yet not submissive.

My heart screams in a convulsion of love, longing and hate. Love for my sister, a longing to die in her place, and a hatred for those who put her there. I suddenly catch sight of Malintaret's blank face as she stares at her dying daughter. Her own daughter, whom she carried, and must have loved, once upon a time, a long time ago. The Emperor stands beside her. May's grandfather, who used to chuckle as he watched her play in the meadows.

All of this exaggerated anger and public violence. But for what? For entertainment? Or to assert their dictatorship over a Country that already hardly allows itself to breathe in fear of them?

The Nobles are like children, insecure and afraid of losing control, maintaining it only through blind violence and deliberate cruelty, as if they know no other way to be rulers.

I feel May breathe. The putrid smoke that fills her lungs like the blackness of a storm covering a mountaintop. How long now? How long will it be until they drag her limp body onto the cobbles of the courtyard for all the Country to see. Will they bury her in the meadow where the children play? Or is the heat of the fire so intense that by the end of it she will already be cremated.

What comes next? How long will it be until it's dad, or me with our faces plastered across the Screens? A month? Six? A year even?

A year without May? In Rente, after she'd been captured, I couldn't go a day without crying. But I can't cry this time. I mustn't. It's the ultimate sign of weakness to the Nobles, and whatever I do, however else I might disgrace myself before them, they will not see me as weak. I will not cry.

Suddenly, I hear a loud crash. A boom that shakes the ground and sends the cameras falling to the cobbles, where they smash into unidentifiable glass shards. The air erupts with shouts as I cling closer to dad, hardly able to move as the ropes around me tighten.

The soldiers on the edges of the courtyard start to fall, buckling to their knees before collapsing on the stony ground as men and women with faces covered by black masks hold guns to their heads.

One marches almost jokingly towards dad and I. I shrink, bowing my head in fear, some parts of me fighting to flee death but other parts embracing it. The soldiers behind us drop to their knees and fall with a thud as the masked man cuts our ropes and unties our gags, a smile playing on his lips behind the black cloth.

He hands us both a gun. I stare at mine in horror, paralysed by the idea that this figure is asking me to kill. The Nobles are murderers, if I take this gun don't I become one of them?

"It's a stun rifle." The minute I hear Sokk's voice emerge from behind the black mask I want to laugh with relief. "Killing them would be far too messy."

Chapter 52

"Sokk." I gasp as he pulls me to my feet.

"Shhh." He whispers. A pained look decorates his eyes as his gloved hand touches my cheek. "What have they done to you?"

I hear dad clamour to his feet beside me, struggling to find the trigger on his stun rifle as several armed Noble soldiers run towards him. Sokk leaps to his best friend's side, his strong arms, and dad's weak ones threatening the soldiers with a gun that they don't know doesn't kill.

No-one seems to notice me. It's like I'm in a bubble - detached from the fighting that seems distant, almost like a digital projection, as one lonely thought absorbs my mind.

May.

I run towards the flames that are still burning stronger than ever, hardly noticing the scene around me as my feet pound down each level of the basin and I reach the furnace. My hands push through the flames, not caring when my skin erupts in seizures of burning pain. May's limp body falls into my arms, the ropes that tied her to the stake now nothing more than dust.

As I drag her away from the fire and lay her down on the cobbles, I almost scream. Her body has been blackened by the flames, and her mouth hangs open, as it was when she took that final, poisonous breath. The white dress has disintegrated around her, and her head is completely bald, decorated with ugly red, purple and yellow patches.

Still, I hold her wrist, then her neck, then her chest, looking for a pulse, for a miracle. A part of my heart hoping that the scars will fall off like paint as I touch them, and she will sit bolt upright, alive, a playful smile dancing over her lips as she tells me it was all a game, a practical joke. That even the flames weren't real, and I was silly to believe that she, my sister, would lose even an ounce of her life and joy.

But she lies still, her eyes wide open, but empty. Full of nothing. No joy. No sorrow. No love. No hate. Nothing. Her hands are curled, and I delicately place my index finger on her palm, her thin and wispy fingers wrapping around mine.

"I love you May." I whisper, but she doesn't hear me. Her eyes don't fill with joy, or even annoyance at my soppy affection. "I'm sorry."

Sokk gently taps my shoulder, his eyes hovering over May's corpse for a moment, filled with all of the emotion that she will no longer feel.

"We need you to fight." He says apologetically. I nod silently, and carefully place two fingers on my sister's eyelids, closing her brilliant blue flames, and putting her to sleep.

I take the gun from the floor beside me and turn around to face an onslaught of Noble soldiers marching in painfully synchronised waves.

My hands shake on the trigger as I step forward to join Sokk, I raise my gun several times in an attempt to shoot, but each time the weapon returns, unfired, to my side. It's almost like I'm invisible, a spectator to the warfare, unable to interact or help in any way, incapable and almost unwilling to touch, and fire a weapon.

Resistance workers are battling all around me, with their guns, and even their bare hands, knocking their enemies' unconscious, but still careful not to wound them permanently. I wonder what we will do when they wake up. Kill them? Lock them up as prisoners? That is more humane I suppose, but I'd rather be killed than left in a prison to rot.

A Noble soldier runs towards me, seeing my weak body and reluctance to fire as an easy target. He smiles in grim excitement that churns raw anger in the pit of my stomach, bringing my gun to his head as his expression turns to one of fear.

"Sorry." I whisper in a voice that could be either earnest or sarcastic. I fire. A strange exhilaration shoots through me and I feel powerful, like for the first time in months, I have control.

Is it wrong to have enjoyed that? After all, they're not really dead. Sokk said that the guns wouldn't even hurt them.

I look over to Sokk now, and see him struggling to fight against Yepole Carrinte's army, the Grangers, who carry red lasers pointed at Sokk's head. On instinct I fire, catching the Granger nearest to Sokk on the back of her neck. As she falls, the others turn towards me, giving Sokk an opportunity to escape and shoot at another who falls, unconscious to the floor.

Together, we sentence all seven Grangers to the cobbles, where they lie side by side, eyes closed, almost tranquil in their deep sleep.

"When you can't see their eyes, you can almost pretend that they've never killed." Sokk comments as we survey the battlefield around us.

Resistance soldiers, still clad in black with masks covering their faces, sit on the cobbles, exhausted. Some lie dead on the ground beside the unconscious Noble soldiers, while others swarm around the injured, producing medical supplies to save whatever lives they can. But the fighting has only paused for a moment, and though my heart longs for it to be over, I know that the worst is yet to come.

The Noble's themselves are nowhere to be seen, probably hiding inside one of the mansions with the Destructors standing guard.

Dad runs towards me, looking strong and alive despite his malnourished and weak body.

"Here." Sokk takes three pouches of what looks like white powder from his pocket. "It's Energy Starch." He hands us both a packet before quickly shoving the remaining one back into his pocket, biting his lip as we all remember who it was for.

I glance over at May's body, lying still on the cobbles. For a moment, I think that she is smiling. But it is a trick of the light, a figment of my imagination that dissipates when I blink, and her mouth resumes a solemn, flat line.

Gravely, the remaining Resistance soldiers gather around Sokk, dad and I. Silence fills the courtyard. Silence that is there for a purpose, which it would be wrong to break.

What now? The Nobles and the Destructors are meters away, plotting our assassination, and the entire Country depends on us and whether we can defeat them. I understand now, that if we win this battle the Nobles will never rule again. But if we lose, this world, already lost in darkness and oppression, will never recover.

Slowly, with a manner and a voice so commanding that it seems even the clouds in the sky lower themselves to listen, Sokk begins to speak.

"Our only goal is to achieve a society that is built on peace, hope and love. A place where our children can live in safety, and where we do not fear for our lives, but enjoy them. We want to be free, in a world where there is no violence and punishments are humane, with the grace of understanding and forgiveness.

"We didn't want this to be the final solution. But too many people have suffered. Too many innocent lives have been lost to those whom we have forgiven and will forgive. But for the sake of this Country, it is our job to remove them from our society and give them a second chance - somewhere that love might be successful, but the risk of its failure won't damage our own livelihoods.

"We run into the fire for the good of this Country. So that we do not have to live in fear any longer. If we die, we should be proud to have done so for the freedom of millions."

People cheer, and I join in, despite that I don't quite understand everything he said. Somehow fuelled by a new type of energy, I follow the crowd as we march into the Emperor's mansion.

Chapter 53

Before we even reach the golden encrusted doors, I hear a shot, and then a scream as a Resistance woman crumbles to the cobbles in front of me, a bullet wound piercing her chest. Glancing upwards, I see rows of thin windows on the third floor armed with guns, manned by the Destructors. I quickly count seven weapons. There must therefore be seven more of Antario's army hiding on the inside.

Without any kind of plan or strategy, I run into the building and up the first flight of stairs I see. I hear footsteps behind me, but they soon dissolve into the distance as Resistance fighters race down different alleyways in the maze of corridors.

My stomach lurches when I suddenly realise I am alone. No. This is what they wanted. To split us up in the catacombs so that we are outnumbered in enemy territory.

My pace has slowed to a walk, edging down the red carpeted corridor as my finger constantly teases the trigger of the gun. I press my ear to the first door I come across. Nothing. Gently, I turn the handle and push my way into the room. Still nothing.

The room is empty. Carefully, I check every corner before finally moving to the window. It is small and sharp, shaped like an arrow slit, but as I look through it my eyes pull towards the courtyard below and a deathly combat scene between a Destructor and a Resistance soldier.

The Destructor has pinned the soldier against a wall, wielding a knife in his other hand.

Instinctively I raise my gun, aim at the Destructor and shoot. I don't think about what will happen if I miss, but just let the bullet fly, where it thankfully hits the enemy square in the back of his head. He falls to his knees, then onto his front as the Resistance soldier stares at the unconscious murderer with a mixture of confusion and relief. I see him smile and laugh as the tension of the situation escapes him. He doesn't see me but runs towards the mansion with a new surge of confidence.

I hear noises behind me, and as the door creeks open I turn to face it, holding my gun poised to shoot. Two Resistance workers, a man and a woman, enter the room, both fighting to be in front and to protect the other. I nod and lower my weapon as they do the same.

"No one in here." I whisper, as they open the door and the three of us slip back out into the corridor.

As we do, another door swings wide open and the third Noble, Yepole Carrinte, leaps out of it, chased by a Resistance soldier. Carrinte doesn't notice me as he passes, and I push his cloaked shoulder so that he loses balance and falls to the floor, where another Resistance soldier instinctively shoots him.

"Take them to the courtyard." The Resistance soldier gestures to the room that they appeared from.

I look through the open door to see Carrinte's wife and only child lying on the plush lilac sofa, now lined with streaks of red. The woman beside me takes the wife, and I slowly pick up the little boy who can't be more than five years old, the bullet of the stun gun still lodged in his arm.

As we make our way to the courtyard, I can feel the boy's sedated breathing against my shoulder and wonder what will happen to him. After all, he hasn't done anything wrong, only been born into a family who taught him that it was right to kill and destroy. But he's not dead, and I know and trust that no matter what the Nobles have done to us, the Resistance will never fight fire with fire.

When I reach the courtyard, I can barely stop myself screaming. Rows of Noble soldiers lie in motionless order across the cobbles. Twelve of the fourteen Destructors are grouped together on the first level of the basin, and on the second, five Noble's and their families are scattered, looking vulnerable and anything but treacherous. We lay Yepole Carrinte and his family to rest, slowly, as if we are placing babies in their cradles, and as I step back from them, I realise I am standing on the platform from which the Emperor made his grand, public speeches.

It's almost ironic. Once they towered above me in my pain. Now I stand over them in their sleep.

"Two Destructors, Antario, Malintaret and the Emperor to go." Someone says, as an eerie silence settles.

I hear a scream from the opposite side of the courtyard and turn around to see a sickly row of hundreds of Resistance workers lying dead or injured on the ground.

I stop short when I find a face I know among the massacred. The memory of his sharp, witty smile and dashingly dark hair is now caked in blood and dirt as I hardly recognise Bant's sullen features. The mysterious boy in the woods has become just another casualty to this fight, and any anger I once felt towards him rapidly dissipates into a mixture of pity and pride. I wonder if his father has joined these ranks too? Or did Bant desert him and his manic schemes in the hope of a better life? Either way, I forgive him. Bant's death has paid the price of his father's misguided ambitions. As my eyes trace the creases of worry on the boy's forehead, I wonder if his mother is still in the prisons, set free to find her first-born permanently locked away in the cage of death? I hope that her husband, whether he is a part of this fight or not, is still alive, and the broken family can be at least partially reunited.

More casualties file out of the mansions, some hobbling and others carried by weeping comrades. The dead sleep on the left, the injured on the right, as a new flurry of people I don't recognise swarm around them, trying to save as many lives as they can.

These people aren't disguised or dressed in black like the Resistance. They are all wearing heavy white belts carrying contraband medical tools as they shout articulate instructions and perform complex procedures which suggest training and experience. Confused, I take a delicate step towards them. What citizens of this Country would be able to handle life threatening injuries so professionally? It is almost as if medicine is their…profession.

Now I can see them more clearly, I realise that they are, or at least were, The Noble's servants. The only people permitted to be trained as medics, to administer to the only people worthy of good health. I suddenly see them everywhere, crowding the courtyard with a dreamlike sense of hope. The Noble's abused and dejected slaves, weak and tired, yet smiling and free.

I glance around at the standing Resistance soldiers, less than thirty of us waiting, exhausted, in the courtyard. We outnumber them easily, but are we really a match for the deadliest killers in the Country?

I don't see Sokk, or dad, and my heart immediately starts to beat an all too familiar rhythm of panic.

Not them...They couldn't have... I couldn't bear it if they... No.

My eyes skim the isles of the dead and injured but there is no sign of them there. With a wrenched heart, I imagine broken bodies thrown across the torture chambers, or crumpled in the corners of the pompous bedrooms. The mansions are lethal. Every room promises a different demise. Not everyone is going to survive.

I close my eyes to stop the childish tears that threaten to escape, but when I open them again the courtyard has morphed into another nightmare.

The two remaining Destructors charge out of the mansion, shooting and dodging bullets as blood gushes to the ground, followed by ugly splashes as soldiers follow its decent.

A mob of surviving Resistance fighters gather around the enemy, but the Destructors don't instantly murder them all, like I know that they could, but battle almost in slow motion, as if trying to delay something or waste time, shielding themselves from oncoming attacks, yet deliberately missing the Resistance with their own.

I run. Not at them, but around them, to the concealed space behind where I now see Antario, Malintaret, and the Emperor sidling past the mob, towards the road leading to the main gates.

I follow them, softly mirroring the pattern of their footsteps, until we are away from the main party. They don't see me, but edge quickly forwards with their heads bowed, and regal furs covering their features as if they would make them any less incongruous. When we reach a small alcove near the mansion that once belonged to the third Noble, they pause to catch their breath.

Like a leopard, I jump towards them, knocking Antario to the ground where I shoot him in the foot, though the fall has already knocked him unconscious.

As I stand over his body, I relish the revenge. But the feeling of power soon dissipates as my gun is knocked out of my hand.

Malintaret and the Emperor press me against the wall of the alcove, crowding me with no escape. Fear boils like a cauldron in the pit of my stomach, as from her boot, Malintaret draws a knife, and from his belt, the Emperor pulls out a gun with a silver-black barrel gleaming bright and deadly.

"Well my child." He says, his voice sly and malicious. "What a joyful conclusion to this final battle. You told me only yesterday that you wanted to die, and now you shall. I hope your satisfied."

Without thinking, I scream. A loud noise that pierces the skies and spreads like a siren.

"You shouldn't have done that, Willow." Malintaret slides her knife across my throat, teasingly. "We'll have to act more quickly now."

I glance around, feverishly, looking for a way to fight. A way to escape. I try to dive under Malintaret's arm but fall to the ground as she kicks me in the stomach.

"Goodbye Willow." She whispers as she pulls me up and pins me against the wall so tightly I can hardly breathe. The Emperor holds his gun to my temple.

I close my eyes and wait. All I can think about is May. Her truth and innocence. Her ability to forgive the monsters who lit the fire beneath her feet. Can I forgive them? These people who are now disposing of my life, like they have thousands of others. I don't think I can. Not because they've hurt me, I forgive them for that, but because they killed you. May.

I hear a shot but feel nothing. As I open my eyes, I see first the Emperor, then Malintaret fall to their knees. I blink, before my father's arms wrap around me, holding me tightly the way an egg shell surrounds and protects the chick nestled inside of it.

Sokk kneels beside Malintaret, tilting her head to the side and injecting a pale blue liquid into her neck.

"What's that?" I ask, leaning against dad's side, and clutching his right hand in both of mine.

"Memory serum." Sokk places the syringe back in a metal case before taking another filled one and moving to Roberto.

Memory serum? Is that what Sokk meant by a 'fresh start'? Deleting every thought from their brains. Every cruel deed. Every pulse of hatred that existed inside of them. So, when they wake, it is as if it never existed?

So, what now? Will they simply wake up and create a new government based on kindness and honesty? As easily as that? Can we really take that risk?

My mind burns with questions, but I'm too tired to ask any of them. I can't cope with more responsibility, with more emotions or answers. I just want someone to tell me what to do. I don't need to understand.

Once the Emperor has been cleared of his conscience, we silently carry one Noble each, holding them in our arms like babes, back to the courtyard.

When we reach it, I gasp, I would be shocked if I had that much energy left. A large, bird like mechanical structure sits in the centre of the basin, whilst on either side, Resistance workers and ex-slaves, carry Destructors, soldiers and Noble's onto it, up a narrow set of stairs and through a wide-open door.

"It's called an Aeroplane." Sokk says. "Three years ago, we found it in the ruins of an old town in the North and started to renovate it. The Noble's found out, and bombed the town, but not before we managed to get it to fly. A team of Resistance flew it across the seas until they found a new land."

"Land?" I say. What land? What could there be other than this? This is The County. There can't be anything else.

"Another Country with enough resource to sustain life. There are animals there, which we thought were extinct, but no humans. Not yet."

"Yet?"

"They came back, in the aeroplane, three months ago. Since then we have been planning this attack. The Nobles now have no memories, no past at all as far as they will be concerned when they wake up. Everything will begin again. We're taking them all to this new Country, where maybe they will evolve as a peaceful community. They're getting a second chance."

"But, isn't it in their nature to kill and hate everyone? Isn't that in their genes?"

"No. It's what they've been taught, what they've grown up to believe. They can change. You proved that."

We walk towards the aeroplane, and slowly climb the steps and through the wide doors. Sokk turns right, and I follow him into what looks like an auditorium, rows of chairs lining each wall and a third column flowing down the centre, separated by narrow aisles and a worn, red carpet. Hundreds of Nobles, Destructors and soldiers sit in the chairs, looking peaceful in their empty sleep, and for the first time I truly believe that they can change. That when they wake up, they will see the beauty of this world, and take from it, the kindness and goodness that is so much stronger than pain and violence.

We lay my mother, and my two grandfathers, to rest in high backed chairs that are tattered, but secure. As Malintaret's hand settles on the armrest, I almost feel her fingers cling onto me and have to consciously pull myself away. I glance at her face, but it is still peacefully asleep. It was only my imagination. I almost smile.

Before I leave the aeroplane, I catch sight of May's dead body outside, her charred flesh now the only casualty in the courtyard's basin. Grief rushes through me, but it's not violent, just sad. She shouldn't have died, not like that, not at all.

Slowly, I turn to take one last look at the villains who put her there. But instead of anger or hatred, I feel pity. They're murderers, cold hearted killers, but I'm not perfect either.

May is dead, and her killers lie vulnerable and exposed within meters of me. I should be at their throats, crying and screaming in vengeance as their blue blood pools onto the floor. But instead, I'm simply staring at them, heartbroken and desolate, but somehow at peace.

I gaze upon the faces of the sleeping beasts. The vampires who massacred the only light in my life. But before I seal my heart, and jump into the carnage of the battle, my lips mouth words that they will never hear, but perhaps, one day, they will feel.

"I forgive you."

About The Author

Hannah Kawira is a debut author from the Brecon Beacons in South Wales.

Having been born in Kenya, she is passionate about standing out against social injustice and infringements of human rights. Hannah believes wholeheartedly that every experience has something to teach us about the world around us, and how important it is to love and care for those who share in the earth's wonderful creation!

As well as writing and, of course, reading, Hannah is a singer and musician - playing French and Tenor horn. She is about to commence professional actor training, having enjoyed being a part of many productions in South Wales, and more recently touring with a Christian theatre company to Churches, prisons and schools.

.